Michael Ford is the pen name of Mig\
Azorean writer, born in Rhodesia in 1y/3. He grew up in a conservative English seaside town, a place which could have inspired the song *Everyday Is Like Sunday* by The Smiths. His education, relationships and work have taken him to many places around the world, and his studies took in forestry, landscape management, journalism and radio, geography and history, philosophy of science and environmental ethics. He wrote and co-wrote numerous books, articles and studies on sustainability policies and practices, and spoke on these subjects in Europe, Africa, Asia and North America. Wishing to take his enquiry into human experience and behaviour deeper and wider, he now writes fiction as Michael Ford. His stories explore themes relating to relationships, identity, spirituality, sexuality, morality and the nature of personal reality.

First published February 2013

The right of Miguel Mendonça to be identified as author of this work has been asserted in accordance with the
UK Copyright, Designs and Patents Act 1988

Cover design by Miguel Mendonça

A catalogue record for this book is available from the British Library

ISBN 13: 978-1-482-09217-2
ISBN 10: 1-482-09217-4

For Dean, an actual angel

Acknowledgements

Being my first published work of fiction, this book is 40 years in the making, and I am immensely grateful to all those who helped me travel this road, principally my parents: my mother, who taught me to read at an early age, and hence fall in love with the written and spoken word; and my father, whose preoccupation with world affairs bred in me both a fascination with, and deep concern about, humanity's capacity to endlessly trip over its own shoelaces instead of doing them up.

And there are many more. I want to thank D.B., Mike, Dennis, Lindsey, Chris, Herbie, Marc, Ania and Lou for always being ready for a deep and meaningful discussion these last few years, and thus helping me to explore the themes of these stories.

The many artists, thinkers and spiritual figures who have made me want to leave a positive mark on the world, chiefly Williams S. Burroughs, Hunter S. Thompson, Woody Allen, Chuck D, Henry Rollins, Jimi Hendrix, the Dalai Lama and Thich Nhat Hanh.

Frankie, for her heart, her spirit and her example.

George, particularly for his early encouragement, and being the first author to tell me I can write. You'll never know how much that meant.

A complete stranger I met online who went out of her way to help me: Susan Harkins, an IT guru who generously helped me solve some of Word's more infuriating issues towards the end.

Dave, Keith, Stephen, Ania and Lou for letting me read you some of the stories, and for your feedback.

MrsThinkyThoughtHead.com for creating michael-ford.co.uk

Ania, for her social media know-how and moral support.

Judith and Dean, whose help and support have been invaluable. This book simply would not have happened without you.

Ravi, for your integrity, and for letting me concentrate on this.

Maria Gentlewhispering for helping me get to sleep every night.

Stephen, for your creativity and energy, and for an inspiring conversation just when I needed it.

Dexter: I miss you every day, but you are always with me.

Joe, for the laughter and the perspective, and for being you. Believe it or not, you've been my greatest inspiration.

And finally to Louise, for everything, always.

CONTENTS

Quick! Act Normal

12 short stories by

MICHAEL FORD

China Dolls

My name is Francis Alan Jefferies. Frankie. Frankie the Harp. AJ. Franny J. Alan Franks. And the rest. By the time I was out me teens I thought I'd seen it all, inside and out. Rucking and thieving landed me up in approved school, then borstal, then prison. Slow learner, maybe. I didn't think about nothing except getting what I wanted, and God help you if you got in my way.

I was born in Hackney in the East End, but got dragged up in a tower block down the Elephant in the late 60s and 70s. Dad liked to drink and knock us about, till I got old enough to return the favour. Me mum and younger brother just tried to keep out the way. I was a bit of a face from when I was young, which had its advantages, but the downside was the local copper, who had it in for me, big time. Once they reckon they've got your number, that's that. Contrary to what most people think, It wasn't me mates who lead me astray. They was all I had. That, and anything I could get me hands on in under five minutes. At seventeen I was driving a brand new 3 litre Capri. The geezer who paid for it must have wept. I had nice threads, birds comin' out me ears, days in bed, nights on speed – when I wasn't banged up, that is.

Eventually I calmed down a bit, after some advice from an old lag I respected – Old Arfa – and I started thinking about going straight. Or at least getting caught less. He taught me to play the blues harp – the harmonica, that is. I got right into the old Chicago and Delta blues players, Sonny Boy Williamson, Little Walter, Howlin' Wolf and all that lot. Our own Cyril Davies too. I love it. There's nothing like being locked up for months at a time to learn what the blues are all about, and 'specially when you get out to find you got no home, no job, no one. Being in the nick, you need *something*; whatever gets you through. Inside it's nothing but long days and longer nights.

That was donkeys ago. Since I hit fifty I've pinched less, and been more savvy when I do. I make a few quid on the horses, do the door at a couple of places, a bit of collecting, knock out a bit of gear. Nothing heavy. I live alone, never got involved. I've tried to keep things simple.

So, life was fairly calm, you might say. Predictable, within reason. But then, when I really *did* think I'd seen it all, I found out I truly hadn't. I found out that things ain't always what they seem, that the hardest heart can be softened, and that there's definitely nowt so queer as folk.

The whole thing kicked off less than six months ago, the middle of last summer. Where I live, it's on the third floor of a big place in Notting Hill, divided into flats. Respectable. One night I'm playing the harp and I get a knock on the door. It's not late, so I imagine no one's coming up to try giving me a bollocking about noise. I open the door, and there's this gorgeous little Chinese girl standing there. Obviously I'm caught out. In the second before I opened me north, I thought: wrong door? Wants to score? Kissagram? And, would you Adam and Eve it, fuckin' Jehovah's Witness. Shows what I know.

'Good evening. It is you who plays the harmonica?'

'Er, yeah love, that's me. Is it botherin' ya?'

'No. I would like to learn to play it.' Pronounced every word clear as a bell. But I'm smelling a wind-up. Women like that don't just come knocking on your door, and *definitely* not for harmonica lessons. Doesn't happen. But I don't play too badly as it goes, so the old ego steps up. Anyhow, I'm standing there, looking boss-eyed at this bird, then I remember me manners and invite her in. We have a cup of tea, and she tells me her name's Gong Lin. Medical student from Shanghai. This girl can't have been more than 25, and she's an absolute picture: skin like porcelain, stunning brown eyes, cupid's bow lips, fine black hair tied back. I was tryin' not to laugh at times, it was mad. Like I said, beautiful women just showing up at your gaff is the sort of thing you dream up when you're in the nick, cock in hand, not the sort of thing that just happens one night out of the blue.

But, over the years you learn to roll with the punches, go with the flow and all that. She tells me she wants to learn the harmonica, paying customer, like. I say fine, but you don't have to pay me, I'm happy to teach. She asks what harp to get, and where from, so I write some stuff down for her, and we arrange something for the next night. She's keen as mustard. Me too.

Took me hours to get off to kip. Kept picturing Gong's face.

Nothing like the mares I usually end up with after the club's kicked out. Most of them stink of booze and fags, and what comes out of their mouths in bed'd make a sailor blush. Trying to picture this little China doll hanging round me … it was hard, but … lovely. I got nothing but hard edges, and I reckoned if anyone could help smooth a few off, it was her. Of course, I knew I was building it up, blowing it out of proportion, but it's the kind of chance that when you're inside, you tell yourself you're going to grab with both hands if it ever comes your way. Trouble is, I could see meself grabbing *too* hard.

In the morning, me head was clearer. I took it all less serious. In the shower I gave meself a once over, saw what the years had done. Too much was curved where it used to be flat, and vice versa. What would she want with a lump like me?

Anyway, I bollocked meself for thinking that way, and got on with things around the flat. Went down south at lunchtime, ended up in a café, talking with a few of the locals, then called in on me old dear. Didn't say nothing about Gong, though I wanted to. It's hard on your mum, being in and out of the nick. They still see you as their baby, even if you're tattooed up, broken nose, scars from half a dozen bottles on the back of your head. Of course she wants to see me settle down with a good woman. She's never quite given up hope.

The evening comes round, and I'm nervous as a virgin on her wedding night. Bit me nails to fuck, then cleaned the top of the oven, filed some papers, dusted a few bits in the front room. I seen I had fifteen minutes before she was due, then I really went to town – cleaned the bathroom in ten minutes flat, all around the bog. Women notice that sort of thing. I quickly hoovered, and chucked all the crap by the side of the couch in the box room. Opened all the windows, even though it meant you got the noise of the traffic.

I was sweating me cods off by the time the door went. Threw some water on me boat in the bathroom and had a quick word with meself in the mirror; then I opened the door, and there she was. I actually felt light-headed when I saw her. Beautiful. Perfect. Smiling, asking how I was, showing me the harp, still in its box.

I got it together, and stuck the kettle on. She'd bought me some Chinese green tea, so we had that. Bit weird having tea with no milk, but it was lovely as it goes. Anyhow, we kick off, and I'm trying to teach her how to hold the harp properly, meaning I have to place her hands right. Touching her hands was like touching … I dunno. Never known anything else like it. Her skin was so soft, her hands so delicate, these fine little bones that felt like they'd snap if you squeezed even a little bit hard. I was having so much trouble concentrating on what I was trying to tell her, 'cos me mind was having a conversation with itself the whole time.

I was getting her to make the right mouth shape for getting a good note out of it, and watching her lips pucker up. She had this tiny pink tongue flashing about in there. It was mesmerising. I defy any straight bloke to give this woman an harp lesson and not think the exact same things.

She could get a note out of the thing, I'll give her that. I was showing her how to get a nice bluesy slur, putting on a few tracks to show her what I meant. Didn't occur to me that she needed a reason to be interested. I've seen blokes inside getting into some pretty unlikely stuff over the years, so it didn't seem that funny to me. When you've seen one of the most dangerous men in the country teaching another of 'em to knit, you've learnt something about human nature.

When I was explaining this or that to her about the harp, she'd just look me straight in the eye. Her eyes *shone*. Felt like I was pitching headfirst into 'em, like I was melting inside. I kept hearing meself saying 'I love you,' over and over again. Couldn't control it. It did me head in, in the nicest way possible.

Well, she's round for a couple of hours in the end. Really up for it. I told her I was playing with a few blokes the next night down the pub, and asked her along. She says she'd like to very much. I'm nearly swooning. *Me!* I let her out, and all I want to do is kiss her. Wasn't till afterwards, when the spell was broken, that I started giving meself an hard time about it. Told meself I was a dick'ead, I was a fuckin' creep, that I should of respected her more, and meself. All that.

In bed that night, though, it was all different again. I wasn't being a creep, I was smitten. It happens every day, on every street, in every city in the world.

Next day, the Wednesday, I get a call from a bloke I do a bit of work for sometimes. Waldocks, a rich Jew in the north. I have to run around a bit. Place a couple of bets here and there. Then I drop by to talk with him about some other things. He wants me to pay someone a visit, collect a debt from a Mr Price. He'll make it well worth me while. No worries, he says, easy job, no kicking the door in or crackin' heads. Fine. He gives me a letter and off I go. It's a nice gaff in Pimlico. I announce meself through the intercom, then an Asian codger collects me at the door and we head up the stairs. Well, the room I get taken into doesn't look like the sort of place you live if you owe people money. But if I've learned one thing over and over again in life, it's to never assume. The butler sits me down in this book-lined sitting room, I s'pose so the man of the house can make an entrance. Big himself up a bit. Finally, in he comes. Fat bastard. Portly, I s'pose *he'd* say. Sixties, English, done up to the nines.

'Good afternoon. I understand you are a representative of Mr Waldocks?'

'That I am. He said you'd be expecting me?'

'Indeed. We have an arrangement, and now he would like to collect?'

'Indeed he would. He's given me a five-figure sum.' I got up and handed him the letter from Waldocks. Price grunts, excuses himself, then comes back after a couple of minutes with an envelope. I flick through it; I can see the money's there, as much from his body language as my maths. You can't do what I do without knowing how to read people a bit.

'Good enough.'

'You don't wish to count it?' I smiled.

'You've got an honest face.'

Waldocks got sorted, and he sorted me. Better than working for a living. That night, business was forgotten. I knocked for Gong at her place, and we headed down the road. She was chatty, excited about seeing me play, she says. I'm trying not to get a big head; I tell meself I'm just a jailhouse harp player gigging in me local. Nothing to get too excited about. I love playing, that's all. I give it some welly, I put me heart and soul into it. That's all you *can* do in life.

It's only a quarter of an hour's walk, and it's a gorgeous summer evening in Notting Hill. The streets are busy, but laid back. I'm feeling good about life. We get inside and it's already buzzin' in there. I keep Gong close, and heads are turnin' – a few smirks. The DJ's playing blues tunes from all over the last seventy-odd years. I love it all. We get a beer each, and I take Gong up to meet the band. They're a grizzled lot, as blues bands tend to be. Been drinking, smoking and getting up to no good their whole lives. You can picture what's going on in their heads when they catch sight of Gong. One or two of 'em, their eyes are popping out. It don't bother me, blokes are blokes.

We kick off with *Mustang Sally*. Wilson Pickett made it famous, but it was originally recorded by Mack Rice, in '65. Every blues band in the world knows it. Then we go into *Rollin' and Tumblin'*, a real favourite of mine, especially Muddy Waters' version. Even Dylan did a great cover of it. Clapton, Canned Heat and Jeff Beck too. Some songs will always be covered – they're just too good, and it feels so good to play 'em. Anyhow, I'm well fired up. Picture it: dark room, blue and red lights, hot air, cracking snare, thumping kick, rumbling bass, sweet piano, fierce guitar, the whole lot going, and me on the harp, ripping right through the middle of it. Billy, the guitarist and singer, was giving it loads, and whipping the punters right up. We done *Sweet Home Chicago*, *Boom Boom*, *Smokestack Lightning*, and Billy's favourite, *Bad to the Bone*. The crowd were regulars, and a few of them discerning blues hounds. They knew we knew our stuff.

We done a few more standards, then took a break after an hour. I went up to where Gong was sitting, and she was still by herself. I'd tried not to eye her up, but had seen a couple of geezers try it on without success. I asked her about it, and she said she just politely spoke Chinese until they gave up. She's no mug, this one. I was so pumped that I weren't feeling as soppy this time, but I knew this had to get messy at some point. I tried to distract meself by jokingly asking if she wanted to get up and blow a bit, but she politely declined, with the cutest smile you've ever seen. Madly, I could see her up there, ripping it out, throwing shapes, the whole lot.

Second half was great, we really went for it. Did lovely versions of Jimi's *Red House* and B.B. King's *The Thrill is Gone*. For some reason me head got filled with memories from being inside. Kept seeing faces of old lags, young offenders, couple of screws who weren't too bad, some of me old cellies. Was a bit weird, how strong it come over me. Still, made Gong's face all the sweeter when we finished. I wanted to help pack up the gear but the lads told me to fuck off, not keep the lady waiting. I wasn't gonna argue, was I?

I took her for a late-night curry in Brick Lane. I asked her about China, and all the human rights shenanigans, the amount of prisoners they top each year, and blow me down – she just couldn't find it in herself to have a go at the lads at the top. Kept saying it's complicated, hard for outsiders to understand and all that. Still, she said she'd rather be here for the time being. No surprise. I wondered whether she'd have to marry a Chinese bloke, 'cos of her parents, their customs and that. Couldn't bring meself to ask. Didn't want to hear about some other bloke she'd eventually go off with.

Waiting for a cab back, I stood there, all warm and fuzzy after a couple of Kingfishers and a brandy, thinking about how proud I'd be if she was on *my* arm. It's in me nature to be a gentleman, that's just how I was brought up, even if I *was* a bit naughty. So, I kept me hands in me pockets, and just let meself feel protective over her. I thought it's the nearest *I'll* come.

I walk her to her door and she thanks me for a lovely night. She says she'll see me for another lesson tomorrow night if I'm available, then leans up awkwardly to give me a peck on the cheek, and I nearly fainted! Lost for words I was. Made some silly noise and waved her off, feeling like I was twelve years old again. I stumbled up the stairs to me front door, this mad sort of half-smile on me boat. I couldn't believe it. Everything I've done, every horrible thing that would make most people sick, and this little angel turns me into a mumbling idiot with just a peck on the cheek. Life's full of surprises.

The next surprise came when she didn't show the next night, the Thursday. Of course, I give meself grief about it, thinking I shouldn't have asked her about China, all that nonsense. I was getting more and more wound up, and the old habits kicked in. I went out looking for trouble, and found it in a pub in Highbury. I just kept going till I found somewhere I wasn't known. Not much to say about it, just a ruck with a few blokes about nothing. They weren't little blokes, and looked a bit handy, but I was sober and more up for it than they was. Smacked the biggest bloke first, while he was still giving it loads of verbal. Bust his nose, and he's pissing blood and staggering about and yellin'. The other two are just staring so I whacked one of 'em, then went to town. Fighting on a regular basis, as you most likely will if you're a criminal from day one, teaches you what matters: speed, getting in first, and being ready, willing and able to do some damage. Test their bottle. I fucked off before the old bill got there, and hoped there was no CCTV. Don't need any more chats with that lot. Most scrappers don't want to talk to the law, so I assumed I wouldn't have to worry about getting a knock.

Next day, the Friday, you'd never have known, 'cept for a bit of colour on the cheek. I went down and knocked for Gong, but nothing. That night, no word either. Or the next day, the Saturday. I kept telling meself it weren't my fault, I didn't do nothing to piss her off. By Saturday night I was going mental, and I did something naughty: I let meself into her place. Breaking and entering was an old specialty of mine, and it's particularly easy when it's your own building. In my defence, I was worried. She'd disappeared into thin air without a word, and I was just tryin' to be Mr Helpful.

I always loved that sense of time standing still when you first break into a place at night; waiting in that black silence, letting your eyes adjust, listening. Then, moving about, quiet as a mouse, looking. It's a buzz. It's not the same since night vision come along. I checked the bedroom first, and she still had a few bits on the bed, told me she'd been packing in an hurry. Drawers were still open. In fact there were a couple of pairs of her drawers on the bed. I stared at them for a few moments, then sighed and mooched off out again.

She had a very basic little life, this one, which made it easy to find things. She had one pile of post, and a notepad by the phone. I looked about for a pencil, then did a rubbing of the top page. It's an old trick, but works every time. I got an address in English, and the rest must've been Chinese.

I couldn't find nothing else that looked interesting, so I left. Upstairs, I looked up the address on the computer, and got no clue whose place it was, but I knew exactly *where* it was. I got a route map there, got me stuff together. I drove to the lock-up, grabbed me piece, night vision and one or two other bits of kit, and hit the road, west.

I'm on the outskirts of Bath, it's just after one in the morning. Everything's posh round here. Massive gaffs. I have a look on me phone at a map of the area. I know I've got the place, but I ain't going up the drive, so I go off down the lanes and park up. I get me tools, strap up and stick on the night vision. Nothing but fields of cows. Bit different to creepin' around Peckham. Even for these parts, the gaff's a big'un, you can see it from a mile off, between the trees. I trudge through the fields and get to an eight-foot wall running round the estate. I can hear music at this point. Good chance they got CCTV, but I reckon if I hoof it, I can be in before the shit hits. Have to chance it.

When I look up at this wall I'm wishing I was younger, fitter and a stone lighter. But I get up onto it in one piece, and have a look. There's a big do on. Music and lights, security out front, a load of pukka motors on the drive, and further up, it looks like the side doors are open. It's a big fucking place, and it's in full swing. I ask meself whether Gong's really gonna be in there somewhere, but I'm positive she will be.

There's too much open lawn between me and the house, and too much light. No good. I drop down and nip along behind the wall till I'm round the back of the place. I get up on the wall again. The doors are open, lights are on, but no one's about. Between the back wall and the house there's an hedge maze. I can't see no one, but it's too risky to just waltz in. Have to get in upstairs. So I tell meself: in for a penny, in for a pound, and I drop down. I creep around the maze, and I spot a drainpipe going up to a balcony. It'll have to do. I finally get up the bottle and run across to it. Me heart's beating like a rabbit's. I get hold of the drainpipe and start climbing. Lucky there's so much going on, 'cos I'm out of practice and I'm making a bit of a row.

I get up to the balcony and climb over. I'm knackered already. The room's dark, and I try the door. Locked of course. I get a lock pick on the case. I picture, just then, Old Arfa. He'd got done for all sorts, but it started with a B&E. I shake me head, and decide I'm acting in defence of a friend. I know I wouldn't have a leg to stand on in court, 'specially against rich nobs like this lot, but you have to tell yourself you're doing the right thing.

Just before the lock gives, I can hear humping. Unmistakable innit? I pause, pull down the night vision and try to see through the net curtains. A bird riding some bloke, jumping about like a nutter. I look over at the next balcony, and it looks like a job to get to it. I screw me fists up and silently mouth the word *fuck*. They're both getting well animated, so I decide to crawl past and chance it. No choice. The music coming from downstairs should be loud enough, and if they clock me, will they really give a monkey's? They got better things to do.

The door gives, I ease it open. They ain't noticed. I get right down on me belly and start snaking along the carpet. I'm nearly through, and the fuckin' thing gets caught by the wind, and bangs off me boot. I curl up, hoping for the best. I hear a giggle from above me; seems the bird's more interested in banging cock than banging doors, God bless 'er.

Then there's the matter of the bedroom door. Closed. The door to me left is presumably the bathroom. The balcony door bangs again, and the angel says, 'Take me on the balcony!' The geezer's tryin' to protest, he sounds off his nut, but she just jumps up and dashes out there, starkers. What choice does he have?

When they're ensconced, I nip over to the bedroom door and quietly open it a crack. It's light in the hallway but I can see a switch. I take a moment, then have a look. No one about. I go for it, slip over to the light switch and flick it off, then close the bedroom door. God loves me, so far.

I'm sneaking down the hall, and the place is dripping money. The wallpaper probably cost more than my flat. The music's fucking loud – banging dance music. Don't ask me what kind. I'm trying to come up with a plan, but can't think of anything besides grabbing someone and asking if they've seen a Chinese girl appear in the last couple of days. Sounds mad even to me, but what else am I gonna do? I'm up to me nuts in it by now.

I follow the music to the balcony at the top of the stairs, and I get me first sight of it. At the bottom of the stairs there's a big foyer which is buzzing, packed. It connects to what I imagine is a ballroom, where most of the noise is coming from, and there's a load of other doors leading off of it. Everyone's dancing and falling about, in skimpy little costumes, mostly with their cocks, tits and arses hanging out. And in amongst it all – blow me down – there's Gong, done up in a tight-fitting Chinese dress. Me ticker nearly stops ticking. She's wandering about the place serving drinks, pills and powders to this lot off a tray. Looks like most of them have had their fill already. Except, I'm staring, and I get the feeling it's just a bird who *looks* like her. But I'm sure I'm getting to the bottom of all this. I keep looking, and I realise there's an handful of Chinese birds serving drinks in there.

I hear a door go and someone's on me. I spin round and it's a skinny, youngish geezer, wearing stilettos, a mask and fuck all else. 'Say nothing mate,' I tell him, 'I've gotta do me bit in a minute. Bit of cabaret.' I wink at him, and he's swaying around looking off his tits anyway. He looks like he wants to ask me something, but can't work out what, and turns around to wander back down the hall. I roll me eyes and go back to staring at this lot. Then I get an idea.

Five minutes later I'm wandering about, right in the middle of it all, stark bollock naked, except for the mask I pinched off the geezer. I've stashed me gear in another bedroom and hoped for the best. First thing goes through me head as I start walking through 'em, is that maybe they all shag each other every other weekend, and'll get suss 'cos they won't recognise me todger. Most of the accents are pure upper crust or foreign, so either I'd have to keep shtum, or fake it. Fat chance.

It's hard to make your way through without constantly bumping bums, or more than once, cocks. Bit weird. I've seen the Chinese girl from behind, and just keep going. Must have been six feet away, when some woman behind me says, 'That's quite the tattoo you have.' I pull up. First, I know that she's looking at this stupid tat on me arse, of a naked bird sat in a champagne glass, and second, I know that if I don't perform right here and now, it's all over. All I can think to do is turn around slowly, look her up and down, then nod towards the bedrooms and raise an eyebrow, like old Roger Moore used to in Bond films. Well, this bird's class, and just smirks, winks and fucks off in the opposite direction. Phew.

Then I see something mental, even for this place. Some tubby, drunken old twat grabs one of the Chinese girls, pushes her up against a wall and he's trying to get her tight little dress hiked up. Nearly impossible, but that don't stop him trying. She just stands there looking freaked, and a little crowd stands around watching! Me eyes are out on stalks, I can't believe it. I think of Gong, and I can feel the red mist coming down. I want to whack the fucker, but no one else seems to give a toss. It's doing me head in. If I let it go I'm as bad as him, somehow, and if I jump in I'll be rumbled. Well, it gets even more weird. Some other bloke comes storming over, yelling at the old cunt to leave her alone. I recognise the voice before I see him. It's only the geezer from Pimlico, Price.

I do a quick about face and head over to a drinks table near the stairs. Can I find a glass of water? Nothing but bubbly. I look over again, and Price has his arm round the geezer, and he's leading him across to some other sort, who's wearing nothing but a huge pink feather boa and laughing like a drain. Price is running his hands over her tits like she's a second-hand motor he's trying to get shot of. I've seen a lot of nasty business, but the upper crust seem to be particularly twisted when they put their minds to it. That's what too much money does I suppose. You end up thinking you really do own people.

At this point, the plan is to find Gong and whip her out of here quick. I know she's going to be here somewhere. Price's appearance leaves me in no doubt.

I decide to have a touch of Dutch courage, and grab a glass of bubbly off another Chinese girl. I throw it down me Gregory just as the room goes dark, and a red light hits a fuck-off great disco ball hanging down from the ceiling. Straight away everyone just hits the deck and starts grabbing handfuls, sticking this and that in wherever. It's mad. You think you've been around, and then a few hundred toffs in masks and boots start rumping right in front of you. I defy anyone to take that one in their stride. I'm thinkin', no one ever talks about the *smell* of an orgy. But believe you me, it has a smell all of its own. I just step over them to the far side of the room and slip off down a corridor.

So, I'm legging it about, checking all the other unlocked rooms I can find. Me tackle's bouncing up and down as I go, and I can't help laughing at the nuttiness of it all. Part of me wishes I had it on tape.

As I get to the kitchens, I can hear a woman's voice, obviously the guv'nor, doling out instructions. She's English, and speaking very clearly, like she wants to be understood by idiots. Or foreigners. I look through one of the round windows in the double doors, and sure enough, there's a bunch of Chinese girls being addressed by this

English bird in black leather gear. I shake me head and mutter, and then I clock Gong, stood at the back. No doubt about it.

I do believe my heart skipped a beat.

I'm wondering what to do next, when this woman's boat appears in the window, staring at me. She opens the door, and all I see is her leather getup.

'May I *help* you?'

'Nah, you're okay love, was just lookin' for a glass of water. I'm spittin' feathers.'

'I wonder *why*.' She has this mean look, and I'm wondering if I'm gonna have to twat her and leg it with Gong.

'The drinks are back *that* way. I hope you weren't fishing for one of my girls. Several of your number have *already* transgressed rule number one this evening.' Still givin' me attitude, but she ain't going to stop me.

'Okay love, you do *your* job and I'll do *mine*. Gong? We're leaving. *Don't* make the mistake of getting in my way, miss hard bollocks.' Gong's looking at me with fear in those pretty little eyes. 'It's okay love, come on. We're leaving this madhouse.'

In the end I've had to yank her out of there by the hand, and the leather bird's just stood gawping. Gong's dumbstruck too, but I get her to lead us back upstairs so I can get dressed and grab me gear. She's looking like she's in shock. We get back to the door I'd come through in the first place; it's open, and no one's about, thank fuck.

We're on the balcony and she's just shaking her head, rambling to herself in Chinese. I reach down and take her heels off, fling them over the side. I just grab her shoulders and give her this look, and she gets her head together; gets down that drainpipe quick as you like.

I make it the ground, and we peg it round the maze, heading for the back wall. And all hell breaks loose. All the security lights go up, on the house, in the trees, on the wall; dogs start barking, people are shouting, and I do believe I hear the sound of shotguns being loaded. Heard that before, once or twice. We get to the back wall, and I near enough throw her over it. It did flash through me head that I could have asked if she was happy to leave or not, but it's too late.

We're well into the fields, me with the night vision on, leading her by the hand, when I hear the dogs behind us. I spin round, draw me Glock and aim. First one's a clean head shot, dead; second needed three. The thing's practically crawling up me leg, claret everywhere.

Gong's in tears by the time we get to the motor. I put me foot down at first, then ease back after a bit and head us onto the main road. I'm trying to find the words.

'So, you wanna tell me what that was all about?' Gong looks at me, then away again.

'You have dog brains on your face.'

'So I have.' I wipe me boat with me sleeve and sigh. It's gonna be a long drive back to town.

After a bit she calms down and starts talking about the whole thing. Seems Price had me followed. Making sure I dropped the wedge off to Waldocks I s'pose. At some point they must have clocked Gong, and his taste for little Chinese beauties would have had him dribbling when the lads reported back. They got hold of her number, called her up, saying they was friends of her old man, and invited her to a party at the manor, promising some good introductions. But, when she arrived they turned the screw, threatened her with deportation if she didn't perform the Chinese waitress bit.

Poor mare looks shell-shocked when we get back. When I go to drop her off at her door, she just pushes me towards the stairs up to my place. Inside, she gives me this look. She wanders into the bathroom, starts running the shower and peeling her kit off, with the door open. I do likewise. Well you would, wouldn't you? If I thought she looked good with clothes *on* … anyway, we get in and she starts off soaping me back. A minute later I'm standing there hard as a rock, but I'm too spent to worry about it. She says nothing, just keeps going, head to toe, and finally starts soaping me tackle. Could have married her on the spot. After a bit she says quietly that to her, British men all smell like cheese. There's no answer to that, is there? I'm trying to think of things to say, as you do, but it don't seem necessary. I soap her after that. It's heaven. Just running me big rough hands over her perfect skin was erotic beyond belief, but at the same time I'm still feeling really protective towards her. It's a weird mixture.

She got into me bed straight after, and I had an education. I learnt something about making love that night. I'd always thought it was like fucking, but slower. Bollocks. Making love is evidently something you just can't do with people you don't feel a certain way about. I can't even describe what that means, but I can say that at times she made me feel like *I* was the woman, somehow. Vulnerable. Open. I know how that sounds. But I felt like I was falling in love, and just wanted to keep falling, to never hit the ground.

And I haven't. Not yet. After what happened, there was no way I could stick around town. If Price was wanting me either permanently shtum, having seen all that nonsense, or if he was wanting revenge for fucking up his do and half-inching one of his prize China dolls, then I was in trouble. Blokes like that have enough clout to have anyone sorted. So, Waldocks did me a favour, and me and Gong hoofed it overseas to where some of his lads could set us up for a bit. Can't say where. Best we just get on with it here for a while. The old man said he'd do what he can to make things right so's we can go back, but nothing yet. Not that I mind. I do local jobs for him which pay the bills, and Gong's studying medicine here for the time being – and getting there with the harp.

Every day I come home to this amazing little woman who makes me light up on the inside. She's hard and soft, she's sincere, honest, and diplomatic when need be. She makes me think before I act, and she's making a better man of me every day. I dunno what comes next, but I feel okay about it. A good woman'll make an optimist of you. I recommend it.

Most of All, I Miss the Sky

The thing I miss the most, being out here, is the sky. Look at it: an endless black vacuum. The void. It's our very best description of nothing. It gets painful to look at on a bad day – the human soul is not made for it. You feel too exposed, and too alone. The sun is hot when it comes, but it's not the same without a blue sky, clouds. Just another dead rock in the infinite immensity. And without ceremony, without poetry, it is soon to be gutted. After being marooned out here for nearly a year, the guys with the machines will come. They will make this place deader, even less whole. But they will breathe life back into *us*.

I don't do the prospecting or the mining. I'm a botanist. I set up the biodomes for the company, ploughing my tiny furrows a few feet from silent airless death, the most lonely farmer who ever lived. Jesus Christ. I'm feeling sorry for myself again. I should be happier. I should be skipping around the damn room; it's going to be over soon.

Anyway, I look after food production, and work with another guy on atmospherics, to make the place liveable for when the Big Team brings the gear down. The company mines these rocks, and the workers need a living space. We set up a few domes, creating enough organic life, and enough room, so the people can survive, and not go nuts. Usually they come about 12 weeks after we get everything up and running, but the company went bust, after one of the directors embezzled a fortune to fund bad investments and bad women. It's taken this long for another corporation to buy the company, and to decide to get to work on this place, LV-427. If they hadn't, we'd die out here, eventually. Probably we'd take a walk outside without our suits before we ran out of food and O_2. I don't think it takes long at all. Ten weeks is not so bad, certainly at the rates of pay you get. But a *year* ... that's a long fucking time on a dead rock with no sky.

Picture our canteen. A perfectly white room, with white furniture. A table and six chairs, and a single, small round window. You take a seat, have some coffee. You gaze out of this window as you drink. All you can see outside is black sky and white planet, and the sun or the stars, depending on the time of day. No clouds, no fog, no rain or snow, no rainbows, no sunset lightshow, no trees or grasses waving in the wind, no birds, no insects.

Now picture the interior of a little diner. It's raining hard outside, a cool, grey Autumn day. The streets are awash, cars splashing pedestrians with dirty water. Most hurry past, heads down, umbrellas, maybe just a newspaper to keep the rain off. When the door opens, the couple of dozen people inside get a sharp blast of damp air. Inside it's warm and humid, the windows are steamed up. The diners are a mix of tradesmen and office workers mostly. There's a gentle hum of chatter, cigarette smoke curls up to the ceiling. The diner orchestra plays: the arrhythmic drone of conversation, the ker-ching of the cash register, the hiss of the coffee machine, the rustle of newspapers, the occasional clink of a spoon stirring a cup, the thud of a palm against a ketchup bottle, the rattle and clang of knives and forks.

The little scene might seem greyed out, sickly, maudlin ... but compared to *this* reality, it's like spring break in Florida, all colour and action, booze and tits. *Life*. Here, it's *lifeless*. Even the air in these domes sits on us like a weight, as does the silence, and the slow tick of time.

Our base is tiny, just the two domes, about the size of a football field all together, and a handful of small cabins linked up by thin corridors. We could have invented cabin fever here, all by ourselves. We had four goats and a dozen chickens at the beginning, but we ate the last of the motherfuckers nearly three months ago, and it hasn't been the same since.

Now, we pass each other like ghosts, Norm and I. In the corridors, we barely acknowledge one another. He sees me as his one and only staff member. He needs to feel superior to me. I don't even report to the guy. He asks me if I've done certain things around the place, asks if I could *just* do this, *just* do that. I call them Norm's 'just' jobs. I think psychologically he needs to keep a sense of structure, of hierarchy. Not me. I rebel. Whenever he asks me to do anything I tell him to fuck off. Our relations have broken down.

A couple of months back I took to walking the dog. I get in my suit and go out there. I throw a bit of old tubing as far as I can and pretend my old boyhood dog, Cappie, is fetching it, bounding through the tall prairie grasses that surrounded our house for a mile in every direction. In those memories, it's always summer. He'd get the stick every time, no matter how long he had to hunt around for it, his tail wagging like crazy. I loved that animal, more than any person, ever.

There's a range of hills not far from the base. I go up there on the rock rover, *Doofus*. You can really get up some speed in that thing, and the low gravity means you get some great air off the berms. I picture Norm, staring at me in disgust from one of the little round windows and I shout, 'Suck my dick, Norm!' and laugh my ass off.

Up on the top of the ridge, you can see for 20 miles or more. A huge expanse of nothing. Man was not meant to live in places like this. It's why the company sees them and has to start planting life. Nah, I'm kidding. They just want money. Mostly they mine moons and planets, and sell whatever they find wholesale. They create new life on some, on a contract basis. The ultimate real estate developers. My old division did paraterraforming; we'd rig up huge domes and create life under them. The domes get linked up, and gradually extend over the planet's surface. It's faster than terraforming, which takes generations, and once they're self-sufficient they can be used as stepping stones for further exploration. The domes themselves are largely constructed on the planet from local materials. We have a 3D printing process which is actually really neat.

As part of my training I stayed in a place like this for a couple of months. Hated it. Never dreamed I'd get stuck on one. I couldn't look up, that first week. It made my mind squirm, to look into total nothingness, just stars and more stars, never, ever ending. When you look straight up you sometimes feel like you're actually stuck to the bottom of the planet, looking down, and if the gravity was switched off, you'd just fall forever. Now I look, and I feel calm. Even when the lights in the sky come. I've counted at least five different types of craft since we've been here. They appeared way off at first, then they kinda zipped past, then started to wander by slowly. Now, they even hover nearby. When I'm up on the ridge sometimes these smaller ones come and do these crazy little lightshows for me. Kinda remind me of cheerleaders for some reason. I don't know what in fuck they think they're saying, beyond 'Check us out, we can do *this* shit.' Don't even know if there's anyone *in* those things. Never seen anyone. Norm won't even discuss it. He just shrugs and wanders off in silence. I rather musically shout, 'Fuck *you*, Norm,' and he doesn't even turn around. I guess he's heard it a time or two by now.

And after all this time out here, climbing the fucking walls and praying for rescue, out of the blue Norm just leaves me a message on the fridge door. You believe that? No big announcement, no games, just a note telling me that we have confirmation that the first ships arrive in three days. That means that in around 65 hours from now, I get to see *other people*. I can't talk to Norm about jack shit, so I'm making these logs, for the sake of saying *something* about it.

I spent this morning going round the gardens, primping. We have no weed seeds, no contaminants at all, just perfect fruits and vegetables. But I needed something physical to do. The biodomes are the only decent place to be on the inside. When I first got here I made a hammock out of a tarp and strung it between two poles – sort of a tradition of mine. I rock myself there, listening to a recording of the ocean. Norm just snorted the first time I asked if he wanted to try it. Fuckin' Norm.

I guess as they expected us to be here a few months at most, they didn't think to match us up in terms of personality. I let myself into his room from time to time, when he's in the bathroom. He always takes the *exact* same amount of time to shit, shower and shave, so I go in for a snoop, just to *check*. You want to know *something* about who you're living with, am I right? I found his diary: paper, bound in leather, written with a pen. Old school. In it, he is disparaging about me. Just refers to me by the initial C. That's the initial of my last name, Chalmers. He can't even treat me like me a whole person. He's perfect for this place, this necrophiliac business. I *think*. Hard to figure him. I've decided he needs a good woman, someone to listen to all his little insecurities in the midnight silences. Someone to tell him he's interesting, that he's valid. Attractive even. We all need that.

Tomorrow, they come. Today, I went over all my data from the last month, did my charts, wrote the same report I've written every week for the last year. I needed something to focus on. I'm *so* excited. Even Norm's spoken to me. Didn't look at me, but said, 'Good morning,' as he sailed imperiously past. Jackass.

Now, I just sit and type. No lights in the room, just the glare of the monitor. I can picture it: my eyeballs in close-up, reflecting the tiny movements as text jerks its way across the screen … you can hear the thudding of my fingers on the virtual keys, the faint hum of the electronics and the AC, and nothing else. My mind keeps flicking back to the ships, three of them, on their way here. Like a kid before Christmas, I can't get it out of my conscious thought for very long. I get that tumble of excitement in my gut. I sip at my private reserve, and wince as it burns down my gullet. I hope the inbound crew thought to bring some good whisky. It was a tradition in the old company. These new guys, who knows?

I wonder if there will be any women on the ships. I actually can't remember the sensation of touching one. I know what to do, in my mind, but I know that the next time, it's going to be a shock to the system. I was in love once, a long time ago. Making love with her was unlike anything else I've ever known. *That's* the feeling I want again. But honestly, just sex would be fine right now. Yeah, put me down for that. Remind me I'm alive, and a man. Remind my dick that it's not just a hose. Back home every song, film, advert – *everything's* about sex. Here, it's like it doesn't exist. Only the plants and insects get lucky. Lying in the hammock in the biodome, amid the silent orgy of pollination and procreation, that's the nearest I've been to sex in a long while.

They didn't say I would be going back on one of the ships. I couldn't bring myself to ask Norm, who's done all the talking. But they *must* have brought someone to relieve me. They can't expect me to stay. Maybe a few weeks, to train someone. I can't think about it. I'd crack if they said another six months. I just can't think about it. I should sleep.

It's the middle of the night and something wakes me. There is someone in my room. I click on the light, prop myself up in my bunk and squint into the dark corners. Movement. I take a breath, and ask who's there. Something moves again, and stands up, still obscure. It takes a step towards my bunk ... I can see a little more ... it looks *alien*. I can make out a dark, lean, ribbed and ridged torso; sinewy, muscular limbs, glistening skin. Its head is large, oval, bulbous at the back; it has smooth features, black eyes with tiny white pin points at the centre. A tiny mouth, almost a beak. It's expressionless, I think. It looks powerful and fragile at the same time. I ask what took it so long. No response. It won't come closer. I can kind of see it, but not properly. It watches me. It reaches back into the shadows and pulls out ... my head swims ... I feel sick ...

I wake. I look around the room. No blood. Nothing. I lay back, laughing. I shout '*Shit!*' and laugh some more. Relief. And then I remember: today's the day. I get up, go shower to celebrate. We don't do it very often – have to recycle and ration water. I soap myself, still shaking my head and laughing. I dreamed an alien brought me Norm's severed head. That's funny. I wonder what it meant. Obviously, it's because today's the big day. The ships arrive. It's about us being separated, and me being happy about it. I guess.

My mind wanders … I think of women again, imagine the ships bringing a smorgasbord of gorgeous scientist chicks. Lab coat cleavage, short skirts and stockings and high heels … brunettes, blondes, red-heads … all shapes, colours and sizes: Scandinavian amazons, petite Asians, curvy Africans, pale Celts, wiry French, lean, big-breasted Slavs, painfully beautiful South Americans … I grab a fistful of cock and indulge every detail until I burst. I get a flash of Norm's severed head again just as I shoot, and I'm standing there, wobbly-legged, dripping come and laughing at the insanely unerotic mental image of his severed head in the hand of some insectile alien creature. I wonder what my mental state would be after five years of this existence. Surely no one lasts that long.

Out in the corridors, there's no sign of Norm. I go to the canteen for breakfast, nothing. No sign. I sit down to eat my bowl of fruit and stare out of the window a moment … then I bolt for the changing room, cursing. I'm spitting with rage. In the hangar there's no Doofus. I have to fucking walk. I leave the airlock, bounce across the surface a few feet, and slow to take it in. The flat plain around the base is now a bright, bustling spaceport. Three huge ships dazzle the area with their floods, their storage bays open like gaping mouths, loading ramps like tongues, vomiting people and equipment with gusto. There are all kinds of buggies, trucks, flashing lights; everyone moves with purpose, with precision. And all silent, in the void. Your mind fills in the sound. I wander through it all, looking around at all these fucking people. They go about their work without expression, ignoring me, and I suddenly don't feel like trying to make conversation. This moment is the biggest anti-climax of my life. I spot Norm's suit entering the airlock of a cabin, along with a few other folks. I bound over there angrily, tripping over some canister en route like an asshole.

The door closes just as I arrive. I knock, wave, hit the buzzer. The suits turn around in the airlock and I can see them roll their eyes. The door slides open after a few, and I join them. Norm stares straight through me. Right then I feel more anger towards him than at any time in the last year. But this is not the moment to lose my shit. The airlock opens into a small room, and we all step in. There are five of us altogether. We remove helmets and there she is. Blonde, smiley and cute. But, it's all business. A tall, greying dude with a square jaw and gravelly voice introduces himself.

'I'm Dr Leonard Stein, head of operations. And you must be

Chalmers.'

'Y-yeah. I, er ...'

'Doesn't matter why you weren't here to meet us.' His eyes are steel. Norm coughs, as if to underline the shared embarrassment. I wanna drop the motherfucker. 'Your part in this project is nearly over. You'll be going home tomorrow once we have *The Nautilus* unloaded.' He gestures to the other two people, one male, one female, well groomed and kinda straight. 'You'll brief your replacements in one hour.'

'S-Sure. Howdy. Not much to know. I'm ready when they are.' I smile at the woman, she smiles back. My little heart flutters, a red bird in a white cage.

I manage to avoid looking at Norm, and go back to my room, carrying the image of the cute botanist carefully in both hands. I hit my bunk and inspect her in detail. Pixieish. Short blonde hair, bright blue eyes, poiky nose and ears, two perfect rows of straight white teeth, full pink lips. My cock insists on being worked again. I picture her in her suit, stripping, holding my gaze the whole time. Slower, I tell her. She's throwing gloves and boots off, almost angrily. A glove smacks me in the face. I laugh, and try to focus again. She hauls the top off to reveal nothing underneath, not even a bra. She has pert, ski-jump breasts, nipples erect and pointing confidently at me. She pushes down the thick white trousers, still staring at me. I lick my lips. I see her flat, milky belly revealed, her hips, then the very top of her ... and God *damn*, that's all she wrote.

I lie there for long moments, my mind a perfect Zen blank. I close my eyes and see the blackness of space, but suddenly it seems to have less presence. Less power over me. The psychological relief of getting back under a real sky will be huge, I know. I will get up in the morning, and I will love the weather no matter what. I will see dirt and grime, and drop to my knees, work the grit into the tiny furrows of my fingerprints. Nothing sterile, nothing contained. I will gulp the shitty air down into my lungs. I will cough and I will feel alive, even as pollutants stream into my body. I will eat every kind of food there is. I will eat meat that caused suffering beyond anything we would allow on humans. I will sit in church and sing along with the congregation, feeling their desperation to fit a comforting framework around their minds, to quell the incessant itching of the Questions: Who are we? Where did we come from? How did we get here? What is our purpose? What happens when we die? I will leave the church and go fuck a prostitute, maybe two. I will open my heart and soul to every woman I meet. I will get a dog, and live the simplest, richest life I can. Then maybe I will start a cult, have thousands follow me, painting images of me fifty feet high – and the look in my eye will say it all. Everyone will know that I *know*. I have *been there*.

The hour passes in this philosophical manner, and I feel happy. I calmly head out to meet my replacements at the main biodome. They are actually called Jack and Jill. Total coincidence, they say, with the world's smallest laugh. But you have to wonder if someone with a modest sense of humour engineered it. I smile gently when they tell me, and lead them off. We walk around, me pointing things out and giving a running commentary, a guided tour, Jack taking notes and Jill recording it all on video. They ask questions and I answer as straight as I can. I just want to burst in with my own questions, ask them everything about what is happening at home, and importantly, how's the fucking weather? No, I *mean*, how is it on your *skin?* How does it *feel? Well!?* But I keep going. Doing my job, for the last time. If I do it well, and quickly, maybe I can get the hell out of here sooner.

I show them the computer set-up, the records, comms, crew quarters, medical, galley, canteen … and most of the time I'm hard as a rock, my dick pinned upright by my belt. It feels really quite jolly to have an erection in the company of a woman. Jill seems real nice … I can imagine that she wouldn't mind a bit if I told her. She'd probably say, '*Awww*, you just go *right* ahead sweety!'

I ask if they want to stop for a drink and a chat in the canteen but they say they have a tight schedule. I say fine, and stay to have a herbal tea. My own brew. I watch them stride off, clipboards clasped to their chests like eager schoolkids. I haven't seen anyone else in all this time, and now that they are here they are still like ghosts. There must be a hundred people arrived. All quartered in the ships I guess. Norm has instantly adopted the role of superior, assisting the head honcho, following him around like a puppy. Fuckin' Norm. He's an asshole, but he's *their* kind of asshole. I don't even make *that* grade.

The rest of the day I spend going over data, checking stocks of seeds and equipment against records. Stuff that needs doing if you're going by the book, but I just do it for the sake of something to do. And maybe I want Jill to have an easier time of getting to grips with it all, and not find herself saying, '*Fuckin'* Chalmers,' several times a day. I feel like I owe her that.

Later on, Norm and I are invited to dine with the crew. It's a big dinner, held in the belly of *The Pequod*. Stein addresses the gathering, talking about the mission as if it's the first time this has been done, like he's fuckin' Columbus. Another asshole. I count 19 women among the crew, and all are eminently fuckable, on a space freighter or anywhere else. Because the dinner's a big deal we get wine. I drink as much as I can, and after dessert I make the rounds, introducing myself to the women, with the excuse of wishing them well with the next stage. I don't give a shit what I look like. I only really connect with one of them, Shanice. She's petite, black, also drunk and tonnes of fun. I suggest a ride out in Doofus to show her around, and to my surprise she thinks it's a great idea. We grab a bottle of wine and sneak off, as the tables begin to break up and people start mingling. There's an air of slightly forced gaiety, and I get the impression that Stein is not universally loved and admired.

In five minutes Shanice and I are in the changing room, and we're half in our suits, half naked, tripping over our clothes, laughing our asses off and grabbing each other all over the place. We end up kissing and my heart's hammering. She's grabbing my ass and looking right into my eyes. She asks me when I was last with a woman. I say, 'What, a *real* one?' For some reason she finds this incredibly funny, and is laughing so hard she says she has to go pee. I say ok, and thinking about her question, I realise I actually can't remember the year for sure.

She comes back, tells me to hurry up before the booze wears off. We suit up, head out the airlock with the wine and take a little buggy of theirs back to the base to grab Doofus. Then we're heading out, top speed, giggling like crazy as I take us over the jumps. It's my last time, and I'm so happy. She keeps leaning back, staring drunkenly at the blaze of stars overhead, shouting about how cool this is, how she never gets to have fun any more. I don't say anything, but in my mind I'm picturing me and her in a park back home, wandering along with a dog, playing fetch and stopping every once in a while to neck. Just looking at each other, able to lean our foreheads together without the dull thump of our helmets getting there first. Still, these are the best moments of the last year, and I try to stay in them.

'Hey Shanice, you wanna see the sights?'

'You bet.' Her eyes sparkle. Crackling, hissing static, punctuated by human voices, interacting, excited by one another, on a lonely rock in the middle of space. It's totally unreal to me.

We drive for maybe 30 minutes, shouting back and forth, her asking questions about here, me asking questions about there. I tell her about the last year, and apparently she hasn't been briefed. When I finish she tells me she can't believe I just kept going, not even knowing if we'd get rescued or not. I shrug, tell her you do what you gotta do.

Finally, we crest a hill and there it is. The main comms tower. It's five stories high, a bare-bones structure, little more than a gantry with a sealed control room at the top. On its roof is the huge dish antennae for deep space transmissions. She looks at me with wide feline eyes, this incredible grin. It's almost overwhelming. I tell her to bring the wine. We reach the base of the tower and head for the lift platform. I pull her on board, and hit the button. The gears turn and we're pulled up, every few feet giving another mile of nothing much to look at.

'It's actually kinda beautiful,' whispers Shanice. I look at her with eyebrows raised, saying nothing. 'You don't think so?'

'I ... it's just been a lifeless *rock* for me ... all the beauty I've seen here in one *year* is in my biodomes ... and your helmet.'

'*Ha*! You're kidding, right?'

'Nope.' Deadpan. She smiles and looks around again at the view; we're almost at the top now, about 60 feet up. When we stop, I lead her off the lift and we take a slow wander around the walkway that surrounds the control room. I sweep my arm across the horizon.

'Look around you kid, look around you. One day, all this will be yours.'

'How long before you got over it?'

'About a week. It fuckin' gets to you.'

'I guess.'

'How much longer are you here for?'

'Another few hours. Back tomorrow.'

'Huh. Me too.' I'm nervous. I'm buzzing. I laugh, then say, 'We should hang out.'

'You're leaving tomorrow? You must be *ready* to leave, huh?'

'Come on.' I take her huge gloved hand in mine and lead her to the cabin door. I punch in the code and the door opens. We step into the airlock and just look into each other's eyes. Her mouth curls slowly into a smile. Mine too. I'm still getting used to smiling a real smile.

Inside, I turn on the oxygen pump and heating. The room is about twenty feet by ten, dominated by a huge window and a bank of equipment for manual transmissions and data collection. There are a few chairs, and at the back there's a bunch of cupboards. I get out two blankets and spread them out on the floor. After a few minutes, when the temperature and O_2 levels are good, we take each other's helmets off, and climb out of our suits. We sit opposite one another naked, just looking, nakedly. God *damn* she's beautiful. I crack open the wine and we pass it back and forth. The room's totally silent, but I hear music in my mind. I start humming. It's an ancient piece of orchestral music, called Eine Kleine Nachtmusik. Shanice knows it, and joins in. We lay on our backs, humming, drinking and staring out at the stars.

After a while she props herself up on one elbow and leans over to kiss me. I put the wine down and we get to it. I was right, I knew it would be like something ... *new*. Shanice seems to get exactly where I'm at, and takes it slow. We're alone, together, in our own private universe. At one point she's riding me, and I'm looking up at her, and I look out, at the millions of suns strewn across the blackness, made tiny by context; humbled and beautiful from here, but close to: certain death. It's an amazing way to say goodbye to this place, to end this year without a sky. I've suffered here, it's been stressful, mentally bruising. And this is like some kind of payoff. Shanice is a kind person.

By the time we've both finished we know it's late.

'Won't you catch hell for this?' I ask.

'This ain't the military, and they can't do shit without me.'

'How come?'

''Cos I'm the damn pilot.'

'*No* shit.'

'No shit.'

'Alright then.'

We're not even dressed, still lying together in silence, when it starts. Something's wrong. The comms light up and start bleeping. I hit the master mic, which routes straight through to the base, and ask what's up. There's a snap and crackle, static and a voice cutting in and out. I think I hear the word attack, but can't be sure. Shanice and I stare at each other, stunned. Attacked? It's unknown in the company's history. The alien from the dream flashes through my mind.

'What should we do?' I ask her, more for the sake of saying something than for practical reasons. If the base is being attacked, we can assume it's game over immediately. 'Are any of you guys armed?'

'We have a small security detail, a few weapons. But if they got caught with their pants down ...' She holds up her hands.

'Do we head in and probably get wasted *too*? I don't know what *we* could do to help.' I just keep shaking my head.

'Me neither.' She starts chewing the inside of her mouth, scratching at her knuckles. How long will the air last in here?'

'There's a machine that makes oxygen, but it works slow. We don't come up here really. We'll have maybe a day, between the two of us.'

'Fuck.'

'Yeah.'

I know we both want to head right back and find out what's happening, but if the enemy is armed, we're a gonner as soon as they spot us.

'Let's see. I can send a distress call to HQ. Tell them there's an attack, and to send in the fuckin' marines.' I try to look reassuring.

'Will they do that?'

'You tell me. You know this company, I don't.'

'Well, we have military contracts. We can only tell them what's happening, then it's up to them. They'll either send the cavalry or they won't.' She shrugs nervously.

I send the message, which'll bounce across a series of relay stations, and be picked up in a few hours. We pace around. In terms of a plan all I can think of is fucking again, but neither of us can get up for it. We give it an hour, then we hug, suit up again, and set off. We decide to just take what comes, as any back-up from home won't get here for days, if at all. There's nowhere to run, nowhere to hide. We drive on.

As we near the base there's no smoke or airborne debris, no sign of a heavy weapons attack. Shanice is leaning forward in her seat, gripping the top edge of the dash. She's saying nothing, but her thoughts are deafening.

We get within a hundred yards of the nearest dome. Nothing. No sign of any people. The ships beyond are towering above the base, and we drive around. By the time we round the final dome between us and the ships I can hear my heartbeat in my neck. Shanice grabs my arm and there's just an intake of breath. I look over to see what she's looking at.

A pile of bodies. No marks, no sign of violence, but there are at least six suits, heaped up next to a loader. We get closer and there are more by the loading ramp of one of the ships, sprawled like rag dolls. We look at each other, both waiting for the other to make the decision. Without a word, I climb out of my seat and approach the nearest pile.

'Keep watch,' I whisper. She just nods, eyes wide. I get right up to the pile laying between the loader and the main building. The bodies are all face down. I look up and around, trying to see what happened, who did this. Surely they're still nearby, meaning I have minutes to live, tops. I reach out to the body on top of the pile and haul it over. It looks– '*AAARRGGHH!!*'

I jump back as the whole lot of them leap up and flail at me; I shit myself and try to run but I can't. I trip and fall flat on the ground.

Long moments pass. I look up and can't see anything. I sit up and turn around and all the bodies are now standing up, they then collapse in hysterics, most of them. Some just point and laugh like drains, hissing in my ear over the comm. I'm speechless. Then it catches up with me, and I'm caught between rage and relief, and total fucking embarrassment. I get up, shaking my head, and stagger back to Shanice, who's looking just *crazy*. I smile and go to put my hand on her shoulder but she bolts out of her seat and bounds towards the nearest crowd, they turn and try to scatter but some are still on the ground. She jumps high into the air before landing on one of them. They get a flurry of slo-mo punches and a stream of stunningly filthy language, before she stands up and walks away. They stagger around, no longer laughing, looking worried. She winks at me as she walks past.

An hour later we're in my bunk. Her skin smells heavenly, and I breathe her in, over and over. Just lying in her arms is the most peaceful thing I can imagine. My last night here, it's like part of me is dying, and a new part of me is about to be born. I whisper this birth and death thing to Shanice and she places a finger on my lips. She leans over and kisses me, a fragrant gale into my mouth. I can't even describe how she makes me feel, so there's not much point trying. It's enough to say I feel safe with her. Like I matter. I wouldn't even know what else to want.

Early morning, an hour before dawn. I pack my few things, and head for the galley for a bite. As I'm collecting a picture from the fridge door, Norm comes in. He puts the kettle on, without even getting a mug out, or trying to make a drink. He stands there awkwardly, then blurts out, 'So. You're shipping out.'

'Yep.' We hold each other's gaze for the first time in months. '*Wait* … you're *not*?'

'No, not yet. I'm going to stay for a while. Help them get settled in. Make sure things get established properly.'

'*Fuck. Wow.* I … I don't think I could take another *day* of this place.'

He sighs. 'Ah … *look*, Bill. I … I *regret* that … well, *you* know. That things got so shitty. Cabin fever I guess. We all have our little coping strategies … and … well, mine was to behave like an ass. And

I'm sorry that that's the way it went. I … I know you're a good guy. A hell of a botanist. You kept us alive. Don't think I don't know that. Or appreciate it.'

'Look man … it takes two. I was … having a hard time of it. Cracking up pretty good. I mean, this was a straight fuck-up, right? Wasn't meant to happen. But … well, I'm sorry too.'

'It was what it was. We're still alive.'

We both shrug, and we laugh. Norm walks over and shakes my hand. I clap him on the shoulder. He hugs me. I hug him back. We look each other in the eye one more time, nod, then I walk out of the room.

It's ringing in my ears as I head for the ship. Of all the things I could not have expected in the last 24 hours, that would have been way up there. I'm actually kinda touched.

The ship is meant to leave in 45 minutes. I head up, and into the winding corridors. I ask my way up to the flight deck, and Shanice is going through pre-flight with the co-pilot, another woman. She smiles as I enter, and nods to a chair at the edge of the cabin. It's exactly as I imagined it: banks of lights, dials and screens, with a huge segmented window in front. I've never flown up front before, and it's neat. She's checking readings, evidently following a sequence, talking back and forth with the co-pilot and someone on the base that sounds like Korzibsky. It's technical talk, another language entirely. I ease back in the big leather chair and close my eyes.

I'm woken by a rumbling. The flight deck is way up, and I look out the windows to see a huge dust cloud being kicked up by the engines, obliterating the base. I don't even get one last look. But it doesn't matter, I'm going to see the sky again. They radio the base, and then we're lifting off.

In my head there is classical music playing, the string section is describing the strange mix of relief and melancholy I feel as the planet starts to shrink away, faster and faster. Again the feeling of part of me dying … I look across at Shanice and she's steady at the helm. The waiting is over, and the tension oozes out of my bones. I melt in the chair, my shoulders slump, I let the tears well up then flow. I can picture the teardrops, shimmering with the dull vibration of the engines, each reflecting the planet, and the sun, just cresting the horizon, flashing into fire across the gulf of space.

Nudity is My Business ... and Business is Good

My name is Crispin Teller, and I achieved something of which I could scarcely be more proud: I got millions of people to get naked in public. And given half the chance, they'll do it again.

It all started back in the mid 1970s, as a child. Running around the neighbourhood with no clothes on was a) very naughty, and b) very pleasant. I would wander out of my parents' view in the garden on a summer's day, quietly slip out of my clothes, and go sprinting off up the road, knees and elbows pumping, racing as far as I could before being caught. It was the wind and sun on my skin, but I think it was also the freedom, the symbolic shedding of authority. My parents said dress, so I undressed.

The neighbours, well, they *mostly* seemed to think it was funny. Everyone knew everyone around there. But that was nearly four decades ago. There was not the same hysteria about paedophilia, the basic mistrust that has swarmed through our society, set loose from the pages of the reactionary press. In those days, people still took pictures of kids without someone freaking out. It was, it seems, a more sane time. Or am I just being romantic?

I grew to find the wearing of clothes an absolute bore. No so-called 'dress sense' ever developed. I had a total disinterest in fashion. I would buy things that didn't suit me, didn't fit ... mostly because the whole idea didn't suit me, didn't fit my idea of myself or how society perhaps ought to be. When bodies are such wonderful things, I thought, why hide them? What's the problem?

I took to nudism in my teens, heading for those blessed beaches with nudist friends wherever and whenever I could. While this did occasionally lead to an enjoyable liaison, I did not pursue it for that reason. It just felt right to go about my day with no clothes on.

There came a day, however, when I became radicalised. I was

laying in a little cove on the south coast of England, naked and minding my own business, just reading a book, when I was approached by two police officers. They spoke of a complaint about my nudity, but declined to say from whom it originated. I was in a secluded place, miles from anywhere, by myself, and didn't think I could even be seen. What in God's name someone could complain about, I had *no* idea. The officers almost apologetically asked me to keep the peace by getting dressed. I humbly obliged, but anger boiled inside me. I stewed and I plotted, I raged and I schemed.

Fast forward to three years ago. I had gone into acting, become known for my willingness to undress. Somehow this garnered me the respect of my peers, and helped attract increasingly demanding roles. It took surprisingly little time to win my first Oscar, but a great deal of effort, and all manner of frantic bullshit with industry types. But, it was worth it. I was not out for revenge, but for … perhaps entertainment, at the very least; a contribution to contemporary culture at most. I had given up the notion of trying to teach society anything.

So three years back I staged a coup. I hosted a nude benefit dinner with every game luvvie from stage and screen – and there were many. It made headlines around the world, and just the calendars we shot during the evening made millions. The tasteful coffee table book we produced is a genuine work of art.

I raised the stakes by opening the first naked restaurant, in Amsterdam of course. Then another in NYC, then L.A., Vegas, Berlin, Paris, Sydney … on and on it went. London took a bit more doing. We did the hugely successful film *Skin* just over a year ago, and last month it went *really* big. International Skin Day. For charity, naturally. Not a goer in the Muslim world, but that's okay. We ask people to donate the equivalent of at least one item of clothing they would have worn – anything from a sock to a designer dress. There were bike rides, fun runs, sporting events, dinners, celebrity telethons, concerts, workplace collections and God knows what else. Globally, we raised the better part of £400 million. In one day. And not one arrest. The money goes to a mass of charities, mostly targeting poverty, at home and abroad. I believe it's important for me to do this, in part, because it shows what you can achieve if you believe in something enough.

There are few things in life that one can be truly proud of, and this is mine: I live to get people naked. The fact that they happily pay tells me that it is more than just the charity, though we have undoubtedly done great things because of this. I think these millions of people who get out of their clothes when given a half-decent reason, do it because somewhere in there, there's a child who wishes to run around naked, feeling the elements on their skin. That is a freedom we rob ourselves of, and tell ourselves cultural stories about 'decency.' Really, it's a collective decision to be ashamed and embarrassed, as though we never come to terms with the loss of our child bodies. They grow into big hairy ones, with fully operational genitals which we try not to talk about. Certainly we joke about it, but somewhere in there is a shame and confusion that seems unnecessary. But people have begun to embrace it, and I hope it continues, beyond the backlash, where the reactionaries flap, as they can't help doing.

Reclaiming our bodies feels like the first step to something greater. Something about losing fear, and embracing a true freedom. I do it every day. In fact I'm typing this naked. Feel free to read it over again with no clothes on, and see how you feel. Maybe you'll see what I mean, and maybe you'll like it.

Too Posh for Porn?

I was once asked if I had any sense of a missed calling in life. I believe so, I replied. A pornographer. That was a conversation killer. Well, my parents were disappointed enough in me already, and I probably shouldn't have been so honest. But it made me think: *why not?* All you really need is a bit of business savvy and a passion for what you do, and I had both. So I counted my pennies, made a few calls, and it began.

After about a year I had converted a warehouse into a fully-functioning pornographic studio. I had a good business partner and film director in Rodd Steed (an ex-porn actor himself, as you may have guessed) a small crew, a steady stream of actors, a good solicitor and accountant, and the time to develop 'scripts.' A couple of years down the line, I was carving out quite a lucrative niche in intergenerational lesbian (IGL) flicks. The website was doing very nicely. We also had websites for the stock hetero, bi and gay stories involving men and women of the trades, emergency services and military, and babysitters, teachers, bored housewives, the occasional dominatrix and anything else we could come up with.

But *this* story ... well, it was something different. How it started was, I'd come up with a story wherein an aristocratic type, the domineering Lady Filchington, instructs her two maids in the art of making whoopee. That delightful old folk tale. Problem was, no Lady F. I tried out a few of the regulars, but no one could get near the accent, or the *bearing*. I'd told the story here and there to various associates, put the word about, but no joy. I wasn't that obsessed with it, so I let it go. However, a few months pass, and I get a call from a friend, a jeweller in London, who *knows people*. He reminds me of the Lady F thing, and tells me that he's heard on the grapevine of an *actual* Lady, down on her luck. But where it gets interesting is that apparently, she'd been selling intimate favours to high rollers for a year or more. The family had nearly gone bankrupt in the recession, and the estate was on the chopping block. Seems it was left in her lap to sort it out. I could picture myself, saying what a pity it would be to lose the estate and have to move to the suburbs. *Ouch*. But I could imagine that if she was already fucking for money, then how much of a leap could this really be? I got Paul to have a discrete word, and almost entirely to my surprise, he said she'd call me. About a week later, the phone goes.

'Hello?'

'Mr Diamond?' No mistaking that accent.

'Call me Eric. I take it you are Ms Rathbone?'

'Call me Penny.' I *loved* her accent. Her tone was difficult to pin down though.

'Penny. Thanks for calling. Look, I'll get right to it. How do you feel about doing an adult film?'

'Needs must. How much do you pay?' She was straight to the point too.

'Depends what goes on. Basic would be a couple of grand or so, then there's extras.'

'Such as?'

'Well, such as … ahem … such as anilingus, strap on … ahem … *that* sort of thing. But it's all negotiable.' Her accent was doing my head in a bit. It just doesn't feel right talking to a posh middle-aged women about this kind of thing. If you doubt me, *you* try it.

'I see. Well, I'll just have to cross that bridge when I come to it.' I thought for a moment.

'Penny. Are you *sure* you're up to this?'

'Quite. As I said. Needs must.'

'Right you are, Penny. You know where to find me?'

'Your friend gave me your coordinates.'

'Er, right. How are you fixed for the fifth?'

'The fifth is fine. I'll see you then.'

And that was how it started. In this business, you are constantly living in a world between worlds. Everybody's thinking sex at some point in their day, untold people watch porn, or sleep with prostitutes … but it's so very hush-hush in our nation. That means it's peopled by those who are able to *embrace* that world. So, you get used to fringe characters, you get used to strange. But this was a new one on me.

Penny Rathbone's big day rolls around but I can only get her fixed up with Astra Starr, a gorgeous young woman who is to sex what a ninja is to assassination. It means a change of storyline is all. So we're sitting about on set; it's a nice living room, huge red Chesterfield sofa covered in sheepskins, everything's lit, crew hanging about, we're having a cup of tea. Penny arrives in a gale of fragrant charm, like some West End luvvie. I have trouble keeping a straight face when she sails over to say hello.

'Well then, Penny! Good to see you darlin'. You alright?' I give her a peck on the cheek; she smells like gold bars.

'I'm very well *indeed*, thank you. And this is ...?' she indicates Astra.

'Ah yes, your co-star, Astra. Astra, this is Penny.'

'Hiya Penny, you alright?' Penny gives a polite wave and smile, then looks around, eyebrows raised. It dawns on me that she's looking for a bloke.

'Ah. Indeed. Er ... Mr Diamond? A moment?' She drags me off out the room, smiling at one and all as we leave. Outside, she fixes me with a look.

'Am I to understand that you would like me to ... *have sex*, with *this* young lady?'

'That's right.' I smile as encouragingly as I can, trying to make it all seem perfectly normal.

'Hm. This wasn't part of the arrangement, now was it?'

'Well ... I don't see that we'd discussed any *specifics* on the phone.'

'But I am not a lesbian, Mr Diamond.'

'Call me Eric. And nor's she. She's bi as it goes, but this is *work*. I imagine you never heard the phrase 'gay for pay' before. Loads of blokes do it. So they say. Think of it that way if you must.'

'Good Lord.'

'You'll be in good hands, I assure you.'

'I see.'

'Look, would it be worth it for 5k?'

'Well ... I imagine it most likely would be.'

'And this is just the start. This goes well, you'll make a killing. This is easy money. You do something for the punters, they do something for you. As long as you look after yourself, you'll never look back. But it's your decision, no one else's. It all comes down to what's most important to *you*.'

'An associate of mine gave me much the same speech.' I never saw a human being actually thinking *elegantly* until this moment. Then she just gives me this little look, a subtle shift around her features that says she's on board.

'Penny? I think you might even enjoy it, if you let yourself.'

'*Do* you.' I smiled.

'Suck it and see, eh?'

Half an hour later we're into it. The script, which I'd had to write in the two minutes after Julie Sukk phoned to say she couldn't make it for the Lady Filchington shoot, becomes an issue from the word go. Penny's 'outside,' about to enter the lounge. Astra, playing Jenny, is moping about on the sofa, waiting for Penny to come in, as Miss Cuthbert, her piano tutor. Jenny has to tell her she's gambled away her tuition money, then Penny's supposed to offer her money for some sexy favours. But.

'Mr Diamond?'

'Call me Eric.'

'Eric … I'm not sure about these lines.'

'Lines?'

'Yes. It says here, 'Ooh yes, *eff* my pussy with your tongue.''

'And?'

'Well … *Eric* … I'm just not comfortable with bad language.'

I was caught *right* out. 'Err, this is *porn*ography, Penny. This girl is going to *fuck* you with a strap-on dildo, *after* about twenty minutes of oral sex, fingering, and possibly arse-licking if you're up to it. At what point *do* you think that bad language might get to be appropriate, in *this* particular context?'

'There's no need for sarcasm Mr Diamond.'

'Well *look*, just do your best, okay? Do what comes naturally.'

'*None* of this is coming especially naturally, I assure you,' she says icily. I look at her beautiful eyes, those fine bones, that poise, effortless elegance, and I want to comfort her, tell her she looks radiant, but to be honest I'm as lost as she is. It'll be whatever it'll be.

We finally got them rolling, and to be honest, I begin to see the funny side of it. Penny walks in from left of frame. Acting is atrocious.

'Hello … *Jenny dear!* I hear you've got yourself into … rather a spot of bother.' She's standing there, one hand on her hip, this mad look on her face. Astra's a shit actress too, but for porn, she's right where she needs to be.

'Oh yes, it's *terrible* Miss Cuthbert.'

'Oh, call me … er … um … Imelda.'

Astra's face is a picture. She knows Penny's forgotten her lines already and is just waffling. Somehow though, they seemed desperately locked in some weird alternate reality where their lives depended on them getting this done in one take.

'Well, *Imelda?* I lost my tuition … *gambling?*'

'I see. Horses was it? Lost a packet on the derby this year myself.' Astra's eyes are like saucers – I'm wondering if she's about to get the giggles. Penny's so nervy she's just letting any old bollocks come out.

'Er. Well, *anyway* … I lost the *money.*' She gives Penny a significant look.

'Yes. That really is too bad. Shocking. Awful. Tut tut.' She's gone totally blank, shifting from one foot to the other, looking miles away.

'Sssooo … is there *any*thing *you* can think of … that we could *do* about that?'

'Hm. Er. Such as?'

'Well … we could … *you know.*' Astra's waggling her eyebrows like a lunatic, making faces at her ample cleavage and short skirt.

'*Oh! Ah yes!* Of *course.* Why did *I* not think of that? How silly of me! We could just have sex and you could have some money orf of me in return. Problem solved! *Well* then!' She suddenly claps her hands and rubs them, making Astra and the entire crew jump. 'We should get started then, should we not?'

'Shh-sure. Er, do you want to come over here?' she pats the sofa with a look of faint horror.

'Well, *of course!* I'll just sit there, by *you!*' She strides over, elbows pumping like she's power walking. It was easily the weirdest porn I'd ever shot. Already.

'Do you want me to take my clothes off?' Astra's desperately trying to be sexy, but the strain is making her perspire.

'Oh Good *Lord* yes! Get 'em orf girl! Wa-*hey!*'

'O-okay.'

Astra strips off her top and bra grimly, climbing onto Penny's lap, who's still grinning inanely and looking jolly enthusiastic and completely uncomfortable about everything. Astra leans down and kisses Penny, who starts making loud *mmm* noises, the fake way a parent does when eating a mouthful of vegetables off their kid's plate. I don't know whether to laugh or cry. But it's riveting.

Astra finally sits back, and looks Penny in the eye. Penny looks back. Astra's expression hardens into one of icy determination. It's *on.* Penny's eyes widen as Astra swoops on her and forces her tongue into her mouth. As she tries to *mmm* Astra kisses her harder, stroking and squeezing her right breast. She suddenly leans back and rips Penny's cardigan off, then reaches round amid the gollies and goshes and unzips her dress. She yanks it down with a look of triumph and leans back a little. Sitting facing her co-star, she gives a Penny a look that says: you're *gettin'* it.

After a few minutes of insistent kissing, stroking, and nuzzling of neck, Penny's in a sort of trance. She goes limp while Astra explores her breasts, which are amazing for her age, then makes her way south. She pushes Penny down onto the sofa and licks her from head to toe. It's not often I get hard filming these days, but this has a remarkable weight of reality about it. Penny's now panting, soaking wet and utterly at the mercy of Astra, who's smiling to herself I notice.

It goes great until it's Penny's turn, then the nonsense starts again. She's kissing Astra's body like she's kissing a family member. Silly little pecks here and there. At least she's stopped the *mmm*-ing. After a few seconds Astra knows what's up and starts to wriggle. She's gyrating and undulating enough to make Penny seasick. She then grabs Penny's head and pushes it against her right nipple, growling '*Suck it*, for fuck's sake! *Suck* my *nipple!*'

Penny sits up, looks at her blankly for a moment, then her eyes screw up and she just *flips*. Total. Wild. Animal. Poor little Astra – like a kitten on a rollercoaster she is. I'm trying not to laugh. This fifty-something member of the landed gentry, trying to save the family castle by getting a bit of cock in front of the cameras – now letting all her frustrations boil over on a 19-year old woman and her every erogenous zone. She bites, sucks, scratches, swearing like a salty sea dog – it's an incredible show. Might be the first time in my life I felt like I was actually exploiting someone.

Astra, with fear in her eyes, motions towards the strap-on on the sideboard. Penny lunges at it, then swears and curses as she tries to get the thing on, then, with a flourish, she rears back on her knees, hissing, 'Well then, how do you *want it*, girly?' She's like the wicked witch of the west. Except with a 9" black plastic cock strapped to her pubis.

The next 15 minutes is eye-watering stuff. On the plus side, we get two fantastic orgasms out of Astra. Penny gets a standing ovation. She leans down, kisses Astra on the cheek, then walks over to her dressing gown saying, 'Now, where's my bloody cup of tea?'

After patching them both up, we film a very moving cunnilingus scene, and Astra coaxes a hefty, grunting orgasm out of Penny. By the time it's over we all feel like we've sat through the porn equivalent of a Liszt piano concerto. I had no idea what the punters would make of it.

Two days after putting Old & Young IGL Fun 17 (Astra Starr vs.

Anna Belle) on the site, we had a flood of emails like I've never seen. The amount of downloads crashed the servers – it went viral. Everyone wanted to know who this new actress was. They wanted to know how it happened. Was it a spoof, a hoax? We had to post a new intro, explaining that this was indeed a new kid on the block. The pleas for more rolled in. A star was born.

The first call to Penny afterwards was strange. As expected. She still seemed to be in shock. She refused to see herself in action, and actually talked litigation until I told her we'd pay her £7k for one with a guy. It took only a day for her to say yes. She was in her comfort zone there, and most enthusiastic about Jonny Buck's equipment. We did two more movies before she quit. She was being offered crazy money to go and shake it in the U.S., and off she went.

I didn't hear from her again until a couple of years later. Called me up and asked would I like to visit her at her home, the estate that had set these particular wheels in motion. Naturally I was fascinated.

And so it was that we found ourselves on a huge patio overlooking the landscaped gardens, sipping Pimms no.1 on a warm summer evening in Bucks. She had a faraway look in her eyes, and spoke slowly. I got the sense she wanted me to soak it all up, to really appreciate why she'd done it all.

'This house ... was built by my great great *great* grandfather. A looong time ago.' She stopped, and I nodded ... waiting for her to continue.

'Oh yes?'

'Hm?'

'Oh, I was just saying. You said it was built by your great great grandfather.'

'Yes.'

'Mm.'

'Do you know ... *how* many women have run this house?' I opened my mouth to speak, but she said, 'One. Me.'

'Right. Hm. That's, er ...'

'I *saved* this house. To do so I had sex with ... I'm not *sure* how many people. In the United States I became a partner in an adult film company, as you probably know, and am now in talks about buying into a documentary film company. I never have to lift a finger again. Ever. This house ... *stays* the Rathbone house.'

'That's good, Penny. I'm glad you worked it out.' She turned to me, looking sincere.

'Thank you, Mr Diamond. *Eric.* It would not have happened

without you. And do give this to Astra. She was also … instrumental.' Penny reached down and took from her bag a small gift-wrapped box.

'I'll see she gets it.'

'And for you.' She passed me another, just like it. 'Just a little something.'

'Penny. I don't know what to say.'

'You needn't say anything.'

'Well, thank you. You're very kind.'

'Did I do the right thing … do *you* think?' she asked, absently.

'Well, *look* Penny. I've been in the game for a while now, and I've seen untold people do it for the same reasons, over and over again. If you're cut out for it, why not? People can clean up, get themselves set up … to do what*ever* they want. Never have another money worry, or *boss*. If they don't get a habit, that is.'

'Hm?'

'Coke?'

'Ah yes. Met a few friends of that powder in America.'

'You *would* do, yeah.'

'Indeed. Well. Would you care to stay for some supper Eric? We have a first rate chef these days.'

'You know, I think I'll hit the road, if it's all the same. Get back to *my* castle. Long drive.'

'Surely. Well. Don't be a stranger.' She smiled, and it was a joy to see that smile.

'You too, Penny.' I reached down to give her a peck on the cheek, and took the gifts with me. The last image I have of her was that sort of faraway look she had, a sort of quiet satisfaction. I can't quite put my finger on it. Heading down that drive, I felt a swell of something unusual. I think that in that moment I actually felt good about what I did with my life, and it was strange to feel that way. We all bump up against one another, in a million little ways, and we all change the course of each other's lives as we do. I didn't get into porn on some mission to make people's lives better, but I helped Penny help herself, and that felt good, made me feel humble, not the way I usually feel about my profession. I mean, there's nothing wrong with helping people get off, but it's not exactly noble is it? I'm good at it, is all. When you find something you're good at, it's hard not to see if you can make a living at it.

However, you never know, maybe this is the year I look at doing something else, maybe something genuinely noble. What, in this world, might suit an ex-pornographer?

Agent, I Stab at Thee

If you've ever worked with the general public and had to deal with some sort of aggressive drunk, or raving bag lady, or young hooligan, you will know that feeling of dread, as they make their entrance. The discomfort that crawls through you, spreading the ugliness to your brain until you want to shriek. You just want them to leave, to go far away. But you may also want them to get help, enter therapy, take the medication, or do whatever it takes to make them better. Not just because it means that they won't bother you again, but perhaps because it may feel like the whole word just became a little more sane.

Because we could all go mad, if driven there. I myself hover seemingly at the brink of lunacy at this very moment. It takes surprisingly little to push one there. It's actually quite appealing in its way. It seems to promise an end to all cares, the way I hear heroin described by wistful junkies. On paper, that is.

And how did I get here, you may ask. But I've already hinted at it, have I not? Dread is central to events. But the idea of dread that formerly constituted my sense of the word lays dead at my feet. Dread is now something *truly* visceral. Like the difference between looking at a photo of a landscape, and being part of it, breathing it, standing surrounded by its immensity.

Why? Why should this happen to *me?* Yes, why indeed. This is a question I am asking relentlessly. Not just because we are born to question, to engage in some level of philosophical enquiry as we move through life's chapters, but because it can mean our very survival. But whether I survive or not, I may just get an answer to the why of this, and in the end, that may be enough.

Although the *very* beginning could be anywhere, from the philosopher's point of view, it is most relevant to say that about three months ago I received a short story. This happened because I am a literary agent. If you look at me now you will not see the highly successful, confident and generally happy man that I was, just that brief moment ago. My life was all pinstripes and chrome, champagne and cigars, private clubs and hard-bodied young women; for I sat atop my profession, and had no reason to suspect life would ever be otherwise. Where I sit now, perched eagle-eyed on a dusty plateau above a windy, winding dirt road on a little pebble in the Adriatic, I am *very* far from that world. I am brutalised, caked in sweat-streaked dust, exhausted from weeks of adrenalin-soaked madness. And I am sad, because I miss the hard-bodied women in particular.

But I was speaking of a story. One which – most pertinently – I did not read. I know that I did not read it because a follow-up letter was sent to me, referring to the previous, with a new story enclosed. The letter said something to the effect of, Dear Mr Lewis, I note the esteemed cohort you represent and I wish to be numbered amongst them. My place is assured, but I must trust that your keen eye recognises my gift with the written word, blah blah blah. I tried not to read the story, having given up on the letter almost immediately, but then I noticed the title, and was, quite understandably, compelled to investigate.

The story was entitled *Agent, I Stab at Thee*. Though one reads many things, including offerings from the occasional deranged mind, this had a personal ring that wrong-footed me, and I would have to investigate, in order to steady myself. I took it home and climbed into a hot, foamy bath with the pages. He had not had the decency to double-space, but so be it. My eyes bored into the paper.

The style was surprisingly engaging. It had a raw, grubby quality to it. The writer, who signed his name only as Briggs, was either a talented mimic, or a genuinely raw, grubby man. He described a writer, bashing away at his black, sit-up-and-beg cast iron Remington, squirrelled away in a decrepit bedsit in South London. He evoked a forlorn atmosphere, a life barely worth living, a life of subsisting on stolen milk bottles, a world of broken windows stuffed with newspaper, of fighting in the shadows to protect the nothing he had from junk-sick thieves … a man driven to stare at the world through mad, reddened eyes and write down what he sees. My mind reeled, because I drew the conclusion that this simply could not be invented. One gets to recognise when people have lived their words, and when they have not.

Then, the writer in the story seeks out a measure of recognition. Like Bukowski, the so-called laureate of the low-life, he sought some measure of exposure, a degree of participation in the fine traditions of the Arts. So, he approaches a top agent with a sample of his work. He receives nothing. No word. Not a single solitary sentence suggesting that any commercial relationship may now, or ever, exist between writer and agent.

The writer broods, and he scowls, and he slowly screws himself up into a tiny, infinitely dense ball of hate and frustration. And then he uncurls, and patiently writes a new story, and sends it to the agent. It is called *Agent, I Stab at Thee*. It concerns a low-rent writer who wishes to be recognised, and so approaches a top agent for representation. In the story, the agent ignores him, and so he harasses the agent. More letters, strange phone calls to his house in the middle of the night, messages appearing in the pockets of his mistresses … on and on. Finally the agent decides to contact the writer and put him off. He sends a letter saying he has talent, but is not producing what the agent feels suits the market at this point. This, it would seem, was an error.

The campaign begins in earnest, with rats being released in the agent's apartment, his car being sabotaged, one of his mistresses being harassed by threatening phone calls. The agent finally tells one of his Mason friends, who soon meets a sticky end. He does not wish to invite the writer into his life with a contract, so he tries again to suggest by letter that he join another agency, and suggests he obtain a copy of the current *Writers' and Artists' Yearbook*. Finally, the writer sends another letter saying he doesn't quite know how to end the story, asking whether the agent should live, by doing the right thing and representing the writer, or should he refuse to give in, due to false pride, and die in circumstances both mysterious and seedy?

So, the main story, not the story within the story, abruptly trails off. *What*? I leapt naked and dripping from the bath to find the covering letter on my dining table, and I read it. *Of course*. It said, 'I have yet to decide on an ending, but my hope is that you recognise a talent commensurate with a formal contract of representation. I feel you are of a calibre second to none, and thus the ideal man to work with, to our mutual benefit, in the hard world of the professional wordsmith. I await your thoughts.'

I stood in the dining room, staring into space, a puddle forming at my feet. Time passed quietly until my phone rang in my jacket, and I became instantly aware of the cold, of my nakedness. I ignored the phone and went to dry off.

At first, I felt trapped. But I was not *quite* the spider in the web – I had *some* hope. After all, I was *not* in his story, and could avail myself of the many benefits of the real world, which included the police. I had no intention of being sucked into this man's reality. I would keep my head, my boundaries and my protocols. After a few minutes I started to relax. I took my phone into the lounge and curled up in a thick dressing gown with a large brandy. I returned the call, to an occasional lady friend. I thought of Briggs' story, and the mistresses. My skin crawled. I started to wonder if perhaps a meeting with a private detective might be the best move.

When one reads a great deal, there are certain characters with which one feels familiar. They are stereotypes, caricatures even, but nonetheless, we feel a certain sense of reasonable expectation when meeting them in the flesh. However, on meeting a private detective named Norris, I was *mightily* disabused of that notion - an experience no doubt common to anyone actually encountering these standard literary characters.

I was confronted with a fat, hard man who in no way impressed in terms of charisma, physical appearance or wardrobe. He was no Philip Marlowe. He was more like the kind of stolid, typecast character actor who always plays the not-too-bright cop, the one with no people smarts, the one who we never learn anything about as a person. Perhaps it was his occupation, but this chap, Norris, didn't seem inclined to give away too much about himself in any case. At his down-at-heel office in Victoria, he received myself and my story with straight-faced disinterest.

'And so you feel you are in danger?' His accent was pure London cabbie. The white English type, at least.

'I may *well* be. I don't feel inclined to take any chances.'

'I see. Here's what I can do for you. This guy Briggs was actually stupid enough to give an address. Even if it's false, it may give up something, *some* connection. Or he may in fact *be* there, in which case I'll have a word and suggest this kind of behaviour could be read as intimidating, and that he should cease and desist forthwith.'

'Yes? And then what?' I was eager to feel reassured. But I did not.

'Well, Mr Lewis, *usually* by this point the gentleman concerned has taken my *meaning* … if you take my meaning.'

'I see. Well. We'll just have to hope so, won't we? And how much do I owe you for this service?'

'I'll bill you after, but it won't be much more than a couple of hundred if I find him quick. Depends on how long it takes to track him down.'

'Fine. Here's my card, you'll call me with any information, yes?'

'Indeed I will. I'll get right to it. Don't worry.'

'No, I won't worry.' I nodded good day and left, worried. If he wasn't the real deal, his office certainly was. I made a mental note to have my clothes dry cleaned that evening.

I drove back through steady July rain, the drops one by one washing the colour from an already grey city. I toyed momentarily with moving to Tokyo, Berlin or Barcelona, somewhere with distance, colour ... and hard-bodied women. The very idea brought me levity. At the next lights I whipped out my phone and scrolled through names until I found one to get excited about. I used the hands-free to dial her.

''Ello?' Her unmusical Essex accent cheered me instantly.

'Hi, *Mel*. It's Duncan. How's tricks?'

'You, *Duncan*, can fuck *all* the way off.' Ah, I remembered.

'I see. Mel, dearest, in my defence I was in a rather *awk*ward position when last we met.'

'Don't give me *that* old bollocks. You can't bullshit a bullshitter. 'Aven't you worked that out yet?'

'Darling Mel, let us skip past all this unpleasantness, and make a date. I wish to wine and dine you as soon as humanly possible. If not sooner.'

'You mean you wish to explore my skimpiest of nighties with 'ands and tongue, and make your way slowly and deliberately inside me?'

'Ah ... well ... you certainly present a rather-'

'Stop gabbling, you twot. Make a reservation so stunning it brings tears to my eyes, then we'll see what happens. You get nice, maybe I'll get nasty.' Clunk.

You see? You see what I mean about something to get excited about? She could turn any man to jelly. Quivering, stupefied jelly. My God. She has done things to me that I would be prepared to go to hell for. Or if not go to hell, then at least receive a serious telling-off from a member of the clergy.

That evening, we nestled in a soft, lipstick-red leather booth in a fabulous restaurant in Chelsea. By dessert I had charmed my way back into Melinda's good books, and had an erection like a lead pipe. She was sticking her stockinged foot in my crotch and grinding along my length, giggling filthily, eyes twinkling in candlelight. I was breathing hard, the blood pounding in my ears, the wine sloshing drunkenly through my veins. Briggs was by this point a ghost, a fading, laughable idea. I was safe. I was safe and secluded behind layers of opaque, bulletproof exclusivity, untouchable, in a whole other glossy dimension, utterly separate from his miserable, seedy, monochrome world.

Mel and I giggled at each other and poked fun, we drank and we flirted, we exchanged strokes and pinches beneath the table, we made obscene oral gestures with our food. We would have romped like chimpanzees on ecstasy, had we had the place to ourselves. She said she had to visit the lady's bathroom, squeezing my crotch as she left.

I sat back and sipped the wine, closing my eyes and breathing it in, letting its delicate flavours play their music. After a minute I revived, let my gaze leave the booth and wander across to the other diners. It came to rest on a gorgeous young thing who was evidently with her mother. Blonde curls fell down her dark purple dress to her laudably plunging neckline. I could touch her generous breasts with my eyes, I knew precisely the feel and heft of them. Only the nipples remained aloof and mysterious. I wanted her desperately. The waitress approached, offering a fresh bottle. I agreed, just to engage her. This one dark, full-figured. I mentally clasped her hips and pulled her down onto me, pressing into her with delicacy and restraint, before ramming myself-

'I'm *back*, darling!'

'Ah! *Good* Lord! Indeed you are! My sweet. My one and only. My juiciest of morsels.'

'I can't be bothered with coffee. Let's get back to yours. My enthusiasm was running down my leg when I went for a pee.'

'How delightfully awful of you, sweetness. Let's away.'

I sent Mel out to hail a cab while I paid, rather than wait the extra two minutes for one to be called. We jumped in and agitated for the driver to take the fastest route possible. As Mel bit my neck and twisted my nipple, my phone rang. I wrestled it out of my jacket to find it was one of my main clients, a relentlessly top ten author who shall remain anonymous. Let's call him Ryan.

'*Ryan*! A very good evening to you! How *are* you?'

'How am *I*? I assume you are going to deny all knowledge of the jiffy bag full of *shit* I received today, that had one of *your* business cards sticking out of it?'

I went numb, the blood and wine drained from my skull. I couldn't hear anything for a few moments, then my system burned with adrenalin. 'Um, I don't … I don't know what to *say*. Ryan, you couldn't *possibly* imagine this had anything to do with me?'

'No, rationality says you had a peripheral involvement at best, but you had better find out what is going on! *This*, I *don't* need!' He slammed the phone down so hard that I felt as though he'd done so on the top of my head.

'S-sorry darling, just give me a moment, would you?'

'Whass the matter?' She looked dishevelled and, to my suddenly sober eyes, rather a cheap, distasteful wreck.

'Look, I better drop you off and just- *oof*! Dear *God* in heaven!' She had immediately thumped my groin.

'You don't *drop* me off! *Pig*! We've got a *date*!'

'Ah … you're right, of course …'

'*Yes*, that's *right*,' she said soothingly, stroking my cheek with her knuckles. 'Mama's going to take *good* care of you. And you're going to take good care of mama, yes?'

'Oh, indeed … s-sweetness.'

Mel made herself at home, putting on music and dancing around in her stockinged feet, making drinks, eating a cheesecake from the fridge, smoking one of my cigars. I was still nursing my abused groin, head spinning from the call with Ryan, when I noticed that I had a string of missed calls, voicemails and texts from clients. I couldn't bring myself to listen. Neither to my home answering machine, which said it held 22 messages.

Briggs.

Undoubtedly. I was hunched over, biting my nails, when I felt ice pouring down my neck! The shock took my breath away, before I bounded to my feet, shaking like a madman to loose the ice cubes from my shirt. 'What the *fucking shit?!*'

'Fuck *you*, arsewipe!' Mel was holding a piece of paper as though it were a smoking gun. She spat on it and slammed me hard against my left cheek. It stuck for a moment, then slid off, fluttering to the parquet floor as she took her coat and sailed out of my living room door. The front door slammed and I sagged to my knees, then tremulously picked up and read the piece of paper before me.

'Dear Miss, you should know that while you were in the toilet, your gentleman friend was eyeing up every other woman in there, especially the brunette waitress and the young blonde lady with the older lady. He was practically dribbling. He's no good.'

I felt sick. *Briggs*. Could he be *this* proactively demented? Surely he couldn't imagine that this would persuade me? It couldn't be just about me not taking him on. Could he be an industrial spy, sent in by one of my competitors, trying to bury me? Wait – the story said …

After changing my shirt I went into my office and looked up the submissions database. And there he was. I'd never clocked his name until reading the *Agent* story, but he had several stories in there. I insisted that all physical submissions be scanned and added to the database, along with those sent by email. I found the previous one he'd sent, called *The Gatekeepers*. I sat in the darkened office squinting at my computer, nursed by a glass of Talisker. I read with fascination.

He'd described the frustration, the fury, the disempowerment that arose from his dealings with literary agents. Their intransigence, their refusal to deal with people, to talk to them. He created a picture of them hiding in a remote fortress, behind high, thick walls, their battlements lined with P.A.s, secretaries and other intermediaries. He drew parallels with ministers of state, with CEOs, people in the public eye who were almost entirely protected from the public.

I had never had an opportunity to see this point of view, to experience this aching sense of despair he described. In my position there was nothing not open to me. That I could think of.

Briggs' other stories were mostly of the outsider character, living with his nose pressed up against the glass, on the opposite side of which lay the rest of society. One mixed only with other marginalised beings, eking out an existence in the gloomy periphery. This world he showed me was so utterly alien, I could not relate to it in the slightest. I could not imagine the kind of reader who'd wish to indulge in this kind of study. There are many modern ills of which I would hope my children would know nothing, if I were ever to *have* children. But I simply had no taste for his work, and knew no one who might. Certainly not in commercially viable quantities. I could not help him, but I did not deserve to be hounded, persecuted, attacked for this. He was turning my people against me … perhaps hoping to see me fall far enough that I'd see the world through his eyes.

I gave up and phoned Norris to report the evening's events. He took it all down, grunting, asking the occasional question to check details. He said he was on the case, and not to worry. I then retired to bed, after locking every door and window securely. I eventually slept, but not well.

When I awoke, Briggs was my first thought. As long as I could handle the immediate situation, it would surely dissolve. Especially if Norris got to him. Buoyed by my positive thinking, I bounced out of bed and called my P.A., Nessa. I gabbled at her, told her what fire-fighting actions to take regarding Ryan in particular, and said I'd be in the office by ten. I soaped in the shower, and felt better when thinking of her making calls and checking in with clients. She was a devastating creature, picked largely for her capacity, like Mel, to subdue men. Believe me, it is vital when one deals largely with male clients, all of whom are being constantly tempted by other agents. You need every possible trick up your sleeve.

Not entirely to my surprise, there was a suspiciously squishy jiffy bag in my mailbox. I would let Norris deal with it. Outside, I approached my car, and slowed. I looked left and right, then crouched to peer underneath. I could see no obvious bomb – as if *I* knew what a car bomb looked like. I called a cab, and waited rather self-consciously for it to arrive. I thought of hiring another private detective, or calling the police. Just then, I got a call from a number I did not recognise.

'Mr Lewis?'

'Speaking.'

'My name is Christopher Perkins, I'm Mr Norris's solicitor.'

'Oh yes? Is there something I ought to know?'

'Well, Mr Norris thought so. He was arrested at 5 am this morning and taken to a local police station, where he's being held for offences relating to child pornography.' My eyes widened, words failed me. 'Yes, it's a shock. However, he maintains complete innocence. He thought you ought to know the situation, as he said he thinks this may relate to the case he was working on for you.'

'Oh my. My goodness. Yes. Jesus *God*. I ... I find this rather difficult to take on board.'

'I can imagine. However, we'll get to the bottom of it. It just may take a little time.'

'God. Did he say he'd found anything at all on the man Briggs?'

'Mr Norris's home is sealed off. It will of course be thoroughly searched by police.'

'Well, if he has something, maybe they'll find it.'

'We shall see. That's not something I can intervene in.'

'Right. Of course. What should I do? Did he tell you much about the Briggs situation?'

'He said he didn't think you had anything to worry about.'

'Oh good.'

'Until now.'

He rang off, and I stood and stared at my shoes. I swallowed hard and looked about me, with what were by now misty eyes. I suddenly heard the music from Cape Fear in my head and thought of the name Max Cady. I shivered.

The cab dropped me near my office in Pall Mall, and as I walked past a phone box it began ringing. I knew it was Briggs. It was classic. I stopped and stared, and the ringing only got louder. My eyes burned into the receiver, daring it to continue. Finally it stopped, and I realised I'd been holding my breath. I exhaled and then jumped as the phone rang again. I reached and grabbed the receiver. 'Yes?'

'Mr Lewis. At last we meet. You know who I am?'

'I know.'

'I think not. However, the main thing is, I have your attention. Or at least, I hope I do. Would *you* say that I have your attention?'

'You do indeed, Briggs. But *why*? Why all *this*? This harassment? This *madness*! You need to understand something. You have to deal with people honestly and fairly and lawfully, not try to bully them into getting what you want.'

'The irony. Oh! *Mister* Lewis. Do you have any idea what Confucius, Eva Perón and Da Vinci have in common?'

'What?'

'I thought so.'

'*Pleeease* get to the point! You are going to be in a *great* deal of trouble with the police, and for what? Have you just flipped? Are you *mad*?'

'Well, by the standards of *this* society, I hardly think so. My mental state is absolutely consistent with a man of conscience trying to live in a world in which we all tacitly accept brutality, inequality and immoral behaviour, as simply an everyday fact and facet of our socio-cultural fabric.'

'Oh *God* in heaven. *Really*, Briggs? What *is* this about?'

'Didn't you just hear me?'

'I heard what you said, but what do you want from *me*?'

'I wanted you to *listen*, Mr Lewis. It seems you are incapable of even that. Well, perhaps that is why you are the man you are.'

'Look. I've had *enough* of this. I will *not* be toyed with! I shall go to the police and they will see to you. I am fairly sure you have committed a number of serious crimes already, and-' Clunk. He hung up. I stood transfixed for I don't know how long, before slamming down the receiver myself.

In the three weeks between receiving that call and finding myself sitting here on this rock, I've been nearly run over twice, had a formerly amenable prostitute tie me to my own bed and leave me until the maid arrived the next morning, come home to find my walls spray painted with men copulating – for some reason – and, let's see … had my bank account defrauded, my office raided by the vice squad, I have made some extremely ugly headlines, and been dropped by all but two of my clients, both of whom are, I believe, senile.

I finally got a note telling me that it would all end, if I came here, to this place on this island, on this day, alone. And so I sit here, upon a brass map of the area, set into a flat rock, and I meditate on dread, feeling half crazed. And I dread what comes next.

And surely, we will soon know. A car approaches, curving around the thin roads, dust thrown up and immediately pushed sideways by the breeze. It feels cartoonish, like he won't *really* get out of the car. It draws near, pulls up a dozen yards away. I can see someone in the driver's seat. Out he comes. Medium height, jeans and t-shit, sunglasses. He's in his late twenties perhaps, dark, unshaven, walks with a kind of animal pride.

'Hello, Mr Lewis.'

'*Briggs.* You're much younger than I expected.'

'You look a state.'

'Mm.'

'So, go ahead.' He looks cheerful, self-satisfied.

'What?'

'Ask me.'

'No.'

'What?'

'No, I'm not going to indulge in any more of your bullshit. Whatever you have to say, whatever speech you want to give, just get on with it. This is obviously personal, you're obviously a *monstrous* fuck-up. So get the hell on with it, then *fuck off.*'

'Are you trying to upset me?' I just look at him levelly. He'll not draw me in. 'Still the man behind the fortress wall.' He snorts, then purses his lips in thought. I relax, feeling that whatever is coming has already lost its power. What more can he possibly do to me? 'Mr Lewis, there is a *reason* I wanted to meet you *here*. Can you think what that might be?'

'No, of course I fucking can't, you madman.'

'Then I'll tell you. I was conceived, just over the water there, in Venice.' He stares at me from behind those dark glasses, casually pointing over his shoulder with his thumb. He comes closer and sits before me, cross-legged on the gravel. He waits for the moment when I should say something, then cocks his head to one side and raises his eyebrows. I wait, and he waits, then raises his eyebrows again, and now I feel it. Ice water, trickling down my spine. Cramp in my bowels. He sees it. '*Yes*,' he says gravely. I feel nauseous. I know what's coming. I wave a hand at him, trying to swat it away; I feel the weeks of torment catching up, a dam breaking, my mouth fills with saliva. I get to my feet, legs weak, and stagger over to the lone pine that stands with us. I take a deep breath and vomit noisily at its base. The words are tumbling in my head, tumbling in my stomach, the images rise up and I vomit again, as if to purge them. 'I see it's all coming back to you.' He takes his time, a note of satisfaction in his voice. '*What* was it you said? We must deal with people *honestly … fairly* and *lawfully?* Not bully them into getting what we want?'

'Jesus …' It's all I can say. A flashback of me singing in the school choir … then of raven hair spread out on the bed, full lips, my arms, muscular in my youth, my laughter, her head shaking, her voice saying No, over and over again. I try to make that voice say it playfully, I scream it in my mind, I *need* her to want me. And I want to find some moral high ground to clamber upon … I cast around, my gut aching. I fall to my knees. Everything is pain.

'Maria Fanucci.' The words twist inside me, I can't believe my ears. Surely the past is the fucking past. It should stay there. He reads my mind. 'That's the thing, Mr Lewis. The things you *do … stay done.* I was swimming around in those nuts of yours a quarter of a century ago. And there I should have stayed. But you clapped your eyes on Maria Fanucci, and … well. The rest is history.'

I look back and he's still sat there, half smiling at me from behind those sunglasses. I get the mad thought that I've imagined the whole thing. That of *course* this is not true. I would never do such a thing. I *could* never do such a thing. But there are no words for this moment, if it be true. I think to speak of regret, of apology, but this is not what he wants or needs. He has the self-possession of an African dictator, the calm of a Zen Buddhist. He has closed some loop, and seems to need nothing more.

I feel broken.

A minute passes, and the sound of the insects comes to me, the breeze, whipping dust across the tiny plateau. Out over the Adriatic the sun shimmers atop that sapphire blue expanse. Even in this, the most deeply anguished moment of my life, there is something perfect. The stillness takes me. I spit, the wind whips it off down the hillside. I move, the million complaints of my body go with me, back to the rock, where I slump down again, facing him. He takes his glasses off and our eyes meet. He is my son. But in this moment he feels more like my father. Part of me is weeping. Part of me is dying. The moment hangs in the air, longer and longer.

I see us as two skeletons, facing each other. Two bags of bones. With organs, and the many systems, circulatory, respiratory, limbic, nervous. And the capacity to stop our own bleeding, to heal cuts, to flush toxins. My mind looks out from this biological miracle, at this glorious natural wonder. My soul experiences the world and feels love for it. My heart is joyful, and breaking at the same time.

He stands, looks around us. He looks back at me with an expression I cannot adequately describe. Perhaps redolent of a priest.

'I'm Carlo,' he says, extending his hand. Without thinking I wipe my hand on my trousers and I lean forward to shake his hand. My jaw opens and closes but my tongue does nothing. I want to ask who Briggs really was. I want to tell him why I keep my distance from the public, show him the scar.

My son puts his shades back on and turns to leave. He pauses, for just a moment, then continues.

I want to call out, to tell him I will see to it that he is published, that his stories will be told. But as he gets in his car, starts the engine and leaves, drifting quietly back down the hill and out of sight, I feel that he has done so. He has told the most important story of his life, to me.

The shock of it all is extraordinary.

After some time: Now what? The question asks itself, over and over again, but my mind is blank. I try to think of what is most important, what single thing I should take from this, but somehow it all looks the same. It is as though a reset has occurred, and now I must make my way back to the world and take all at face value, one thing at a time.

Perhaps I will feel compelled to confess, or perhaps I will choose to live with my deeds silent, my revelations secret. I think about this and feel no particular attraction to either option. I am certain only that I desire a little water, to swill my mouth out, and more to drink, and yet more to bathe. And then a meal, then sleep. I am stripped bare, hollowed out by truth. What will reassert itself in the morning, of the self I was before, I have yet to discover.

The Women in the Woods

Ben brushed his way heavily through the densest part of the woods, enjoying fighting through trees rather than people. He shouldered his way through thickets, brambles pulling at him, leaves and branches whipping and slapping at him. Eventually his pace slowed, the need to fight subsiding. He paused to absorb the gentle September rain, the smell of mud and wet leaves, the quiet. He leaned back against a tree and watched his breath condense in clouds before him, wiped his hands on his jeans. Closing his eyes, he allowed himself to *catch up* with himself.

After a minute or two he moved on, picking his way more gently, stepping over or around, rather than through, angst from a week of the city dropping away. His mood lifted, just as the sun began to glow through the thinning early autumn murk overhead. The light shifted subtly, and a break in the clouds sharpened the foreground, the woodland becoming edged and vivid. He came to a small clearing where a tree had collapsed, felled from within by fungi and insects, and from without by woodpeckers, wind and time. He noticed something etched into a tree which stood respectfully beside its fallen sibling. What was it? A symbol, maybe. Or a letter, or initials? He leaned down, squinting up close, but couldn't make it turn into anything he recognised. He pulled out his phone and took a snap of it. A half moon facing right, with another, facing left, midway down, making a kind of overlapping S. The base of the lower curve and the top of the upper curve were connected by a wavy line. There were half a dozen or so dots and dashes around the S, seemingly at random.

He stood back, looking around, trying to give it some context. He turned the name of the woodland over in his mind, trying to think of anything historically that might be connected. He was in Leigh Woods, which ran along the south side of Avon Gorge in Bristol, blanketing the top and flowing down the hillside to the river, which was spanned dramatically by Brunel's suspension bridge. But the tree had to be less than a century old, suggesting that the symbol could have been carved into the bark any time from the 1900s to the 1930s. He pondered it for another minute or so, but came up dry. Nothing. He scratched his head, pulling a comically puzzled look. It seemed appropriate. He shrugged, thought *whatever*, and headed off through the other side of the clearing.

Ben's mind emptied as he walked, making measured progress, parting foliage and stepping over obstacles smoothly, feeling his way into a rhythm, working with nature, rather than blundering through it. Time passed quietly, punctuated only by the swish of branches, the soft squelch and suck under foot, his deep but measured breathing, the soft whoosh and rustle of treetops in the breeze. A sudden movement stopped him still, his left hand shot out reflexively to catch a trunk, and he pushed himself slightly back behind it. His eyes narrowed, picking out a figure crossing from right to left, about thirty yards ahead. It was a woman, walking slowly with a dog, a lurcher. He couldn't make himself move. There was something about the woman that transfixed him. He couldn't place it. She was slim, in a green waxed jacket and tight jeans, her curly, reddish hair falling in damp tresses to her shoulders, long slender legs slipped into black wellington boots. As she passed, seemingly in slow motion, he frowned, trying to understand why he was so captured by the sight of her, by the moment. She glanced briefly in his direction, but if she had seen him, she didn't show it. In moments she was gone, just a flicker between distant branches, then nothing, silence.

He raised a hand to the top of his head, running it over his dark hair back and forth, eyes glazed, more musing than vexed. He peered into the depths of time, but found only an impenetrable, swirling haze, impossible to find anything in. For the second time in a matter of minutes he was baffled. Could it just be the stress of the week catching up? A trick of the light? The shock of suddenly encountering another person after such meditative solitude?

He moved on, his mind gently turning the images of the symbol and the woman over and over. He found the main path after a few minutes, followed it back to the car park. He got into his car and pulled the door closed with a solid thunk, then stared ahead, into the woods, unfocussed. After a while he shook his head, started the engine and headed home.

That night, Ben dreamed of the woods. It was filled with figures which he understood to be a sentient hybrid of human and tree. They pulled vaguely at him as he passed, they danced and swayed, calling to each other, whispering to him. And then, there she was. Crisp and clear and dead ahead. She strode, smiling, slow, sensual, her tongue just visible, running over her lower lip gently, side to side. She looked at him, eyes seeing through him, pulling him forward, a vortex of lust, a look of command, eyes aflame, cold reptilian smile … he sagged, stumbled to his knees, unable to withstand the Look In Her Eyes. He crawled forward, his erection carving a furrow in the mud, the sound of laughter, wind, a cool voice on the breeze calling his name: Ben … *Ben*!

His eyes snapped open, blinking in the gloom; his heart was thudding. He strained to hear, to make sense of the moment, to guess the hour. He reached over and snapped on a low red light, narrowed his eyes, let his mind come clear. He lay back, letting his breath out, still feeling the mood of the dream, seeing her approaching. His mind flicked back and forth, between his memory of her in the woods, and the figure that came to him by night. He felt his erection tenting the quilt, and gave it a reassuring squeeze. At least that was real, neither fleeting nor imagined, but solid in his hand. He pictured the dream woman and squeezed it again, stroked it absent-mindedly, wondering about her, about who she really was, and why she should so affect him after a single, momentary, one-sided encounter. And he wondered what she looked like under the waxed jacket and jeans. In his mind, then, she was the bored housewife, out with the dog, looking for a casual liaison .. then she was a high-class whore, who he could buy, then and there, a hard fuck against a tree while the dog chased squirrels … then she was a lonely widow in need of some measure of intimacy, then a swinging singleton, then the love of his life, his soul mate, who loved fucking him, anytime, anywhere, anyhow. This image, the perfect other, eased him into fantasies that took him all the way, the moments before orgasm electrified with visions of her open mouth, her full breasts, her milky skin, her soft curling pubic hair …

Ben exhaled long and deep, tissued himself dry, his mind suddenly springing free of the bear-trap of desire, erotic thought dissolving in the stillness. He leaned on one elbow to look for anything with the time on it. He grabbed at his phone clumsily, off balance, just managing to stop it sliding off the nightstand. He pushed at the buttons and it blinked on, making him squint. It was just before eight in the morning. Sunday. Ben hmphed at the phone, put it back and rolled over, pitching straight back into sleep.

It was two hours before he resurfaced. His first thought was about what time it was. His second was about dreams, his third: the woman. In the shower, he washed slowly, musing deeply. When he managed to sweep aside the fading curtains of lust, he could see through into the back room, a cluttered, murky, dusty place of old objects, old images: monochrome, yellowed, curled at the edges. He could find nothing of note, nothing to guide him to this woman, or her significance. The question was, why *did* the sight of her pin him to the spot? He could picture high cheekbones, dark eyes, big soft lips, a wide jawline and a long neck, but he couldn't put them all together into a single image. Was he making it up? Exaggerating? Had he *really* seen her that clearly?

By lunchtime he was thinking of little besides. It even occurred to him to try to find his way back to the same spot, see if he could figure out her route. But, that would be a bit weird, he decided. By lunchtime he found himself trying to sketch what he'd seen. He sat at his desk in the attic office, watery sunlight falling through the skylight and onto the page. He sketched and erased over and over, into the gloom of evening, when he lit several candles and crowded them in around himself. Hunger washed acidly around his gut, burning and gurgling its need, until finally he relented. Pins and needles made him wince as he stood; he took a moment to massage life back into his legs. He leaned over the drawing and took it in; a ghostly woodland at the edges, solidifying towards the centre; the woman walked, almost glided toward it from the right, the arc of her dog slipping between trees, just behind her. He stared some more, trying to force meaning from it, but like an itch he couldn't scratch, like a name he couldn't remember, it refused to satisfy him.

The moment he got to the top of the steep attic stairs, something inside clunked into place. He had to sit a moment, and let the thoughts come clear. The memories stirred, spiralling up slowly from way down, coming in waves; the woman in the woods ... something he'd seen before ... something drawn or painted ... it was ... it was on a *wall* ... *some*where he'd been ... long ago ... an old house ... at the bottom of some stairs ... that's *it*! His great grandfather and great auntie's house ... in Broadstairs, in Kent. A hand flew up to rub his forehead as he stared, frowning, into the past ... yes, that was *it* ... a woman in the woods, in a painting, in their house ...

He tried to crystallise the memory into detailed imagery, but it was as if the resolution was too low, and however much he tried to mentally zoom in on the painting, it would not come into focus. So what next, then? Alfred, his great grandfather, had been dead some years, more than ten, surely? His sister, who he'd lived with since the war, was she still alive? He couldn't recall any news that she'd died, but then they hadn't been close.

Half an hour later he was sat in his lounge, curled up in a leather recliner with pizza, and his ipod on shuffle through the stereo. He let his mind drift for a while, trying to take a break from the questions. But, when faced with the option of thinking about work in the morning instead, he voted to go back to the woman, the woods, the painting. He reached over for his phone and sent a text to his mother. 'Hi, how r things? Q: is Great Auntie Jean still alive? I want t get in touch if so.' He let it slip from his hand onto the coffee table beside him. The music had changed to *Farewell*, the soundtrack to the finale of Blade Runner. It gave him pause. He'd wept, the last time he'd watched it. Rutger Hauer's final moments; the illumination, the realisation that life is the most tender, fragile and precious gift. He thought of Alfred and Jean, and wondered if that painting was precious to them, or just something they'd ended up with. He thought about what it must have been like, the siblings parting for the last time, after living together for seven decades.

Moments later the phone rang, and as he guessed he would, he heard his mother's voice.

'Hello dear, how *are* you?'

'I'm okay mum, thanks. And how are *you* doing?'

'Very well, thank you. You were asking about Jean?'

'Yes. It'll sound ridiculous, maybe … but it's about a painting they used to have … I think at the bottom of the stairs, in the hallway. You remember?'

'Yes, the lady in the woods. Great granddad painted it.' Ben sat back. His eyes narrowed, his brow furrowed.

'*Really?*'

'You don't remember? He painted in the conservatory.'

'No, I … oh … *wwaait* … no, I can *pic*ture it … *kind* of … the easel, in the corner. Huh. I just haven't thought of it since.'

'Well, it was a long time ago. You were just a boy when Alfred died.'

'*Really? That* long ago? Well, that explains it. What about Jean?'

'She's *very* old, love. She's in a home now.'

'Well … s*sooo* … *why* don't I know this?'

'Well, there was some kind of falling out. Jean always had a reputation as a bit of a battle-axe, if you must know. When your father and I divorced ... *she* went with *him*.'

'Hm. Hmmm. Hm.'

'What *are* you humming about Ben?'

'Well ... it's about the painting, you see ... so ... well, I'd like to ask her about it.'

'I see. I have the address and phone number of the home somewhere, though I've no idea how much help she might be. Like I said: very old, bit of a battle-axe.'

Ben took the address down, thanked her and rang off. He had no idea how useful she might be either, but he was determined to find out. He rang the home and a Jamaican woman told him she was a livewire on her day, but often just a grouch, and *of course* he could visit. The next day at work he asked his boss for the Friday off; a family matter, he added darkly. His boss looked upon him softly and nodded.

He did his best to concentrate through the rest of the day, but recruitment consultancy was just not able to offer the same mystery as his weekend. The more the desperate faces loomed before him – imploring him to solve their problems by producing a job, any job, enough to save their finances, their marriage, their dignity – the more desperate he felt to escape, to just get in the car and drive. He found himself asking a couple of them absently if they'd ever considered becoming a detective, either with the police, or privately. There's money in it, steady work, he murmured, while doodling a tree behind his computer monitor. He had no takers though, and only succeeded in getting a few quizzical glances from colleagues.

At lunchtime he wandered the shelves of Waterstones, leaving with two Philip Marlowe novels and a Mickey Spillane. He'd thumbed a few by Elmore Leonard, but decided to work his way there chronologically.

Walking around the city centre, the usual hubbub now seemed to be simmering with intrigue; *this* woman: what was *her* deal? That intriguing half smile she wore as she came out of Boots with an eager bounce in her step ... *that* guy: what was he nodding so *seriously* at, as he listened intently to his phone? *This* young lady: surely the guy she was with was *too* old for her? What, he wondered, were these people *up* to? *Were* their lives riddled with drama and intrigue, or was it just his imagination? Was it even *possible* to avoid the black skies, howling winds and driving rains of the human heart? He sighed. It just was *not* all sunshine.

The rest of the week followed the same pattern, and Ben sank deeper into his detective novels, finishing all three, between bus journeys, evening, bath and bedtime. It stopped him thinking too deeply about the women in the woods. Commuting, and his lunchtime wander around town, had several times had his heart leap and sink as he thought he saw her. Often out of the corner of his eye she would stand there staring, or walk past, glancing over at him, but when he looked it would be a woman who looked nothing like her, or a guy, or on one occasion, a post box covered in flyers for a dubstep night. The essence of this torment was tantalising, oddly pleasurable, and when Friday arrived, he was ready to continue into the story.

The long drive gave him hours to ponder it, and he turned it over, and over again. The radio burbled nonsense at him; he didn't take in a word. Chief among his questions for Jean was: Who was she? And, Where had great granddad known her? Why had he been so captivated? Maybe he'd seen her in a dream, or another painting, or just made her up. Was the woodland setting literal or allegorical? Alfred had never been married, so far as he knew. It could be the most crashing anti-climax ... yet he was willing to bet that it would not be. He felt it so strongly, from the moment he saw *his* woman in the woods, that this was something that was going to *mean* something, and stay with him. He'd imagined all kinds of scenarios, many of them non-sexual. Some where he wasn't the object of *her* attention. One or two which didn't even end happily.

Approaching the rest home, just a few streets back from the seafront on the Kentish coast, he felt a sudden lurch in his stomach as he let the thought come: this is a waste of time. His heart thumped as he turned off the radio, then the engine. He paused with his hand on the button to unclip his seat belt. An internal voice counselled a rapid about face. Better the eternal lyrical fantasy, surely, than the excellent chance of it becoming a laughably washed-out, beige reality, a frowsy, bedraggled, unloved thing that would leave him the emptier for having breathed its air. 'Chin up sport, this is *your* time!' counselled another voice, more devil-may-care, more dashing, well-dressed and popular with the ladies. It added a few more mental images, smoothly arguing for the romance of the thing. '*Romance is All!*' another voice exclaimed suddenly, this one sounding definitely feminine. He took a moment to listen for more, but they were silent. It was all on him now. He nodded, cleared his throat, and got out. He took a deep breath, then walked up to the door and rang the bell.

It opened with a gale of bonhomie and stasis; the bright, toothy greeting of Mrs Archer, the portly matron with whom he'd spoken a few days prior. She lead him cheerfully inside, into the grey miasma that surrounds great age, composed of soft furnishings, central heating, pot pourri and very old skin. He grimaced, trying to bully his expression into an easy smile, but instead produced a rictus that eerily mirrored one or two of the more cadaverish visages before him, sat silently running out the clock in high backed chairs. He was out of practice with truly old people, and was finding it hard going.

Mrs Archer lead him to the large conservatory at the back of the home, and Ben tried to spot Great Auntie Jean as early as possible so he could compose himself. But she stopped by a blue patterned chair with a high curving back which faced out into the garden, so he had to come around to set eyes on her, for the first time in two decades. Her face was long and rather grey; her eyes were intelligent, but lifeless, her white hair scraped back in a bun. He thought briefly of the teenage girls he saw in Bristol rocking the not dissimilar 'Croydon facelift' look. Her mouth curved down in perpetual disapproval, her lips a limpid mauve, her skeletal hands crossed in her lap. She gave the impression that she was awaiting the end, with absolutely no feelings about it either way. It was a horror to a thirty year old.

'Jeanie, dear? You have a visitor. Your great nephew, Ben.' Mrs Archer reached down to pat her gently on the hand, leaving it there until Jean returned from wherever her mind had been. She looked up slowly, first at Mrs Archer, then, with a movement that seemed calculated to convey just what a hassle it was, she turned further and peered blankly at Ben. The grin froze on his face, he counted the milliseconds, then couldn't stand it any longer.

'Hi Je- ... *Auntie* Jean. Ha. *Great* Auntie. Great Aun-'

'Hello ... *Ben*. How are *you*? You've grown, it seems.'

'Ah, ha *ha*! *Yes*! Yes I have, Great, er ... Yes. I ... am, *thirty*. Thirty years old.' He grinned, feeling horribly warm.

'You were shorter.'

'I would have been, yes.' He glanced sidelong at Mrs Archer, who was standing there with an encouraging grin which she waved over each of them in turn, luxuriating in the contact between client and visitor. This, she seemed to be communicating, was what made her job worthwhile.

'Why have you come?' asked Jean with apparent indifference.

'I, er.' He realised that getting to the matter in hand was his best bet. 'Well. It's about a painting. It was hanging at the bottom of your stairs, I think. A woman, in a woodland?' He was studying her face intimately as he spoke, watching for the first sign of either recognition or ignorance. So much seemed to hinge on the next few moments.

'The *Lady* in the Woods. One of Alfred's.' She narrowed her eyes and lanced him with them. 'Why do you want to know about it? Why now?'

'Well, to tell you the truth … look, do you mind if I pull up a chair?' He looked at Mrs Archer for help, who finally realised he was asking for a seat. The benevolent smile cooled, and she walked over to the nearest chair, that had been set beside another resident, and without asking dragged it over. She parked it awkwardly so that Ben had to move it the rest of the way himself. The matron gave him a peculiarly childish smile then took her leave. Ben shook his head and sat.

'Jean. I'm interested because I saw someone in the woods last weekend, a woman, just out walking her dog, and I … well, it just stopped me dead. I didn't know why. But then later on, I remembered that I'd seen an image like that in a painting once. And *then* I remembered, that I had seen that painting in your old house. *So*, I wanted to ask you about it.'

'Indeed. Ask away.' There was no warmth there, but she was not exactly cold either. It seemed more that she simply saw all experience as the same these days. Utterly without significance.

'Well, er … what can you tell me about it?'

'Your great grandfather, as I presume you are aware, lost his wife during the war. Pneumonia. But they had a son, your grandfather. I was to be married, but my beau never returned from France. So we shared a home, and raised your grandfather together, just a few miles from here. I never married, and neither did Alfred. That lady was a ghost. She may as well have been. He saw her only once, he *claimed*. He drew her, he painted her, many times, but he did not speak of her. He was an austere man, quite undemonstrative …' Jean paused, her eyes focusing on events many decades past. 'But, he seemed to place all his love in her. She was a kind of muse, I suppose, but … I think he wanted some sort of … *immortal* love, not the flesh and blood that he had lost already. War does *strange* things to emotions, don't you know … makes them disproportionately large or small. An undying love is what he had with the lady in the woods.' She turned a rheumy eye toward him, lit with the faintest hint of warmth. 'Maybe they met in heaven.'

This last stayed with him the whole drive back. He felt quite emotional, strangely shaken. Finding he had drifted into some of the deepest, most sacred parts of his great grandfather's life affected him. He saw a haunting series of images: Alfred returning from the war, not to her arms, but to her grave; of Jean opening the letter that regretted to inform her of the death of her fiancé; of the two of them growing old in that house, just the occasional visit from Alfred's son and family; and images of each of them in their single beds, going to sleep every night with the fading pictures of their loved ones in their minds. The sheer nightmare loneliness and heartbreak of it anguished Ben. He was tortured by the idea of someone living their life looking backward, nursing the fragile past, giving so little nourishment to the present. He resolved to find his lady in the woods.

The next morning, a Saturday, he hatched a plan.

'Hello?' A dreamy female voice, early thirties.

'Hi Cate, it's me.' Ben, at his most self-consciously winning.

''Ello *you*! How you doin'?' A cheerful rise in pitch.

'I'm good. Listen. A favour. *Or*, let me do you one.'

'Ben, you intrigue me.' Game on.

'Ok. I need to borrow your dog. *Or*, to put it another way, would you like me to walk your dog for you?'

'You pick.'

'The latter then. Or, a third option, we could walk Brian together.'

'*When* is this all happening?'

'How about tomorrow lunchtime?'

'Err … should be okay. I have to do a food shop, but I can do that early doors.'

'Alright then. You want to pick up me up at midday? Since you've got the doggy boot?'

'Sure. Well, this'll be fun.'

'Maybe. Just maybe.'

Ben put the phone down, sat back, smiled the smile of the proactive. He even chuckled a little he-he-he for effect. He was terribly pleased with his masterstroke. It seemed to him that the only way that the British engage strangers outside of commercial exchange, structured recreation or faulty public transport, is via the slightly eccentric world of dog walking, and it would be his way in, if he saw *her*. He saw the band of local dog owners in the vertiginous park near his house most days, clustered together in mostly dog-based conversation, while their dogs were having a whale of a time together, chasing each other and sniffing one another's bums. The limitations of it all didn't seem to matter. The fact that social exchange took place was enough, a modern miracle, a hold-out, a last bastion of free conversation among citizens.

Feeling full of it, he had another bright idea: join the library. That way he could get in another few dozen detective novels for free. He biked into the city with ipod on shuffle, turning up a curious mix of songs. First The Byrds' *Jesus is Just Alright*, then a major change of pace to Ministry's *Jesus Built My Hotrod*, and finally easing out with Jah Wobble's *Becoming More Like God*. As he locked his bike up outside the central library he pondered the chances of getting three religious-themed songs back-to-back, wondering if it was the work of some wit who wrote the shuffle algorithm, lacing a joke into its workings on his last day in the job.

Walking up the steps into the beautiful old building he wondered if God and Jesus Themselves might be up there, chuckling over his failure to realise it was in fact a divine joke. It was a deeply uncomfortable feeling, echoing the comedian Bill Hicks' conception of the 'prankster God,' which engaged in various activities designed to mess with the minds of men, such as inventing then hiding dinosaur fossils, in order to test people's faith in the biblical account of creation.

This also gave rise to the possibility, he thought as he wandered among the shelves, to the *likelihood* even, that the devil was just as bored and mischievous. It would explain a lot. If you were all-powerful, there would be nothing left but to mess with people for the pure childish amusement of it. Like that character in Star Trek, Q. It did make a horrid kind of sense, that by now they were so awesomely disillusioned with humanity that they'd decided to just have fun with it. Humanity was an interesting project, it hadn't worked out, so why not just enjoy what they could of it?

Ben observed the folk drifting among the shelves, looking like lost souls. They'd make *great* ghosts, he thought. They've really captured the essence, and they've got the moves down. What must *I* look like, he wondered. The same, or do I look out of place? He mused that pretty much everyone has experienced that feeling at some point, that existential, geographical, temporal, sartorial doubt: am the right person, in the right place, at the right time – and am I dressed for it?

His ruminations were interrupted by the sight of a lurid illustration on the spine of one book, of a pair of glossed, pouting ruby lips, blowing the smoke from the barrel of a .38 snub nose special. It was another Mickey Spillane. He looked along the shelves, and just started pulling books at random. Screw it, he thought, if the Gods are trying to send me along a path that amuses them, I'm going to throw my own curveballs here and there. Mix it up. Have fun with it too. He smothered the immediate thought that perhaps the woman in the woods was just another example of the Gods, the fates, whichever divine figure had him in their sights, messing with him. It was too awful to contemplate. He needed mystery, but he needed a solid fundament upon which to consider and pursue mysteries.

He then found himself marvelling at how they'd turned a person into an ugly if intuitive machine for checking books in and out. A couple of staff members hung about, trying to look as useful as possible, in case they too were mechanised. He briefly pictured a kind of Robocop, calmly checking books in and out, then pulling his gun on a terrified pensioner who owed a fifty pence late fee.

He shook his head and went to engage one of the staff in conversation regarding membership, and allowed her to lead him to a desk where she took him through the joining procedure. Ten minutes later he left with a rucksack full of books, reflecting on how wonderful, and taken for granted, libraries actually are.

He decided to get a burrito and eat it on College Green, a hanging out spot for every kind of person who found themselves in that part of town with time to kill. Tourists, office workers, students, skaters, homeless people, miscellaneous. The grass had now recovered from its time the previous winter as the site of Occupy Bristol. Ben had skirted the encampment with interest but found it all made him feel rather impoverished in terms of his political ideas. It seemed to be about the reworking of society, and he simply had no clue what to suggest. It seemed altogether too much of a responsibility.

The energy of the place was now entirely back to normal. It was fairly busy on the green, but he found a spot and sat, chewing mouthfuls of black beans, rice, cheese, sour cream, guacamole and salad. It was a sunny, clear day. The air of early autumn still wanted to be summer, like a memory you wish you could live over. But the leaves were turning, the sun cool on the concrete and grass. Clothes and shadows were lengthening as the sun began to fall more obliquely on the earth.

He pictured the planet turning in space, a sense of immensity as it passed before him; he saw Asia, the vastness of China and Russia, Europe coming into view, then the camera lurched, hurtling downwards at hundreds of miles an hour, smoothly through the upper atmosphere, the stratosphere, the highest clouds, sharp tingle of ice crystals, down and down and down, accelerating, rain-streaked lens staring down, plunging further, through rushing air, breathless; now the patchwork coming into view through layers of damp cloud,

He kept it up for ten minutes, leafing nervously through the poetry section until he found something that appealed, a stylish Sylvia Plath hardback, *Ariel*. He paid for it, and the assistant bagged it with a delicacy that suggested he approved of Ben's choice.

He then found himself heading left into the big exhibition space, and took in the installation. He couldn't bring himself to go looking for her, but couldn't leave either. He earnestly tried to make sense of the work, entitled *I Have Not Yet Found Myself*. Upon a dozen or so long white tables, were glass cases. Within them was a collection of seemingly random objects sprayed white and mounted on a black background, with little cards beside them, on which was written Dylanesque prose. If it *had* a meaning, it utterly eluded him.

Ben moved to the side of the room and observed the dozen or so people milling around the pieces. None of them betrayed the bafflement he felt. Either they got it, he reasoned, or they didn't expect to. Or they were pretending they did. That seemed to cover it. He was dying to ask someone what they thought it was all about. Presumably one had to examine each piece in detail, then assemble it as a whole and stand back, to crack the code.

Could it be that these people, craning their necks to read each card in turn, accepted – consciously or otherwise – that they could only have an interpretation? Was that the point? Could you just have fun guessing? Did you *have* to be an informed viewer? His head ached at the idea of not knowing. He wondered what was in it for the artist, aside from profile-raising, respect and remuneration. Surely even a mass of public exposure was unlikely to yield *that* many interpretations which would align with the artist's intended message. Maybe it just doesn't matter to the artist. Maybe the point is simply to *be* an artist, to create the most satisfying work you can, then cast it to the winds, and let it fall where it may.

He looked at the punters again and it struck him that each of them now had their own relationship with the work. It was now a part of their lives, and his own. It had been thought-provoking, and, completing that process, of observation, consideration and realisation, felt satisfying to him. Maybe the artist understands this, and *that* is why they share it with an audience. Provoking a reaction, of any kind, is perhaps satisfying enough.

Should he be satisfied with this deep questioning, which had arisen out of living this strange parallel with his great grandfather's life? What would Alfred make of it? Perhaps he would congratulate him, and be delighted that his painting, and his experience, had inspired one of his descendants to seek a happiness that had eluded him. But that happiness felt no nearer, no more real than Alfred's painted Lady.

He sighed, feeling the rucksack and the sentiments weighing him down, and he walked back outside, into the fresh dockside air. He went to his bike, and sat on the railings beside it, looking about him at the people coming and going.

Maybe it was just that simple, he thought. He felt alone, and wished that his lady could be made flesh. In the story in his mind, she had grown from the sensual fantasy creature into the companion, the sounding board for his ideas, the soft landing for his emotions, the home for his heart, the cool hands stroking his head while he quietly speaks his thoughts.

The vividness of his need, his desire, pained him. It hurt to know, then, precisely what he wanted, and to see all the other couples, perambulating around the docks, making it look so easy to achieve. How had they all met? How had they got over every bump and ruffle, and managed to still look so happy? It's like a fucking *magic trick*, he thought.

And just then, as the waterfall broke upon his shoulders, she re-emerged, carrying a paper bag, walking straight towards him. His mind scrambled; he frantically tried to organise the set of his body, his features, but instead his mouth hung open, his eyes wide, eyebrows slightly raised, the image of a man unready for the moment. But it was suddenly upon him: he would discover if she really *was* the woman from the woods.

'I think this is yours?' she said, handing him the paper bag from the bookshop. The instant he computed this, he decided he would keep her before him for every second he could.

'Oh, er, thanks. I better just check.' He flashed a smile, brain racing to think of a way to prolong the conversation, while horribly aware that this was exactly what it must look like. He saw the Sylvia Plath book inside and tried to find the right line.

'Yep. That's it. Thank you *so* much. Very kind of you. You er, you ever read her?' He glanced at her hair; *could* be. And her eyes? Just not sure.

'Who?'

'Er, Sylvia Plath.' He waved the bag with brittle enthusiasm.

'No, no I haven't.'

'Er. Me neither. I just *loved* the cover.'

'I didn't look at it. Someone said you left it in the main room.'

'Oh? You saw the installation?'

'Yeah. It's my work.'

'*Really?* Huh.' Ben leaned back with a half smile. 'It's really interesting stuff. Do *you* mind if I ask you what it's about?'

'Well, *you* know. We have to keep *some* of the mystery. Never spoon-feed art, so they say.' She was smiling easily now. Oh yeah, thought Ben, people *love* talking about themselves.

'You're *really* not putting me on? It's *really* your show?' He was genuinely unsure.

'It's *really* my show. My first in Bristol, actually.'

'Oh? You're not from here?'

'Oh I'm *from* here, I just never had anything *shown* here before.'

'Well, look, I really appreciate you taking the time to give me this. I suppose I'd better actually read it now. I just loved the cover, and seem to remember Sylvia Plath being mentioned in Fight Club. The film.'

'Ha. Yeah … I think you're right.'

'Yeah. But anyway, let me let you go. To meet your public. But you think I could er, *you* know, er … hang on …' He fished a business card from his wallet, handed it over. 'Just … er, *you* know. If you ever fancy er, actually telling me what your work's about, *or*, you want to hear what *I* make of it? Or you want to talk about … well, anything at all, you've got my number. Might be nice.' He shrugged, smiling, nothing to lose. She took the card, her green eyes bright, folding her mouth tight shut as if to contain the smile.

'Sure. Here.' She took a flyer from her satchel. 'It's got my email on there.'

'Okay. *Nice* one. Er, I'm Ben.' he extended his hand.

'Leaf.' She shook it.

'*Leaf?*'

'Leaf.'

'Hippy parents?'

'Bingo.'

'Still a cool name. Alrighty. I'll drop you a line. Drag you out some time.'

'Do.' She smiled again, turned and headed back in. Ben leaned back against his bike, closing his eyes and exhaling slowly, as though he'd just defused a bomb. He wiped his palms down his thighs and felt only relief. But, after a few moments, he felt a smile rising inside him.

The next day, trudging through the mud in Leigh woods, he retold the events of the last week to Cate. She listened intently, with the occasional theatrical 'wow,' 'whoa,' 'no *way!*' or '*cripes!*'

'And *this*, is where it all started,' he said, pointing to the marks in the tree.

'Yeah, *right.*' Cate stared at the tree, stood back, then looked sidelong at Ben. 'Up till now I thought you were just on one. You really weren't making all that up?'

'*What*? No. Why *would* I?' He looked genuinely stunned.

'People *do*!' She laughed.

'Well, *I* don't. Not to other people, anyway.'

'You only make stuff up to tell your*self?*'

'Doesn't *every*one?'

'I suppose *so*. Well, I've got no clue what it stands for.'

'Nope. It just doesn't look natural, or random. I mean, it had to take some effort to get it in there.'

'Yeah. Hm. Nope. No clue.'

'Me neither. You win *this* round, marks in the tree. Well, let's head on, at least go full circle, get back to the spot where I saw her.'

'You're the boss. Come on Brian.' Her dog, an English bull terrier she'd named after Brian the dog on the animated show Family Guy, was insistently sniffing the carved tree. 'Obviously he senses it too,' she said, grinning at him.

After a few minutes' walk, Ben pulled up.

'Okay. I *think* this is it.'

'How do you know? It all looks the same to me.'

'Er. Dunno. It … *feels* the same. Yeah, it feels right.'

'Interesting. And did *Leaf* feel the same as the woman you saw here?'

'Fuck.'

'O-*kay.*'

'No, I mean: I should have asked her if she had a dog.'

'Obviously. 'Cos that wouldn't have been weird.' He looked at her, she smiled benevolently back at him.

'Well, *you* know what I mean.'

'Err,' she said, before catching his look and deciding to keep quiet. A few seconds passed before she whispered. '*Now what?*'

'You know what? I have *no* idea. How about this: we go find somewhere for a hot chocolate, then go home and cook a roast.'

'That sounds genius. We'll do that.'

'*You* want to come?'

'Seriously? You were going to cook a roast just for yourself?'

'You look incredulous. When you live by yourself that's how it goes. You must make stuff with your housemates, no? Rather than a huge effort, you know, to sort of huddle in the corner with. While they all watch, icily stirring their baked beans.'

'I guess so. Anyway, if you *want* some company?'

'Sure. 'Be great. Beats standing here, waiting for … Godot.'

'Mm. It's *sort* of an anti-climax.'

'Story of my life.'

'Ah, Benny, Benny, Benny. I'm *quite* sure you don't mean that.'

'*Don't* I? *Feel* the bitterness.'

'Are you *joking?* You just ended up meeting some swell arty chick out of all this.'

'Well, yes. *Technically*. But I have to work up the bottle to call her now.'

'That's *your* problem. But you can't blame *life* for being boring if you don't.'

''Spose so. I'll give you that one.'

Ben lead them back towards the car park. They arrived to find it heaving with adults, children, dogs, bikers, all in a froth of leisure, pleasure, laughter and chat. He suddenly stopped, squeezing Cate's arm till she squeaked. '*Where?*' she whispered. 'Her in the green?'

'Yep. C'mon.' He took Brian's lead and dragged him across the car park, even as he tried to pull towards a group of dog walkers and their charges in the opposite direction. The coat, hair and lurcher on a lead said it was her, but when he got within a few yards it was evident that she was *not* Leaf, and probably about ten years older than her. She was stood talking with another middle-aged lady dog walker, and Ben just sailed over, all smiles. 'Afternoon,' he nodded to them both. 'Lurcher is it? Used to have one myself. Hello boy!' The ladies smiled good naturedly as he reached down to pat the dog, who managed to look both terribly sweet and terribly downtrodden in a single expression. Brian nosed at its asshole without enthusiasm.

The ladies carried on their conversation while Ben squatted down and talked nonsense to the dog. He inhaled the woman's evidently expensive perfume, and listened to the other lady chatting away about this season's fruit and vegetable crops, bemoaning the fact that they had summered here instead of at their place in Provence, where they produce far superior tomatoes. The lurcher's owner spoke softly, saying she had to get back, and bid the tomato-fancier farewell. Ben stood and smiled, looking her full in the face for the first time. She smiled back, with what struck Ben as gentle eyes. He couldn't think of anything to say, other than, 'See you 'round.' She said nothing, just nodded with that smile, and tugged the lead. The dog gave him one last quick sorrowful glance and trotted after her. He swivelled around to face Cate, who also had an oddly melancholic look about her. She took Brian's lead and pulled him to heel and they walked back towards her car. They stopped to watch the woman put her dog in the back of her estate and head out of the car park.

'Are you disappointed?' she asked.

'Umm, *no*, actually. I've solved a mystery, and *maybe* got a date.'

'You *are* going to write to her?'

'I'll give it another day, then drop her a line. You think that's sensible?'

'*Oh* yes. Not too keen, but don't leave it *too* long either. She might feel like an afterthought.'

'I just think it's all quite funny really.'

'You do?' said Cate, opening the hatchback and letting Brian jump in.

'Yeah.' Ben leaned across the roof, thoughtful, looking around the car park at the chattering, cavorting people and animals. 'Look at us. We're all just people. Doing the do. We read so much into things, but in the end it's just *life*. It means everything and nothing, all at the same time. Imagine if my great granddad had met *his* lady in the woods. Probably he would *never* have painted her. He would have seen that she's just a person, instead of getting obsessed, making her into some kind of *conduit* for all his love ... his desire. *That* lady, with the soppy lurcher, to me *now*? She's apparently just a nice lady who loves her little dog. But, I could make up *all* kinds of things, if she was still the object of my fascination. Every stitch of clothing, every twitch of inferred body language, what she said or didn't say, her facial expressions. If I was an artist I could obsess over it all too, create any number of versions of her, depending on where I was at.' He paused. 'Is this making any sense at all?'

'Kinda.'

'The thing that hit me, when looking at Leaf's installation, and at the *other* people looking at it, is that it's all just *my* reality interpreting other *people's* realities. It's like looking at someone else's dream. It's *all* interpretation. I don't think there's an objective, *absolute* reality of who she is, and what her art is about. Or what any person is all about. It seems to me, that surely each interaction is unique, each experience in *each* moment. And each person involved has their own interpretation of it ... which is all based on their ... backstory. Who they are, and how they are. In *that* moment.'

'But you said your granddad just kept painting the same woman over and over.'

'Maybe that proves the point. He was limited by his ability, his knowledge of her ... but maybe that was enough for him.'

'But not for you,' said Cate with a sly grin.

'What can I say? It broke my heart, his story.' He looked at Cate with a pained expression, then shook his head. 'I don't want to live the way he did. Maybe it's just the times we live in. They're so different. Non-stop commercial propaganda instead of wartime propaganda. We're told we can have whatever we like. No rations here, now. No duty, no sacrifice.' He went quiet, took a breath then held his hands up. 'It all made me want to ... open myself to possibility. I chose to look at this as an *opportunity*. And it *is*. I met someone who seems ... fascinating, lovely, engaging, because of ...' he waved an arm at the woodland, '*this* whole thing. I have no doubt that we'll at *least* have coffee, and maybe I'll tell her this story, and see what an artist makes of it. *And* find out if she's got any closer to finding herself.'

'Eh?'

'I didn't say? That was the name of her installation. *I Have Not Yet Found Myself.*

'Oh. Wow. I should see it. *Should* I see it?'

'Yeah. I guess that's the point. We all just make of things what we will, and we try to get by, in whatever way makes sense to us. We're *always* in the process of finding ourselves, even though that self is always changing. It's like trying to hit a moving target.'

'*That's* why I meditate. One day you're going to let me talk you into it.'

'Maybe. You never know. Life's *full* of surprises. You just have to roll with it. Having said all that, I'll be gutted if she fucks me off.'

'Well, nothing ventured, nothing gained.'

'Innit? I'd rather regret something I've done, than something I haven't. You know, within reason.'

'Right. And on that note, I'm hungry *and* thirsty. I'm buying and you're cooking.'

'Deal.'

Faye

I

There she was again, painting intently. On sunny days she would take her easel into the white painted gazebo, which was covered in blood-red climbing roses, and situated on the north side of the long, wide garden. This Friday she was wearing a long dark blue dress and skinny leather boots with lots of laces. Sel hadn't seen her in that outfit before.

He cut the mower's engine, then went to lean against the thick trunk of the nearest Beech tree. He pulled the tobacco pouch from the top pocket of his t-shirt, which was green, matching his trousers. He slid down the trunk, sat crossed legged, rolling a cigarette with care. He enjoyed rolling them more than smoking them, but once a cigarette was rolled, he felt an obligation to smoke it. It seemed to him that things *want* to express their nature, to fulfil their role, like a spinning top that *asks* to be spun, by the simple fact of its form and function.

For at least a year the internal voice that urged him to quit had been rising in volume, but he gave himself until the end of the summer. Two more weeks, officially. He speculated that perhaps if he found another job that didn't reward stopping quite so much, he'd actually do it. The romantic in him suggested that maybe it went with his brooding complexity. Which he knew was bogus. He got bored of brooding, and didn't feel especially complex, it was just that he didn't have anyone to explain himself to.

He lit the cigarette and blew several inept smoke rings. Fingers with bitten fingernails tapped the cigarette, deliberately, trying to do one a second. Counting off the moments. The tiny plume of smoke wafted into the warm afternoon air as he did so, making him envy its *naturalness*. It just behaved according to the laws of physics, he supposed. It did not have to make decisions … or pluck up the courage to find out all the things he wanted to know about the woman who painted.

For the last four months he had been coming every Friday to do the lawn and the weeding, pruning and tidying jobs around the large gardens. There were a few shrub beds running around the driveway in the front, but most of the work was done in the large back garden, with mature trees, numerous shrub beds, trellises covered in climbers against most of the walls, and a large lawn. On the patio by the conservatory were many pots and planters.

The house was a six-bedroom, red brick Edwardian affair in Hampstead, salubrious and spacious territory in the north of London. An air of easy wealth there, not restless wealth, as in the centre. It took him all day to get the garden done, though he could have done so with at least two hours to spare. She painted all day, so he gardened all day.

Not once had their eyes met. He tried to look up only when he was sure he was unseen. Every stolen glance was a small thrill, payment for a job which demanded nothing of him but fifty hours each week of his time. His youth gave the energy for free. He filled those hours with internal dialogue, with poetry, often unbidden, sometimes with music through earbuds, but mostly with mild levels of regret and worry. Regret about not shaping his present more wisely in the past, and worry about how poorly he was shaping his future.

He glanced up again, and shock burst through him as thought he saw her leaning out to stare at him. His eyes snapped downward and he drew on his cigarette so fiercely his vision went blotchy, then he blew out a thin stream of smoke over his steel-toecap boots. Reflexively, his other hand scratched at his stubble, at the back of his neck, then wiped a film of perspiration from his forehead. Finally, it dabbed at his top lip. He wanted to look up again, to *know*, but he could not manage it. He cursed the length of his cigarette, drew on it busily, then stubbed it out, ready for the compost. He was light-headed from standing too quickly, and pictured the blood draining from his face. I'm ashen, he thought, and he took a few deep breaths. His t-shirt hung loose at his waist and a merciful wisp of a breeze blew up it, cooling the beads of sweat on his chest.

He began to feel slightly better, and looked up to see how much lawn was left ahead of him. At least two thirds of it, which should take him until lunchtime to finish cutting and edging. The afternoon would be quieter, just hand tools and the sound of birds and insects. He went back to the mower, slipped the dog-end into the grass catcher. He took a breath, reached down to pull the cord and start the engine, then lined it up to continue mowing strips lengthways.

As he pushed, Sel felt her gaze on him. He had never examined her face up close, as he always tried to keep his distance, and she would sometimes scuttle away when he was about to head for wherever she was painting. One day he had taken a quick look at her work on the easel, expecting a gentle evocation of the garden in full sun-showered bloom, but instead it was a dirty riot of blood-spattered filth, all ugly angles and nerve-jangling colours. He had tried not to gawp, but he did a double-take, looking longer than he wanted to, before trying to blot it from his memory. Presumably she witnessed this, as since then she'd always picked up the canvas and taken it with her. Sometimes she would take it into the conservatory at the back of the large house. He got a sense of her moving about in there, but he did not look.

He had been told, in no uncertain terms by his boss, Alexander, that he was *never* to look at the house, the people, the cars, or anything other than the garden, and only that which was absolutely vital to the job in hand. The company's clients were only rich and/ or famous, and from day one Alexander had impressed upon him the fact that one only got to work for these people by reference, and it was far easier to lose clients of this type than to gain them. Don't upset anyone, *ever*, was the instruction. *Always* err on the side of caution. Never ask to use the bathroom inside unless it's an emergency, never get caught pissing against their trees or fences, never ask for anything if you can avoid it. In fact, try not to be seen or heard at all if you can manage it.

The warnings climbed the heights of paranoia at times, but Alexander needn't have worried. Sel was a man who preferred to edge his way around the margins of life, doing his utmost not to attract attention. He'd even started smoking partly to blend in at university. In the last week of first year, as exams loomed, the anxiety drove the vast majority of the students to nicotine. They would collect outside lecture theatres, jabbering nervously at one another, passing around the tobacco pouch, fiddling with papers, laughing and puffing and displaying a fascinating variety of nervy tics. For many the habit waned through the year, occasionally replaced by a short-lived regime at the sports centre. Then, as exam time came around again, one by one, they would accept the offer of the tobacco.

All that was more than three years ago. Having no idea what else to do with a degree in philosophy, he did a two year masters in philosophy. Having no idea what to do next, he got a job through a friend of his mother doing garden maintenance. His classmates were now in management consulting, marketing, financial services, new media, some working as interns in the political and NGO worlds, and there was barely an hour that went by that he didn't think about this, and once again chew on what he *should* be doing, instead of pushing a mower and not looking at the house or its occupants.

He completed another stripe, arriving at the end of the lawn, which met the shrub bed that ran along the bottom of the garden. Behind it was the neat red brick wall which bordered another set of large gardens on the other side. He briefly looked over the condition of the shrubs, before turning the mower and lining it up to cut the next stripe.

He caught a movement up ahead in his peripheral vision, and this time he was certain she was looking. His eyes snapped back to the grass, he cleared his throat and on he went, trying to move all his conscious awareness to the engine's relaxing, insectile drone. He focused on it, and on staying straight, perfectly overlapping the previous stripe. He slammed his mind shut to all else, but he could feel the insistent thoughts, like insects banging against a window. Finally one caught his attention, demanding to know *why* she would be looking at him. Why *now*? Had she *always* been looking? And after three, the multitude. Was she painting him? Was she bored? Was he disturbing her? Was he in trouble? What should he do? What would he do if she talked to him?

His heart thudded away in his chest, and the sweat bloomed on his lip as he pushed on towards the house. He drew near to the gazebo but could not see her. He felt the relief sweep over him in a vast, cooling wave, then he jumped as she said, in a tender, musical voice, '*Excuse me?*' Sel pulled up, throttled down the mower and dragged his head around in slow-motion, eyes wide, to look at her. I must look *crazy*, he thought, as a delicate, paint-spattered hand rose to her mouth and a smile peeked around it.

'*Me?*' She just nodded, now biting her top lip. The hand still dabbed at it nervily, but he thought in a flash – she must *know* I'm more scared of her; *she* doesn't need to look nervous. 'Er, yes? Can I help you?'

'*Maybe*. Can I show you something?' His guts churned and he tried to control the nerves. His bowels suddenly felt full and heavy, like he was carrying a bowling ball around in his hips. It flashed through his mind that she might be the first woman who had spoken to him, other than his mother, or salespeople, since he left university. She looked shy, cautious … he could make no sense of it. He nodded, and she beckoned him toward her easel. Her movements, like her words, were quick, darting things, appearing and disappearing in an instant. He edged forward, and she edged around to the other side of her easel, giving him room. He looked at her again, and her eyes shot to her painting and back to him.

'You'd like my *opinion?*' he said, trying to smile, but feeling his facial muscles awkwardly pulling his mouth all over the place. They lacked practice. She only *mm*-d and nodded, biting the inside of her mouth. He stepped up into the gazebo to see, conscious of his big boots next to her fine ones, the sweat dripping down into his eyes. He blinked it away, wiping his face with his arm, and looked. Not the raucous, garish nightmare he had anticipated, but bright-edged swirls of green, trailed in the wake of someone who *had* to be him, with what could *only* be his mower, in what *must* have been this garden. It was abstracted, dream-like, something from a psychedelic children's book, but his brain told him that he had, absolutely unexpectedly, become the muse of an artist. His mouth opened and closed a few times, a little croak escaping. He coughed, put his head on one side, *mm*-d in appreciation and nodded. 'It's er. *Is* it? It's *me?*' He glanced at her for a small fraction of a second, getting only an impression of a coil of long blonde hair piled up on her head, skewered in place with something.

'It is,' she said quietly. 'I think-' She stopped abruptly, shifted from one foot to the other. 'You seem ... *interesting*. And what you do for a living.'

'*Huh?*' His jaw hung open. He felt astonishment, embarrassment, discomfort, confusion, and he heard Alexander's voice in his head, telling him to leave this woman alone immediately. But he was rooted. 'I *am?*'

'Certainly. Don't *you* think you are?' she asked, suddenly grabbing one arm with the other and squeezing it uncomfortably.

'Well ... I ... *pff* ... I can't see *why*.' He squinted at her for clarification.

'*Everyone's* interesting to *someone*. Everyone's beautiful, or ugly, or wonderful or awful ... to *someone*. Six billion people ... that's a lot of opinions. *I* think.'

'True. True enough.' He looked at her, this time for more than an instant. He took in her features, noticing her eyes and lips, blue and pink respectively. He thought them pretty. Not shockingly beautiful, but pretty. Attractive. Nice to look at. Her nose was thin and her chin pointed, her neck swanlike and her collarbone prominent. She was fine-boned and looked fragile, in every sense. He relaxed a little. 'You paint a lot?'

'I do.' She shifted about again, biting the inside of her mouth and apparently looking at his boots. 'It's how I make my living.'

'Wow.' He nodded slowly. 'Well … I'm no *expert* … but … I haven't seen anything quite like this.'

'I have my influences. Some good, some bad. Do you … do anything creative?'

'Me? I play the guitar. Well. I *have* a guitar. Draw a tiny bit. I write … oh gawd.' He groaned, shook his head. 'I *do* write some poetry. If you can call it that.'

'I'd love to hear some,' she said quickly. His eyes darted away like startled fish. 'Or *not*. Only if you were comfortable with it.'

'Mm.' He began mirroring her body language, rubbing his arm defensively. 'They're not really *po*ems. Maybe … *I* dunno. Depends what you de*fine* as poetry. It's just … whatever hits me. I get visions. Moments. I try to just write what that moment *feels* like. But … I don't know who's writing it sometimes.' He glanced off at the Beeches. 'If that makes any sense.'

'Oh yes. Yes it *does*.'

II

Sel stared at the page. It was off-white, rough and flecked with … with, he supposed, stuff that went into the rather DIY paper-making process somewhere in India that had produced his journal. The page *dared* him to mark it. Dared him to attempt to wrangle his feelings and lead them calmly onto the page. But he did *not* feel calm. He felt … a *crazy* mixture of things: elation, a high, an effervescence … and a leaden dread … a fear that this high would be followed by the almost inevitable low, the punishing bout of despondency that would drag him towards self-loathing, brought on by wilfully entertaining a momentary, ill-advised joy. He breathed deeply, allowed himself to focus on the breath … to feel it come into him, pause, and to leave him, naturally … one after the other … just as thoughts and feelings come, and go. Like clouds in the sky, like waves on the shore … nothing permanent, nothing to be attached to … nothing to judge. It helped. He felt an emptying out, visualised the tide going out, leaving an ever-growing beach of fine white sand, glowing in the tropical sun. He relaxed in his chair, feeling the lamplight on his eyelids. He breathed long and slow, and then the words and images and sensations began to come.

A man leans against a wall, tired
of walking, of running
The streets steam in midday heat
Cars like whales, glide past the sidewalk
A bell rings nearby, a customer
enters a coffee shop, hailing the owner
Normality

He sweats into his clothes, they stick
to his back, his chest
He tries to push himself upright
Move on
But where? To do what?
His hands search empty pockets again
Normality

He takes the match from his mouth, squeezes
A drop of saliva onto the sunburned street
runs his fingers down the bitten notches
The wood feels real to him, the street
The people, the cars, they don't
Jobs, families, friends, system, purpose
Worlds within worlds
and His

His hand stopped writing, moved to the page beside it, and began
sketching bits of what he'd seen and felt. He tried to get the
perspective right, the close-up of the man, in foreground, and the cars,
their size, their way of making an impression on the scene. He thought
about where it had come from, and he did not know. It came from
wherever inspiration comes from, he supposed. He thought of Faye.
His hand turned the page.

She made me
With her hands
Eyes
And what else?
Why did she make me?

He looked at what he'd written, leaning both elbows on the front of
the small bureau, his jaw atop on his knuckles. Then he wrote again.

My mother tells me what I am
Not to her, but what I AM
A lady, a paintbrush
Showed me what I am to her
Not what I AM

He sat back, thinking of the painting, and of the painter. He knew he'd be counting the days.

By the end of the weekend he'd filled twenty pages of the journal with words and images. He took it out with him everywhere he went. He stopped to people-watch in the centre of the city, he rode the tube trains, took buses, walked in a rain shower on the Sunday and let himself get soaked. He found himself walking along the south bank to the Tate modern, only recently opened. He studied the paintings and tried to get a feel for it, to place the woman's work in some context. To see if anything about her came clearer as a result. He tried to memorise the names of the painters and their paintings, but it would not stick, Rothko and Matisse aside. Still he saw nothing that put him in mind of her painting. He scratched his head, looking at the other visitors. Many appeared well-heeled and well-versed, quite at ease, silently gesturing, quietly pontificating. He became very aware of his own clothing and manner, then became aware of his projection, of telling himself a little story about how ridiculous he looked: poor and ignorant.

He took a breath and let the thoughts and feelings drift away, instead looking at another painting, and attempting to get lost in the brushstrokes. He felt a presence nearby, and turned to see a young woman looking at the painting, her head to one side, a hint of a smile. She turned and smiled so fast he could not avoid her eye. He flushed and left, wondering, for at least the thousandth time, what was wrong with him.

That night:

Unclean and unfinished,
A shambling form
Not ready for the light

And after a while:

Where are you?
In the paint? In the brush?
Where are you now?
What happens when you are not painting?
Do you paint in your mind?
Is everything a painting to you?
Am I anything more than everyone's image
whether they reproduce it or not?

He cleared his throat deliberately, and picked up his pencil to sketch a paintbrush, and then the coil of her hair. He thought, this is poor. Maybe she'll teach me to draw.

'So you spoke with him. How did that *feel?*' The woman sat back in her chair, staring at Faye with a kind of professional, supportive, encouraging concern.
    'It felt ... *good.*'
    'Talk about ... *good.*'
    'Mm.' Faye was laying on the leather couch, looking at the ceiling. The sun was throwing the patterns of the lace curtain across it, the breeze giving motion to the patterns. 'It was ... *hard*, at first. I think he was more scared of me than I was of him.'
    'Why did you think that?'
    'Body language.'
    'Go *on.*'
    'He's young. He's a shy young guy.'
    'How did his *shy*ness make you feel?'
    'Oh ... *I* don't know ... a *mix*, I suppose? I felt sort of ... oddly ... pro*tective* of him, I suppose. He doesn't seem to have any confidence at *all*. I mean ... he made me feel positively greg*ari*ous!' She laughed, a hand moving to her mouth. '*Honest*ly ... I thought I'd *never* meet someone who'd make *me* feel confident. Comparatively.'
    'How did he react?'
    'Him? He was nervous ... but didn't seem eager to get away. I got the feeling he doesn't talk to many people either. Before you ask *why* I think that ... that was just how he struck me.'
    'Do you think he was attracted to you, sexually?'
    'Oh *gosh* no. *Sylvia!*' she laughed musically, but with an edge of melodrama. Her therapist scribbled something down.

'What *are* you writing?' Faye asked, her eyes dancing with amusement.

'These are my *private* notes. You know that, Faye. So, did you en*joy* this conversation? Sharing your art? Sharing your *self*, with a stranger?'

'Well, he doesn't *seem* like a stranger.' More scribbling. Faye ignored it. 'It felt … like we'd *already* been talking … *before*. I can't explain that. It was funny … but … if you ask *how* I felt about it … it made me feel … a little less alone, I suppose. Six billion people. And now I *know* one of them. Aside from yourself, of course.'

'Do you feel there is a difference between talking to someone and *knowing* them?'

'Well, of *course* … but this was … *both*. He just seemed … familiar. Sort of … *argh*. I can't explain it. It was simply as if … I *knew* him.'

'Will you see him next week?'

'Well, he hasn't missed a week, but it's getting toward autumn, and the hours always drop down for the gardener, after the autumn pruning. They just clear leaves for an hour. This time of year they still do a full day.'

'Would you like to see him again? To talk again?'

'I would. Al*though* … although like I said, it felt as though we had already been talking … known each other … but it *also* feels like we're just getting started. Or does that sound like gibberish?'

'So, would you say you are *pleased* you followed through with the idea that you talk with him?'

'I am. Certainly. I *didn't* expect to paint him. It isn't a major work … it's just … he seems to move in a blur, even though he moves rather slowly, and deliberately. He doesn't *burn* himself into the space, he sort of … *ghosts* through it. But his *presence* is solid. When you're near him. When he focuses on you. There seems to be much more to him up close. Yes, I *would* like to find out more about him. And yes, I *will* talk to him again.' She looked up at Sylvia, who was smiling thinly at her notes. I'm making her day, thought Faye.

By Tuesday, Sel was caught between impatience and anxiety. Soon it would be Wednesday, the week then picking up speed on the downslope, and it would be Friday before he was ready. How to *be* ready? He began to catch the thoughts and feelings as they came, writing his small poems whenever the mood took him. Except when he worked with Alexander on the Thursday. He was helping him break out an old garden path, dumping the old stone into a skip, and carrying in the slabs for laying the next day. He and Alexander were bringing in the last of them when his boss said, 'I might need your help getting this down tomorrow, okay?'

'*Oh*,' said Sel.

'Problem?'

'Well, no.'

'You *sound* like there's a problem.' Alexander was looking at him, a curious smile on his ruddy, sun- and wind-chapped face. He scratched at one of his beefy sideburns and said, 'What's up?'

'It's nothing.'

'It's *something*. Come on, you can tell Uncle Alex.' He sat on his haunches next to the bare, flattened soil where the old crazy paving had been, snaking its way through a particularly 1970s garden, with its ugly rockery and bland shrubbery. The plan was to clear the site and rebuild it from the bottom up. Sel felt as though it was silently thanking them.

'Well, it's just that Fridays ... I do ... *you* know. That place up in Hampstead.'

'Ah.' He sighed. 'Faye. *Now* I understand.' He laughed, shook his head. 'Ah, dear boy. *What* have I told you about fraternising with clients of mine?'

'*Faye*. Hm. Look, *she* asked me ... *she* spoke to *me* ... it wasn't *my* idea. You *must* believe me.'

'Okay, calm down son. I'm joking. Kind of. I *know* you know the score. But I like a bit of gossip. So what happened?' He sat back, making himself comfortable, and Sel uncomfortable.

'*Nothing*. She just asked me what I thought-' He stopped abruptly, as though his mouth was suddenly mugged at knifepoint.

'Come on, don't tease me. *Asked what you thought* ...' his hand made the circling 'and *then?*' motion.

'Oh *Lord*. About a *pain*ting. She was there, in the gazebo. I was just finishing mowing, and she calls me over. She asked what I thought of her painting.' He blushed, looked awkwardly at Alexander, who was clearly waiting for more. He sighed. 'It was of *me*.' Alexander whooped, cackling to himself. Then he stopped.

'My God, you're serious, aren't you? She really *did*. She painted you. I tell you, young'un. She's a ... she's a *funny* one ... you mark my words. I know about these things.'

'What things? Funny how?' Sel bit his lower lip and scuffed the soil with his boot. Then he bit his thumb nail and peered quizzically at the older man, who shrugged.

'*I* don't know, son. She's a lovely lady, perfectly polite, but … she's a bit … *funny*. Artistic temperament, I suppose. Don't look like *that*. I don't mean anything bad by it. But take it from me, that kind of woman is *trouble*. Even if she *wasn't* a client I'd tell you to steer clear. Romantically I mean.'

'But she's *much* too old for me anyway. We were just *talking*. You *know* I don't …'

'Yeah. Sure.' Alexander stood up, dusting his hands against his trousers. 'You're a lovely kid, Sel. I just don't want to see you get yourself chewed up and spat out. Even a girl *your* age'll do that. *Older* ones … well, they'll always think they know better than you. And most of the time, they'd be right. But look … if you promise me you'll … keep your *head* around my client, I'll get Paul to help here tomorrow. I can't stand to see you moping.'

'We're just *talking*,' said Sel quietly. Alexander sighed.

'That's how it starts.'

Those words rang in his ears all evening. In bed, he stirred them around in his mind, along with images of Faye, and tried to put some sinister cast around her eyes. It didn't take. He hadn't known her name until Alexander told him. He tried it on her, and it fitted particularly well. As he pictured her hair, piled up on her head, he heard it sigh the name *Faye* as it fell, undone, to her shoulders. He pictured the paint on her fingers, the way her dress clung to her slender figure, the way she shifted and fidgeted and performed an entire symphony of nervous gestures. He just could *not* see her as a malign influence, as someone ready, willing and able to do him harm.

He opened his journal as he lay in bed; too much light on the page. He reached up to push the anglepoise lamp away. Again, the page defied him. It lay, *again* daring him to mark it, to expose himself, to tell a story about her which was not yet formed. He rolled onto his back and closed his eyes, eventually drifting off with endless snapshots of her playing across his mind.

He dreamed he was in the garden, mowing and mowing, but the grass got no shorter. He couldn't see her … she was only ever a possibility nearby … but he could feel an *idea* of her. He knew he should steer clear, but the siren-song drifted out from the gazebo, and he fought it with everything he had.

III

Sel was glad that Alexander was not in the yard the next morning, when he went to pick up the transit van. He waved to another couple of guys who he worked with occasionally, and pointed up at the flawlessly blue summer sky. They smiled and nodded then continued getting ready for their jobs. Sel unlocked the van and checked over the equipment methodically, starting with the mower, making sure it was clean, and that its oil and fuel were okay. He started it up for a few moments then killed the engine. Then he ensured he had all the tools and equipment, one by one. He had his own secateurs and gloves, and his lunch and water stowed. He got in the driver's seat and took a few moments to clear and still his mind. A short, sharp laugh burst out of him as he reflected on how big a deal he'd been making of this. She might well have pulled up the drawbridge by now, and just wave, from high up on the parapets. He'd just nod with professional cordiality, and get on with his work. He would do every job with love and care, then tidy up and go home for the weekend, leaving Faye, in her entirety, in her home. He took another long, deep breath: in, hold, out. He took another, letting it out slow, and started the ignition.

It was getting warm and humid by the time he reached the house. The wide, curving driveway had only Faye's car in it, and he parked one space away from it. Some weeks there would be a black Mercedes there too, but usually not. He looked at the shrubs that lay in the beds around the end of the driveway, and decided they would get some attention first. An hour later, he was lost in clipping, when her voice startled him. He froze momentarily, then turned to see her in the doorway, in another clingy dress, this one white with a vivid floral print. Scarlet red roses, just like those which wound around the gazebo. She was beaming, her blonde hair in a ponytail.

'*Morning*. Can I make you a cup of tea?' She looked to Sel as though she were *trying* to appear relaxed, casual. But she'd never offered him a thing before, so this wasn't *really* casual. He slung his shears over his shoulder and took a few steps towards her.

'Sure, though I only have fruit or herbal teas. Caffeine doesn't really agree with me.'

'Oh, certainly. I'm just the same. Wait here, I'll bring you a selection.'

'Oh no, please. Just whatever you recommend. Anything at all really.'

'Really?'

'Absolutely.'

She said no more, just smiled brightly and went back inside, leaving the door ajar. He went back to clipping, feeling a pleasant tightness in his chest. Words of poetry tumbled around inside his head but wouldn't fall into any order, so he tried instead to focus on doing his work mindfully. He was just raking up the cuttings when a chinking from the doorway announced Faye's return.

'Here we are,' she said, coming down the steps in bare feet with a tray of tea and biscuits. She stood with it, looking around the driveway and frowning, chewing the inside of her mouth. 'Um. Nowhere to sit …'

'Oh, that's no bother, I can just, er …' he surveyed the options and said, without enthusiasm, '… sit in the van.'

'Well, that's just not civilised. Come in.' She turned and went back into the house, not waiting for an answer. He picked at his fingernails, his heart rate jumping. He pushed his tools out of sight under the shrubs, locked the van, undid the laces and slipped his boots off, leaving them by the front door.

Inside was immediately cooler. It was bare floorboards and colour everywhere, with rugs, sculptures, bits of funky wallpaper and hardly three walls painted the same hue. He could hear the sound of the tea cups up ahead, and threaded his way through the house to the conservatory. He glanced at the rooms as he passed. Doing this work, he'd become aware of what a well-appointed home looks, feels and smells like; the antiques, the leather and hardwood, the sense of taste, of comfort, of security. This house had it all in spades, yet he couldn't quite put it together with his impression of Faye. She didn't seem like the kind of person who was in some way *tame* enough to organise such a living space. She seemed too restless a spirit. There was more to this than met the eye, he was sure. He went through the large hardwood and granite kitchen, to the conservatory.

'*Through here,*' she called loudly, just as walked in. 'Oh my goodness,' she said, startled. 'You *crept* in!'

'We're trained to de-boot at the portals. Er. As it were.'

'We're trained to de-boot at the portals,' she repeated slowly. 'Now *there's* a sentence I didn't expect to hear when I got out of bed this morning. Take a pew, anywhere.' She motioned to the various seats arranged around the conservatory. She settled in a comfortable rounded wicker chair with a large curved cushion, facing the garden. She took her tea and pulled her feet up. The chair was part of a set, with another just like it, and a two-seater settee version also facing out.

Sel plonked himself down on that, immediately looking around at the tall greenery that defined the space. It put him in mind of images of colonial days somehow. This seating, in a house with a veranda, on the edge of a plantation ... he must have seen it in a film.

'Very nice,' he said, nodding. 'You look after all these plants?'

'I try to. This house was left to me. I try to keep it tidy and the plants alive.'

'Oh, by your parents?' he said, leaning forward to take his tea, and a French biscuit.

'I don't know.'

'You ... er ...' He tried to make sense of this, but failed.

She sighed, and picked up her cup, nestling it in her hands and peering into the steam, as if to divine the truth. 'I was living in someone's attic, about ten years ago. I'd always painted. I went to Saint Martins ... what feels like a *life*time ago. Fine art degree. I couldn't *seem* to quite ... *function*, really. I just painted, nothing else. My old tutor, Seamus, had found me that attic room, in the home of some eccentric art patron, and there I stayed. *Finally* Seamus convinced me to exhibit, and ... well, it sort of took off. Everything sold. I didn't even know the prices, Seamus did it all. I suppose he just liked my work, and wanted to see me succeed with it. I didn't know about succeeding at *anything*, I just followed my ... *instinct*, I suppose. And that was just to sketch, draw, and mostly paint. I didn't go out much ... but the show seemed to open something up. Seamus introduced me to an agent, and I painted more than ever, did another show, and another. The prices kept going up. I didn't really spend anything. Though I *do* like shoes. Anyway. One day I get a letter asking me to attend a meeting at some solicitors in the centre of town. This million-year-old guy sits me down in this time-warp of an office and smiles this very *meagre* smile, and tells me that someone has left me a house ... but the will directed that I not be told *who* left it to me. Obviously I just said fine, and thank you. I mean, what *else* do you say? It certainly makes life easier. But after a few months I thought maybe I could get an antique dealer in, and they'd be able to work it out, or a private detective or something, but in the end I just decided to trust it. After all, no one had come looking for their stolen inheritance and chucked me out or whatever ... so here I am. I *still* feel kinda like I'm living in someone else's house. So like I said, I just try to look after it.' She looked at him, shrugged and took a sip of her tea.

'Wow. That's ... *quite* something.' He nodded sagely to himself, occasionally *mm*-ing, and blowing his tea to cool it.

'And what about you? I'm afraid I don't even know your name. Well, that's not quite true. Your boss *did* tell me before you started, but I don't really take *in* names as ... well, I meet hardly anyone for more than a few minutes.' She pulled an apologetic face.

'I'm Sel.' He got up and went over to shake her hand. She took it with a small but strong hand, and smiled. Up close, he saw how her features crinkled along well-worn lines. He was slightly surprised, as he found it hard to imagine her doing that much laughing.

'Sel?'

'Short for Selby. My surname. My first name's Gregory, but no one's called me that since school.' He shrugged and sat back down.

'Sel. Hm. So how did you come to do gardening? Is this your ... *passion*?' She seemed to find it hard to say the word, and he suddenly had the distinct impression that she was acting all this. The tea and biscuits in the conservatory, the polite conversation ... he felt she was but one small step from running back to the attic, locking the door and painting like fury.

'My *passion? No.* Sweet *Lord* no. I mean, I enjoy doing it *mindfully* ...'

'As in ...?'

'Mindfulness. Non-judgemental awareness? Being alive in the present moment? It gets described lots of different ways ... and I suppose everyone has their own experience of it. That's sort of the point, I think.'

'How did you come to that? Sounds ... sort of Eastern, if you know what I mean.'

'Well, yes, it sort of *is*. It's from Buddhism, but may well predate that. It's a name for something that ... I guess most people have forgotten how to do. It's simple to do, but hard to do *well*. Sort of. I'm not explaining it very well. But the point is, it helps.'

'Helps with what?' She asked innocently enough, but he felt like she were making him walk the plank. Another step and he'd be off, into the shark-infested waters beneath. As if by a miracle, his phone rang in his pocket. His eyes flared. It was *only* going to be his boss. He held up a finger and strode off back through the house to answer it. And walked straight into Alexander.

'I hope I didn't get you into any trouble,' she said, standing awkwardly in the doorway when Alexander had driven off. Sel looked flustered, but did his boots up methodically.

'Oh no, not at *all* ... it's just that ... my boss likes to know his workers are *work*ing. He's keen to retain *all* his clients. That's all.'

'Did I do the wrong thing?' She seemed to say it as much to herself as to him.

'No. He just thought it odd that we were suddenly having elevenses, having never spoken before last week.' By the time he was saying the words he regretted them, but it was unstoppable. He felt himself flushing, not knowing what to do but continue doing his boots up.

'Oh. Well. I see his point. Hm.'

'Well, I was enjoying it,' said Sel, standing. He looked at the shrubs. 'But, these things won't clip themselves. That I know of. But maybe we could … pick up the conversation at lunchtime, or whenever.' He knew he was flushing terribly, and his body seemed suddenly *made* to make him look awkward, as he folded and unfolded his arms, pocketed and unpocketed his hands.

'Sure. Anyway, I have to finish my painting of you,' she said, her smile a disarming mix of shy and cheeky.

Sel went back to work with a surge of wellbeing. He became aware of the smells of the garden, particularly the flowers on the more pungent of the late-blooming shrubs, which he'd never learned the names of. That seemed to be for the professionals, and the amateur enthusiasts, not for the youngsters still trying to find their path. But that's not true, is it? he thought. I'm *on* the path. Or *a* path. I just don't know where it will lead. He then mused he was actually *helping* the plants, though it was hard to support when he was trimming them according to human ideas of what constituted attractive form, not what they would naturally grow into. Regardless, he chose to simply be *aware* of this, and continue. He had to eat, he reasoned, and the plants were not *worse* off for his professional intervention.

Somehow he felt like he'd reached some milestone with Faye, and that he need not feel particularly keyed up about talking with her now. He'd been honest about Alexander's comments and concerns, and he felt that this spoke well of his integrity. He had not been honest about all his mixed-up feelings about talking with her, but that seemed okay too. It was culturally appropriate, he decided.

When lunchtime rolled around, he'd timed his work at the front perfectly. He got to the back of the house with his lunchbox and water, to find Faye putting out a spread on the patio table by the conservatory. He was speechless. It was a picnic for two. He looked around, half-expecting to see a group of arty types gossiping and readying for food, but no, it was just his host, surveying their lunch and looking pleased with herself. He looked stunned, in what he hoped was an appreciative way. After a period of wowing and thanking, he asked if he could wash his hands. Eventually, they settled down to it, making up their plates with salads, olives, hummus, salmon, potato salad, chutney and so on, all from Waitrose.

'I'm an absolutely *average* cook,' she said dismissively, opening various lids. 'And I like to be able to nibble while I work, you know?' She nodded at him, buttering a piece of French stick. 'Help yourself to apple juice. It's sublime.'

'*O*-kay, I'm just going to thank you *one* more time, then shut up and enjoy it, if that would be the right thing to do,' he said. He hadn't realised how hungry he was.

'It would, surely. But, you were telling me about your passion.'

'Oh yeah,' he laughed. '*That* thing. Hm. *Well*. It hasn't necessarily revealed itself yet. It isn't gardening, though I think we covered that. I didn't know what to study in uni, so I did philosophy. Undergrad and masters.'

'*Mm. Inter*esting. Hm.' She paused. '*Was* it interesting?'

'Er. Hm. Well, let's see. How does one discuss the study of the subject of philosophy? Well, I suppose by asking that question. It's very easy to get caught up in asking why, endlessly, going around in ever decreasing circles. You get mesmerised by the endless 'ologies. You get into lots of bizarre and possibly pointless arguments. Or *debates*, as we called them in those days.' He looked up from his food to see Faye looking at him with amusement. 'Yes. And so, when you get far enough away from it, it *was* interesting, but at the time it could be murderously complex and ... often seem a big fat waste of time. Eventually, you just get a moment where you go, oh I get it, we're all different. We all walk into the same space through different doors, *perceptually*, and want and value different things, and so we end up with a world that *no one* really wants. Except that, as the Buddha said, everything is as it should be. We all get our lessons, even from douchebags, or *karma angels*, if you prefer that term. And the idea is to pass on those lessons. Make life easier for others, and lead all of humanity, a bit at a time, towards enlightenment. After that, I don't know. I suppose we put our feet up, spiritually. But I'm guessing.'

'*Hm*,' she laughed. 'You'll have to let me digest that lot. To say the least. What was your thesis on?'

'My masters thesis? Okay. Ready? *Being and not being: a comparative analysis*. And that's *true*. It was a garbled comparison of mainly German and Eastern philosophies, but it was very well received in the end. It started as a joke – though I was the only one in on it – and it ended up being a bit of a hit. With very passing month afterwards I thought of ways to improve it, but in the end you have to let things go, don't you?'

'Well, I know *nothing* of philosophy, not academically anyway. I'm not so much the thinker as the *doer*. Maybe the *feeler*.'

'You're a *feeler*? What *do* you feel?' He blushed at the directness of his own question and took another mouthful of salmon.

'You sound like my therapist. Oh no, not in a bad way. You look mortified you poor thing.'

'I'm okay,' he laughed. 'Taking the opportunity to eat.'

'Good. *Anyway* … I *always* felt things very deeply. The sensitive *type* I suppose. I couldn't *think* about things … it was too painful. My therapist would say something about displacement of emotion, or something. Possibly. *Aaanyway*. I always painted, since I was tiny. I didn't need anything else, just paper and paint, and then canvases.' She went quiet for a moment. Then a longer moment. Then she took a mouthful of food. And stopped chewing to say, 'Your turn.'

'Oh, okay. Well, I was never very … *creatively* confident. It seemed to be the job of other kids to be good at that. I liked English, that was about it. Media. A bit of history and geography. Not PE so much. RE … religious education … well, we had a good teacher. He seemed deep. No one wanted to mess about in his classes. He related to us too well for that. There was nothing to rebel against. He seemed to have the number of every kid in the class, and he made things accessible for us. Nothing was taboo. One day all the girls had a visit from the Tampax rep. Had to meet up in the hall, kick the whole thing around a bit, and watch a video. Later we heard stories of vomiting and fainting. Anyway, the boys all had RE at that time. Someone kicked off in our class about how it was ridiculous not to educate the boys about it too. So, the teacher spent the lesson talking about periods. You could've heard a pin drop. We were careful what we asked him after that.'

'Mm. Glad I didn't go for the salsa dip.'

'Oh yeah, sorry.'

'I'm kidding.'

'Right. Anyway, the poetry, or whatever it is, appeared at some point during my undergrad. I was pretty embarrassed about it at first, but since I had no friends, there was no one to laugh at it. So I kept going, and I liked it.'

'Seriously? *No* friends?' She looked astonished.

'Seriously. No *good* ones, anyway. Acquaintances. The usual people you get on with at the beginning, but … I dunno … I just tend to drift off into my own little world, and that's it. I had zero ability to talk with girls. Maybe a result of growing up … just me and my mum. I couldn't … *well*, I suppose it's what happens when you start to need to get your own life, your own space. You get embarrassed by your mum having to tell you everything …'

'It's okay, Sel. You can talk about it, or not talk about. *Either* is okay. No pressure.'

'I feel like I *should* be embarrassed about it, if you know what I mean. No girlfriend. Ever.' He looked up at her briefly, shrugged, then took a mouthful of olives and hummus.

'Gosh. Well you know, Sel, I don't exactly make a habit of talking with other people about *my* life … and it's nice … to *actually* do it … and with someone who gets what I'm talking about. And it's nice to hear about someone else's life. Their dysfunction too. Not that you're … *you* know, I don't mean like *that*. Not *badly*,' she said quickly.

'No harm done. Mm.' He finished chewing. 'One thing I try to let go of, is judgement. Of myself, as well as others. I don't always *succeed*, but …' He smiled quickly, and took a sip of the apple juice. 'Good lord, this really *is* good. I'm going to have to skimp on the food and *live* on this stuff.'

'You know, I have the strangest feeling that we've met before. It's pretty much unheard of for me to be this at ease with someone I've just met. Does that sound odd?'

'No. Not really. I do know what you mean. I think you're a genuine person. It's really nice talking with you. It's easy. Kind of makes the long wait worth it. But, right now I should get back to it. I can only upset Alexander *so* many times in a day. He may well lay me off in a couple of months, and I want to at least get that far.'

'Sure. Well, it *was* lovely talking. I'm going to carry on painting you, if you don't mind. Perhaps we could stop for tea together later on.'

'That'd be nice.' He held her gaze for a moment, and said it again.

He helped her back in with the trays, then they stood looking at them, then each other, then they laughed and embraced spontaneously, and laughed again. They were both surprising themselves.

Sel had the distinctly unusual feeling of approval, as he pushed the mower up and down. Alexander hadn't taken him to task, but just warned him to behave, and be respectful at all times. Sel could see he was conflicted, because he had been telling him to go out and meet some young ladies all summer; that he was at the age where he should be getting experience, and finding out about how awful sex and relationships can be, and occasionally, how wonderful. *This* is wonderful, thought Sel. It's safe. I don't know how I know that, but it is. She's kind and gentle and sort of fragile ... but there's a strength there. And she lets me in. Who'd have thought that, before last week? There must be something about me ... and it can't be just because I'm so obviously a beginner ... she *enjoys* talking with me ... she likes a *real* conversation. These thoughts proceeded through his head as he went back and forth past the gazebo where she painted. He was glad he didn't feel obliged to wave and smile every time – there was no way he'd be able to keep his lines neat. He cut the engine when he was done, emptying the cuttings into the compost. He suggested they take a break then, as he only had the weeding to do after that.

For twenty minutes they drank tea and Faye talked of her upbringing. She knew neither of her parents, having been given up at birth, becoming what they called a 'relinquished baby.' She was adopted by a gentle, quiet couple, but was always distant from them, always very self-contained, closed off. She said she hardly remembered them, as she stuck to her room and would not, or could not engage. She had left home at 16, taking a supermarket job, stacking shelves and watching people. She observed them wandering the aisles anonymously; all together, doing the same thing in the same place at the same time, but few ever shared a word or a look. She lived in a bedsit, just her and her painting, sharing neither with anyone.

She said she had yet to feel – or perhaps acknowledge – any stirring of desire to know her biological parents, and was sure that they had not left her the house. She always had the feeling that they had been far from the types that would live in a house of this kind, in a place like Hampstead. She had never been contacted by any member of the family, so had left it all way off in the past ... though she admitted after a pause that it was with her every day in some way.

Their conversation rolled over into Saturday morning on the phone, and on the Sunday into a Chinese restaurant in Soho. By the evening they had talked and shared until they'd inflated a bubble around themselves that neither wanted to pop. Sel felt they were not just perfectly comfortable, but *satisfied* by one another. Answered, on some complex, indefinable but vital level. Yet in the back of his mind, the fact that neither of them had ever successfully cultivated a real relationship as adults, gave him the feeling that they ever walked the edge of a blade, above a chasm – the slightest gasp of wind could send them tumbling. But in the moment, he found it easy to connect, to watch her eyes as she spoke. Most people, he couldn't hold their gaze for more than a second at a time. It was too intimate – left him too exposed. Her intelligent blue eyes were to him jewels, glinting, nested beneath the wilful blonde curls. Her mouth had a million sets, expressions; her forehead, eyebrows, her cheeks too: they all moved with a music, a rhythm. She never seemed to have quite the same expression twice, giving the impression that she was living every moment of the conversation, that she was truly engaged in it, and *with* him, and giving of herself completely. Sel did his best to both welcome and answer her openness and directness.

She took him to Ronnie Scott's later, and they began to drink steadily, sat to the far left of the stage, slightly behind the sound. They watched the band, a Latin jazz quintet, but talked almost non-stop. She described the performance in visual terms, drawing his attention to the movement, the light, the relationship with the audience, framing and reframing, moment to moment. He talked of the poetry in it, the story, the mood, the questions that arose in him, the totality of the experience, and the finest details, like the glint of freshly painted nails around a cocktail glass, or the tiny ripples in their drinks caused by the bass drum.

During the second half, she took his hand and didn't let go. Their talk quietened down, and tiredness and alcohol overcame them. The faces in the crowd, that had looked so vibrant and wonderful and *important* an hour ago, now looked washed out by the lights, distant, unrelated, and Sel lost interest in them. He and Faye had explored them, drenched them in meaning and significance, yet now they needed only one another, sat in a gradually closing circle of intimacy that did not go beyond the lamplight. He tried to hold her hand causally, and take sips of his brandy and coke as though he did this kind of thing all the time, but it was an effort. The drink was tasting too strong and too sweet now, too much for his taste buds and his throat and his brain. The alcohol, sugar and caffeine jangled thought and sensation. Sometimes she would take his hand in both of hers, and squeeze it, looking into his eyes and smiling. He was sure he knew what that smile meant, but the possibilities overwhelmed him.

The set drew to a close, the energy of the band outmatching that of the audience in the end. And as the silence flowed, the customers sluggishly began going their separate ways, mostly never to meet again.

Sel went to fetch their coats from the cloakroom and watched Faye standing to one side of the room, looking cool in a deep blue dress with black detail. Though he knew she was pretty uncomfortable with it all, especially as people wandered past her, she looked stylish, aloof, and in that light, he could see fashion photographers drooling over her. He didn't know her age, but she looked like she could have been anywhere from early thirties to mid forties, like a dour teenager or a wise elder; her looks came and went like wind across a wheat field. She took her coat from him with a warm and weary smile.

They stood outside, chilly in the cool night air. She pulled him close by the taxi rank and they embraced. He breathed in her perfume, and it made him slightly light-headed. He realised he'd been smelling it all night, without ever paying it attention. A fine rain drifted down, just a mist, hazy against the streetlights. Tiny droplets glistened in her hair, lit by the taxis rumbling by. A few people asked if they were next in line for the cabs, but they both shook their heads silently. Eventually, Sel sighed heavily.

'I hate to say it, but I have to be at work in a few hours.'

'Can't you skip it tomorrow?'

'Er, *nope*. A man's gotta earn his crust.'

'You're the sensible type.'

'I'm as surprised as you are ... but I s'pose I don't want to leave Alexander a man light. I observe that I have some kind of work ethic trying to kick in. This is news to me.'

'You *are* funny.'

'On a bad day it's all I have, laughter. Ha-ha-ha, I'll say. What a terrible day I'm having. Ho-ho-ho.'

'I can pay Alexander off. I'm rich.'

'But you can't pay off my *conscience*. You're not *that* rich.'

'Ooh. *Good* answer. You're quite a catch, you know that?'

'Mm. Well, no one's ever dangled anything anywhere near me ... I mean as in like a fishing lure ... *never mind* ... Point is, I wouldn't know. I assumed I was scheduled to die alone. I'm kidding. But seriously, I have to get going. You want to share a cab?'

'Of course.'

They sat in the back of the cab together, Faye curled up on Sel's lap, his hand running over her damp hair. He thought of Buttons, his mum's cat. The cab dropped her off first in Hampstead, where they parted slowly and sadly, she gripping his hand for what began to be an embarrassingly long time. She gave him a pained smile and drifted off to her doorway, not looking back. He was sure she wanted him to stay with her, but not a single instinct of his recommended he do so. The cab then took him on to his bedsit in Kilburn. In bed, the night was spinning through his head, and as he dropped off to sleep he almost immediately began to dream that the night was carrying on, as they went to more bars and parties, and observed and chatted and laughed, locked in their own perfect little world.

IV

The alarm on his phone smacked him into wakefulness, what seemed like only minutes after getting to sleep. His body weighed a tonne. The idea of work drained him further. He realised he had seen the top of the mountain, and busying himself back in the foothills was, relatively, of no interest. But the fragility of his new friendship was clear in his mind, as was his sense of duty, and he dragged himself to the yard.

The short bike ride woke him up slightly, but she was still with him. He'd listened to her voice so closely for hours, and drank in her energies, everything she put forth, and been locked in her proximity to the extent that … he realised that he felt in some way *bonded* with her … and it had not been lost on him that she had been at pains to stress that she barely ever socialised these days, other than the necessary evil of attending the opening of one of her shows. He felt the swell of secret joy that they seemed to share, but felt it must be a blaring siren, a row of flashing lights on his head, as he entered the yard and saw Alexander turn and fix him with a look. Sel smiled weakly. He locked his bike in one of the sheds and did his best to saunter casually over to his boss, who was talking to Jerry and Stacy, a couple of American kids who were working in London for the summer. He gave them a sheet of their jobs for the day with photocopied close-up maps. It tickled Sel that they always called Alexander 'Sir.' They said hi to Sel and goodbye to Alexander, leaving the two of them alone. The other vans had already gone, and it was just the two of them.

'Good weekend, young man?' He grinned.

'*Yeah*, it was … it was fine. Thanks. How was yours?'

'Oh, *you* know. Mostly DIY. Wife's orders. Come on, you'll be with me today.' He got in the last van in the yard and pulled out onto the road. Sel locked the gates behind them, then got in the passenger seat and automatically pulled his knees up and pressed them against the dashboard, leaning back and settling in for the drive. They said little as they crawled through rush hour traffic, just listened to the burbling of Radio 4. Despite Alexander's knowledge of the back streets it still took them over forty minutes to drive the few miles into central London. He talked about the job they had for the day as they arrived in Marylebone, and said he hoped Sel was feeling strong. They had another garden to clear, everything but a mature Oak and a few selected shrubs to be retained, otherwise it was to be levelled, ready for hard and soft landscaping.

As they arrived they saw the skip had been delivered, which always put Alexander in a good mood. He knocked on the front door and they were greeted by a tall, greying blonde woman in a silk kimono, who looked to be in her mid fifties. She was sleepy but gracious, and left the door on the latch for them to set up. She was quite stunningly beautiful to Sel, and had a solid, curvaceous figure that oozed both maternal strength and erotic power.

He avoided his boss's eye as they fetched the dust sheets from the van, and laid them over the hardwood floors. They then set up a ramp into the skip and took spades, shovels and a few other tools through to the back garden in the wheelbarrows. It was a long, slender garden with new fencing. It was full of shrubs with no real shape to them, and an old pebbledash path that ran to the back. It managed to have no character whatsoever, and Sel was pleased that the owners had decided to make love to the space through their money and someone else's sweat. He wondered why sex was, quite unusually, on his mind. The lady, whose name was Eliza, offered them hot drinks, and Sel consented to a coffee. This was seized upon by Alexander as they stood surveying the task at hand.

'Ah, *in coffee veritas. You*, had a late night.' He smiled and settled himself down on the nearest barrow, and looked up at Sel, who felt himself reddening.

'I'd prefer to fib, or avoid the question, quite honestly.'

'Oh *God*.' Alexander's head fell forward onto his palm, and he sighed. 'Faye?'

'Dinner in Chinatown, band at Ronnie Scott's. It was perfectly enjoyable.'

'Well, my words'll fall on deaf ears, so I'll save them.' He stared down the length of the garden, looking into some other distance. 'But I *will* say this ... or will I? Yeah. I suppose, like most young people, you have to make your own mistakes. I watch my kids do it all the time. Aaron ... you can't tell him *anything*. Fair play, he doesn't complain if he *does* burn or scratch himself, or fall over or whatever, after I've told him to be careful ... and there's no telling *you*, is there?'

'It's hard ... to de*scribe* it, in a way that'll make *sense*. We just ...

hang out, we talk … it's not, you know. Like *that*.'

'Are you sure? Are you sure you'd *know?*'

'What do you mean?'

'I *mean*, that you can't always know what a woman wants. Or what *you* want. Anyway, it's not really my business. Even though it is *exactly* my business …'

'Look, I'd never do anything … to … *you know*. Mess things up for you. With her. She's a satisfied customer.'

'*Is* she? Well, it's not like she'd tell anyone … I used to do the garden for the previous owners, and when I turned up, just after she'd moved in, she didn't question it. We just talked about my rates, and that was it. Seems to keep herself to herself.'

Sel's eyes widened. 'You mean you know who the previous owners were?' His head was whirring with possibility. Should he pry? Would he want to know, and then be burdened with the knowledge?

'Not really. I never met them, just the housekeeper. She took care of the financials.'

'So how did you get the job, if you don't mind me asking?'

'Why *are* you asking?'

'Because … well, this is just between us, right?' Alexander nodded slowly, intrigued. 'She was left that house, and she doesn't know who by.'

'*Seriously?*'

'Absolutely. That's what she told *me*. Can't see why she'd fabricate such a thing.'

'Huh.' He lowered his voice. 'In *this* business … with *these* sort of clients, a lot of the time you don't know who the client actually *is*. They have people who sort these things out for them. Occasionally you get someone who genuinely *loves* their garden, knows their stuff, and on the odd day will actually work *with* you. But no, I'm afraid I can't really help her with that one. Still, she probably doesn't mind too much. Free house. Result.'

'Do you know much about her?'

'Well, I check out my clients a *little*. It's useful to know who you're dealing with. *Oi oi*.' He glanced towards Eliza, who was emerging from the kitchen with a tray of coffees which they took with thanks. Sel's eyes slid to the woman's ample bosom without his permission. He nodded and thanked her without meeting her eye, and took his mug. 'All I know is, she's a highly collected artist these days. Worth a mint. A man could do much worse, if he could make sense of her head. But anyway, how about this garden?' They stood side by side with their coffees, and Alexander held his out to chink with Sel's, who looked up with surprise. Alexander said nothing, just smiled a smile that seemed to come from a long way off.

They worked steadily through the day, saying little aside from what they needed to. They had a neat system, and Alexander appreciated Sel's graft and single-mindedness. By lunch, however, Sel was feeling a little light-headed. They ate quietly at the back of the garden, surveying that quiet corner of London caught for a few hours in the process of creative destruction. It put Sel in mind of a Vietnam film for some reason. He began to feel a little better, and let his mind wander gently, while Alexander read the newspaper and muttered the occasional sarcastic comment. He started to do the crossword and Sel thought he was out of the woods. Just at the exact moment he felt the relief easing out along his shoulder muscles, Alexander said, 'So. How *is* it going with herself?'

'Well. *You* know. It's okay.'

'No, I *don't* know. What does *okay* mean?'

'I am within my rights to plead the fifth amendment.'

'Wrong jurisdiction. Pray tell.' He looked up from his paper just long enough to fix Sel with a stare, who held it for a few moments, then weakened.

'What can I tell you? I mean, I don't know my*self*. We've hung out a bit. We get along very, very well. She ... seems to enjoy my company.' Sel looked at Alexander and held up his hands. 'If you think I *really* get what's going on with her ... well, I don't. I *do* know that if she *chooses* to spend time with someone, it must be with good reason. She seems like she's ... sort of ... *I* don't know ... de*tached* from the world. She just watches it. I watch her watching it, and I can relate. I'm the same. I don't feel ... not really *integrated*. Not quite *here*. With everyone else. To be honest, I'm not quite sure *what* we're all doing here. Five years of philosophy studies and still baffled.'

'Mm.' Alexander sighed. 'That's a young person thing. You'll get there. You'll *want* to be doing what others are, eventually. Be integrated. Tick all the boxes. It's just what happens. You may as well enjoy this bit while it lasts.'

'It's a hard thing to enjoy. Alienation.'

'Good Lord. She *really* enjoys your company, you say? Wow.' He stared into space, shaking his head slightly. After a moment he shrugged, slapped his thighs and said, '*O*-kay. Let's get back to it.' He looked across at Sel and narrowed his eyes. He flashed a smile. 'It's probably good for you to get out of your head and into your body.

Know what I mean?' Sel nodded, grinning sheepishly.

That evening, he ate quickly then got into bed, his sleep-deprived brain and worn-out body urging slumber upon him. But it wouldn't come easily. He glanced a few times across at his phone, wanting to call Faye, but feeling too mixed up to do so. He turned the light out and let the darkness settle upon him gently. Alexander seemed to think that their relationship should be something obvious, something that anyone could understand. Something *traditional*. But even though they were only just getting to know each other, there seemed no prospect of it being something easily pigeon-holed.

He found himself running his knuckles lightly across his temples, thinking of her hair. Whatever she needed from him, there was an obvious echo in him. Some kind of understanding. That felt right. Meeting another person and feeling understood. Accepted. Not having to explain it all.

He started to feel more tired now, his grip loosening on the day. He thought about how he wanted to find, or *make* a reality, a version of his existence that wasn't so underpinned with doubt and loneliness, so edged with the sense that his life was virtually going to waste. But what would it mean, to pin too much hope on Faye lifting him up and out of the quiet sadness that seemed *his* reality? Should he give any one person so much responsibility? Could he avoid it? Was he already on that slippery slope? The last thing he caught clearly, before sleep took him, was the sight of Faye, in his mind's eye, as she watches the band play, twirling her hair, a whimsical look on her face ...

V

'U still up?' read the text. He had to re-read it. He turned over in bed, sat up. He breathed deeply, noisily, staring at the words. His thoughts were in slow motion, snatches of sentences. He rubbed his jaw, looked across at the curtains. It was still gloomy out there, but his phone alarm was adamant that it was the start of a new day. He looked at the time of the text: nearly two in the morning. She must be asleep by now. But she'd wanted to talk in the middle of the night. He rubbed his eyes, carefully brushing crystals of sleep from the corners, then swung his legs around, pushed himself to his feet and stumped off to the bathroom.

The shower woke him a little more. He looked down at his body as he soaped it. Lean, taut, muscular, almost hairless. The thought came:

what does she want with a *boy*? Then: maybe that's all she can handle. Then: if movies have taught us anything, it's that men have a reputation for being dicks to vulnerable women. Is it possible *I* could be a dick? Do I have that in me? Could I manage to mess this up, despite my best intentions?

He watched the news as he ate his cereal. Jesus, he thought. No wonder people like us are drawn to each other. Sensitive types. This place is too much for us. We need the quiet world, the one we make for ourselves, the one with curtains shut and candles lit, keeping all this madness out. But, she paints it out, too. He sat for a few moments, switched the TV off. He reached for a pen and the envelope on the coffee table and wrote:

She could play my heart like an accordion
Squeeze, pull, fingers tapping
Music

He underlined the word 'music' several times, then left for work. By lunchtime he felt ready to respond to her message. He sat in the van and ate half a sandwich before getting his phone out. He texted: 'Soz – got yr msg this am. Had early nite. Exhausted. U ok?' His phone rang moments later, making him jump.

'*Hi.*'

'Hey. How's things?' She sounded tired.

'Okay. Having lunch. Am near the heath.'

'You want to swing by?'

'Can't. Have to get back to it in a few minutes.'

'Ah. Bummer.'

'You sure you're okay? You sound ... *flat.*'

'Nah. I'm alright. Just not a morning person. *You* know how it is.'

'Yeah. I have to be up at the crack of fucking dawn every morning ... and it does *not* suit.'

'Why don't you do something else then?'

'Like what? Teach philosophy? Be a starving poet? I told you. I just can't seem to work *any*thing out.'

'It takes time, Sel. Time.'

'Right. I guess that's about the only thing I *do* have. My youth.'

'And me.'

'And you?'

'Don't sound so surprised.' She yawned. 'Of *course* you've got me. Maybe you're a bit too young to know just *how* rare it is to meet someone you really click with. It's not just superficial stuff, but … you know, the energies are … somehow … *har*monised. Something like that, anyway.' She yawned again and made a loud stretching noise.

'And ours are?'

'You don't think so?'

"Well … it's just that … er, no one's ever told me *anything* like that before. I've never harmonised with anyone. That I know of. I'm sure I would have noticed.'

'Me neither. I didn't know that's what I was looking for until I met you. I don't mean like romance and all that … you know what I mean. Anyway. I want to see you. Come over tonight. I'll cook.'

She would not take no for an answer, and Sel let himself be persuaded. He was still too tired for it, but he wanted to see her too. He went back to work with a shade more energy. He worked in the quiet garden of a secluded property that apparently had once belonged to Peter Sellers. As he clipped a few shrubs he found the poetry coming of its own accord, words bumping up against one another, sometimes heavily, sometimes gently.

A singing voice
Melodious, mellifluous
Way off, in the distance
Across wide and deep fields
the breeze carries the notes to
my ear, grateful, my eye
a single tear
falls

She
The biggest syllable there is
Meaning everything and more than
you can comprehend
It is HUGE
too BIG
to grasp
It is too slippery
You cannot catch a river in your hands
You cannot catch the meaning of She

What use a man
When he is controlled by
A boy

Naked
Wild
Fucking
Fantasy

What if
her door was open
Innocent
I creep inside, remove my shoes
scale the stairs
and the bedroom door wide
a man, six foot seven
twenty five stone of solid muscle
has her bound hand and foot
naked
welts and whip marks
only tears of gratitude
the flush of pleasure across her chest

At this last he shook his head, stopped clipping and sat, rolled a
cigarette. He wondered about all the strange fantasies and supressed
desires that may be sunk to the bottom of his consciousness in a lead
safe. He wondered what might happen if she somehow freed it all.
What might he become? What could happen? Did he really have some
desire for domination? Or was it that something in him feared he was
getting into deeper waters than he could handle? Sink or swim, he
thought.

By the evening he was having to *breathe* through the tension as he
cycled across town. His inner five year-old relentlessly tugged at him,
asking whether she was thinking about sex too. The world of adult
relations seemed so complex, so incomplete in anyone's understanding
that there was *always* the possibility of *any* possibility becoming real.
We are always in the process of becoming, he thought.

'Hey, *flower!* How are you?' She reached her arms around him and
pulled him in tight; he felt an immediate surge of blood to his groin,
and sweat dotting his forehead and upper lip. He tried to keep his

pelvis tilted away from hers, then pulled back with a tight smile. She cocked her head to one side and gave him an amused, quizzical look. He liked that look.

'Sorry, I'm just *so* tired. Need to … sit … before … fall *down* …' He feigned collapse and lay spread-eagled on his back in the doorway. After a moment he said, 'This is actually quite comfy.'

'Well, can I make you a tea while you get comfortable?' She walked off to the kitchen and he took a moment, breathing, trying not to think about her body, before getting up and fetching his bike up the steps and inside.

They sat at the large solid Oak kitchen table, drinking tea and chatting languidly about their days. At one point the conversation drifted into silence and he caught her looking at him in a way he had never seen before. Not on anyone's face, ever. He smiled and took a sip of his tea, marvelling inwardly at the seemingly infinite variety of facial expressions that humans are capable of. He was sure that the more complex the person, the rarer their suite of expressions, and the more they blended them in new ways. He was enchanted and mystified and tired. After the tea she got up and began putting together a chilli con carne, and he helped with the prep. Sel talked about growing up and learning to cook basic things with his mum, then thought of her family background and lapsed into silence.

'It's okay, you can talk about her. It's nice to hear about that kind of thing.'

'Well, enough about me, I'm sure. What do you have in prospect for the rest of the week?'

'Therapy tomorrow. Painting. The usual.'

'What kind of therapy?'

'The expensive kind. I jest, but it really is expensive. Though cheaper than being crazy and unable to function.'

'I see.'

'Yes, thanks for asking. It's some kind of talking therapy. I've done a lot, but this seems to work okay. It was my therapist's idea that I engage you in conversation, in fact.'

'She sounds pretty on the ball,' he said goofily.

'Uh *huh*. The point is, we get along. It's like any relationship, it's all about communication and … you know. Chemistry. The x factor. Whatever it is that makes things work. There's something … that's *really* hard to define, but as long as *that* thing is there, and you are ready, willing and able to talk about things … personal things, with honesty and integrity, you've got a good chance of making the relationship work. So she says.'

'Right. In that case I've not yet ticked the first box, actually meeting someone.'

'You met *me*.'

'I mean someone of my own age. A normal girlfriend-type person. Like everyone else has.'

'I see what you mean. Hm.'

Faye went quiet, mixing the spices into the minced beef and vegetables. Sel felt a flush of anxiety. 'Did I say the wrong thing?' he asked quietly.

'No ... no, it just made me think the same thing. That's all. I finally meet someone I want to be around and we're ... *well*. I mean, my therapist is delighted, and somewhere deep down ... I know that it's possible for me to connect with a man. I *know* that now. But it'll only ever be platonic with us. That means that we will only ever get so close, and we'll never have a life together and ...' She stumbled into silence, and Sel felt the anguish and discomfort again as her shoulders began to shake and the tears came. She clamped a hand over her mouth and sniffed, a tiny sob escaping. He went to her, turned her round gently and embraced her. She held him tightly, letting the emotion out. He felt a great swell of warmth, and caught the thought: I'm helping someone who really needs it.

She wept with dignity for another minute, then sighed into silence. She pulled back, looking him in the eye. Her eyes were blurry with tears but she smiled broadly, sniffing and nodding at some inner comment. He smiled back and reached to catch a single tear as it coursed down her cheek. He saw it absorbing the tiny hairs on her cheek just before he took it. Without thinking he put it to his lips and looked startled that he'd done so. She laughed at this miniature drama. She squeezed him in her arms again. 'You're a lovely, *lovely* man, Selby.' She kissed his neck and the mingled cool tears and hot breath made him shiver.

'*Yikes!*' he pulled back, rubbing his neck theatrically.

'Sorry.'

'Don't apologise to me, Faye. Not *ever*. I just want you to be *happy*. Try not to kill anyone in the process, but just do what makes you happy. If I can help with that, I'm more than willing to. You've given me more hope, and happiness, in a few *days*, than anyone else in my lifetime.' He started to feel choked up himself, and stopped.

'Well, good. We'll call that a win. Let's have music while the food gets on with it. Take a break. You want me to open a bottle of wine?'

'Absolutely.'

It was getting dark outside as she lit candles in the lounge. It was a large room, but the lights created a gentle intimacy. She had a huge brown leather couch which they lay on together, in each other's arms, as Miles Davis rose smokily through the air. He was sure she was doing a lot of thinking, or at least feeling, and his own mind was busy. An inner voice was narrating the evening, and talking about how sweet it was that they'd found one another, found solace, a shelter from the storms of the world, or at least of *their* worlds.

Then the voice started talking about how sexy she was, how beautiful her blue eyes looked, flushed with tears. He thought of *Play it Again, Sam*, the Woody Allen film in which Woody's character is coached on how to score with women by an imaginary Casablanca-era Humphrey Bogart. He could imagine a notional audience telling him to make his move, to kiss her.

He'd heard those voices before. So many journeys on public transport, the little stories would play in his mind, featuring different women; how quirky and interesting they'd be, how their romance would be. He'd examine their faces in detail, looking for every little story written there, in every expression, in their makeup, their habits, their reading matter, their sense of themselves, their life lived in *that* moment in *that* space. And then another woman, another story.

And now he was entwined with a complex, wonderful woman who made it clear that she expected nothing from him other than his friendship. She was giving him most of what he needed, and allowing him to give her the same. He marvelled that life could be so neat, when it made the effort.

And then the question: was life doing this constantly? Was this simply the first time he'd engaged with it? Surely he could start a new story with anyone, anywhere? But that wasn't true, was it? How many would freak if he clumsily pronounced his interest? The tube was a classic case of people making their own space, despite the cramped conditions, or *because* of them. Most people would be too preoccupied to notice him in the first place. Why would they bother? After all, it's not a film, things don't happen that way. Most people are just extras, in the film of our lives. Very few have major roles.

'Huh?' she said.

'Hm?'

'Er, you just grunted and nodded. Looking rather satisfied with yourself.'

'Did I?'

'*Yes,*' she laughed. And kept laughing. '*God* you're a funny lad. Okay, you *have* to tell me now. Don't torture me.'

'I was … I was just thinking that … oh, it was a *long* train of thought. Just a mental ramble. But if you're *really* interested …'

'I am.'

He spent the next ten minutes relating his thoughts, and embellishing them with asides and illustrations. She listened quietly, occasionally *mm*-ing and nodding, with the odd snorting laugh, her head resting on his shoulder. Just as he wound up with a flourish, the timer went off in the kitchen.

'*Mm*-mm. *Very* interesting. Okay, all that food for thought's made me hungry. Let's eat.'

Faye served the chilli with nacho chips and dips, and they ate in the living room, watching *Futurama*. They laughed their way through it, and then watched a second episode, taking them up to nine pm. She suggested a film, and Sel decided to ignore time's invitation and hang out. For twenty minutes they went through her film collection, trying to find something that they were both in the mood for, and hadn't seen for long enough to enjoy it properly. In the end, *When Harry Met Sally* got the vote, which Sel hadn't yet seen all the way through. It was so apposite that he wasn't sure how to laugh, or how much.

They curled up together and kept their wine glasses within reach. Faye had also brought out some chocolate truffles that made her eyes roll up in ecstasy with every bite. It was quite something to see. Sel got more pleasure watching her eat them, than from tasting them himself. He took to feeding her one every few minutes just to watch her do it again. Half way through the film she went to get a blanket and put it over both of them, and let Sel spoon her. They said nothing for a while, but he felt the blood rush to his loins.

'One moment,' he said, and reached quickly down the front of his jeans to pull his erection straight. 'Sorry,' he said primly.

'That's quite alright,' she said, but in a way that didn't really tell him if it was alright or not. Damn, what *is* she thinking now? he wondered to himself. Once more he felt baffled by the elegant mystery that is woman. 'I wish, in *some* ways,' she said slowly, 'that I could give you somewhere more comfortable to put that. But I can't.'

'Oh Lord, *please* don't think that I was-'

'No, it's not that. It's … Well. I can't have sex. With anyone. I just can't. Physically.'

'Look, Faye, it's *really* none of my business at *all*.'

'Well … I'm just saying. It's kind of a big deal for me. I have this thing, it's quite rare. But, it pretty much means that when anything goes near … *down there* … it clamps shut like a vice. Nothing will go in. Nothing. Not a sausage. As it were.'

'Er … I …'

'No, well, not many people *would* know how to react to that one. Like I said, it's quite rare.'

'But I think I've heard of it. I couldn't begin to guess *where* … but I'm pretty sure I have. Have you *always* been that way? If it's okay to ask.'

'It's okay to ask.' She pushed her ass and then her back against him. 'I've *never* had anything inside … *there*. Ever. I don't quite know why. Sylvia, my therapist, thinks it may be because I never had anyone explain anything to me. I was freaked when I worked out where babies come from … and periods were a truly horrid surprise. I just started bleeding one day, and I didn't really know what the fuck was happening. I must sound … *stupid*. But I was sort of in and out of school … I didn't discuss this stuff with Clare, my adopted mother … didn't have friends … I dunno. I suppose I was gifted when it came to not letting anything in. And later on … I didn't have any call to use it anyway. I thought I was so defective that I steered well clear of boys. I had a crush on one or two, and one or two girls in my class … but didn't do anything about it. No one really bothered with me. In college I think I radiated a kind of *don't mess* thing. Well, no one did. The longer it goes on, the less it seems like it'll ever happen, so why worry?'

'Ouch. Painful to hear.' He wanted to say more, but instead stroked her hair.

'At this stage of my life … I realise it's not *so* uncommon. At least that thing of not really … you know. Fitting in. Feeling attractive.'

'Yeah. I try not to care either way. If we make our happiness contingent on external factors, we are doomed to unhappiness.'

'Gosh. Pithy. So speaks the philosopher.'

'Mm. Well.' Sel fidgeted a bit. 'I don't know what I can do for you Faye, but I hope *you* can let me know what that might be … any time.'

'You're already doing it. Being you, being here. Now.'

'Gosh.'

'Yeah. *Whatever* this is … it feels like the right thing at the right time.'

'Mm. And what did he say to that?'

'Well. Just that it made him very happy. That making *me* happy made *him* happy. That sort of thing.'

'Yes. I have the impression from what you say, that he is a sympathetic character.'

'Character? It's not a film. He's one of the most ... *vivid* people ever I've met in my life.' Faye looked stung.

'Go on.' Sylvia encouraged her with a brief, taut, professional smile.

'Yeah ... he's really *there*. Though most people wouldn't even notice him. He's totally *present*. Know what I mean?' Her eyes wandered up around the ceiling. She played with her hair. 'Yeah ... he's really *some*thing.'

'And what is your sense of the nature of the relationship at this time?'

'Why? You think it's going to change? Is that the suggestion?'

'Most do, in one way or another.'

'Well.' She bit her top lip, sucked at it noisily, eyes tightening with concentration. She listened for a few moments to the silence in the room. A car passed by out in the street, and some unrecognisable noise came from elsewhere in the house. 'Um. Are we talking sex again?'

'Is that what you're thinking about?'

'There you go again, Sylvia. Trying to snooker me. I was just wondering if that's where *you* were going, as you always seem to.'

'That was one of the thing you came here to deal with, Faye. It's my job to see if we can find a way *in*to that issue.'

'No pun intended.'

'Quite.'

'Well look. I realise the rest of the world makes quite the song and dance about sex. But you don't miss what you haven't had. I'm nearly too old to worry about it any more. And I don't want to ruin my friendship with this lovely young man over the old Pink Vault Syndrome.'

'I don't suggest that you do, but it seems prudent to recognise that whether the two of you have experience or not, there can be physical chemistry that ... may over*whelm* any common sense approach you may wish to take.'

'Yeah but, *look* who you're talking to. *Neither* of us, *ever*. And we're expected to *both* want to? Long shot.'

'Again, I am merely pointing out that it is *possible*, and that you may wish to be prepared, in the event that it does arise.'

'Sylvia, you've *got* to knock those double entendres on the head. And prepare how? Condoms?'

'I *mean-*'

'I know what you mean. I'm just kidding. Seems to me he'll most likely decide at some stage that sex with a functioning woman would be best … and besides, he'll want to be in *love*. What *we* have … maybe it's better not to analyse it. As, let's face it, your response is to take it to a place that one would ex*pect*. But this isn't … it's not that *kind* of thing. It's its own thing.'

'But nevertheless Faye, it's significant. And worth exploring, wouldn't you say?'

'Sylvia.' Faye paused, began biting at her top lip again, and squeezing her fingertips, each in turn. 'This is the most special thing that's *ever* happened to me. I don't expect to get it right … necessarily … but I want to just *be*. To just be *in* it. For however long. And that's precisely what I intend to do.'

VI

The weeks rolled on, and their relationship grew in intensity as the autumn spread its cool gloom across their world. Alexander kept him on, but reduced his hours as the work thinned out. Faye offered him a room of his own in the house, but he refused, wanting to keep his own space. He began to share his poetry with her, but not his latent desire. It grew steadily in him, as the days grew ever shorter and darker. They had begun to spend nights together, coiled tightly, though always clothed, and Sel found the magnetism of their genitals to be merciless, increasingly unpleasant, and eventually, distressing. After a while he began to see a little less of Faye, and eventually only at weekends, and then every other weekend. She said nothing, but the gap grew, and her heart began quietly to break.

In early November, when their relationship was tethered only slightly, Sel joined a writer's group, and within a fortnight was seeing a young woman who also attended. Olivia was quirky, bright and optimistic, though she wrote of the torment of being too aware of herself and her surroundings at all times. She was heavier set than Faye; she was a curvy, earthy brunette who liked to laugh at virtually everything. She breathed new life into him and made him see the world through her shining eyes, and in particular, excelled at making him take himself less seriously.

She also, to his gratitude, gave him a crash course in adult relations. He was genuinely shocked to discover how liberating and fun it could be to set out on such a journey with someone who didn't judge, didn't compare him to anyone, didn't expect anything of him. It quickly became his new favourite thing. When the moment came to leave his virginity behind he thought of that moment when Faye made him feel like he was walking the plank. As he sank himself inside Olivia, he instantly felt new circuits lighting up, a revelatory awakening. He wanted to give a running commentary, to share every drunken thought, but she shushed him, pulling him into her rhythmically, sighing in his ear. It made him focus instead on the sensations, the whole body experience, and for long moments he suspended all thought. He leaned up on his elbows, peering down to see himself moving in and out of her. He shook his head, surprised to see what it actually looked like, to see that you really are inside someone else's body. It was a kind of responsibility, he felt. Really an intimate thing. How can people do this just for fun, he wondered. It's a *really* big deal. Her hands fastened on his hips and started pulling him in deeper, and the whole experience shifted, accelerated. Her breathing, the soft thump of her hips against his, it took on a music all of its own. Her sighs became moans, and dropped an octave, and he felt like a passenger, trying to remain on board, pictured a rodeo, tried not to think about rodeo clowns ... then felt his whole body tingling, saw and felt arrows all over it, pointing at his penis, which became one big arrow; he looked down again and saw her pubic hair as *her* arrow, telling him where to go: the meeting point.

'*Fuck* me,' she sighed, eyes closed. It was as though her words were a text message, an instruction from far off. He stared down at her, trying to discern how much she actually felt connected to him in that moment. 'Fuck me,' she said again, her breathing becoming deeper and louder. He was spellbound. Her eyes flicked open, a tiny flash of anger in them. '*Fuck* me,' she said. 'Come *on* ... *do* it.' He felt like an actor being prompted. Luckily the stage direction seemed clear enough. He thrust harder, trying not to giggle at the strangeness of it. Here he was, hitting a woman in the groin with his groin, over and over again. If you even mentioned this to a stranger on the street you could be arrested, but here, it's totally cool. Required, in fact. 'That's it ... that's it ... don't stop ...' A little smile amid the panting, coming faster and faster. Her eyes opened, she stared at him, a minute look of pleading, of nakedness, then her face screwed up like she was in deep discomfort, then a groan that rose and rose and became momentarily a look of pain, then a bursting, her face almost empty, vacant, a lost look, then a series of thrusts, grunts, gasps and spasms

that bucked him up and down, making him think of the rodeo again ...
then a kind of falling away, a long fall ... then she hit the ground and
the air went from her lungs. She inhaled with a luxurious kind of hiss,
and pulled him into her again, pushing against him slowly.

'Oh *man*. Thank *God* for that,' she sighed. She swallowed hard and
looked at him, focusing on him. 'Did you come?' It sounded like a
ridiculously personal question, but she asked with absolute
equanimity.

'Er. No. I was watching you.'

'*What?* That's a *funny* thing to say!' She giggled, then shook her
head, like he truly was a prize weirdo she'd managed to stumble
across. 'Okay then, your turn. Come on. Don't watch *me*, this time.'
She laughed again, then started pushing against him, moving her hips
in circles, immediately sighing. She reached a hand up and pinched a
nipple, squeezing it rhythmically. He wanted to laugh, but it actually
felt good. Okay, he thought, you can do this. You know how to come.
It's part of the deal. The minute he thought of his own pleasure, he
thought of Faye, and she drifted through his mind, back and forth,
wearing those tight dresses. Is this wrong, he asked himself. He looked
down at Olivia's breasts, which were large and fairly pert, capped with
equally generous, upstanding nipples. Her breasts suddenly looked like
eyes, and he got a sense of them staring at him, saying, come *on* now,
pay attention, this is *serious*. His mind continued to wander until she
pulled his head down and kissed him, her tongue playing gently with
his. She whispered, 'Come in me, Sel. Come *inside* me.' This seemed
to push some button somewhere, and his whole body lit up again; he
saw the arrows, felt a heat, a tightness in his entire pelvis that became
increasingly focused, then had an image of molten metal flowing into
a mould, and he thrust harder and faster, saw himself running along
the ground, flapping his arms, jumping higher with each bound until
he became airborne, rising with great slow wingbeats way up into the
sky ... then he saw himself as Icarus, catching fire ... and his body
convulsed as the liquid seemed to explode from him like a bullet, and
he went rigid – thinking this is why they call it shooting – then the
juddering, having to slam into her to overcome the almost painful
sensitivity. He thought of her slow fall, and saw himself, Icarus again,
wings crisped, tumbling through the air towards the ground. He
collapsed upon her with a gasp, eventually breathing slower, his mind,
for the first time in a long time, empty.

'Not bad, eh?' she said, a smile in her voice.

'Oh my *God*. That was *totally* worth it. Why didn't anyone *tell* me about this?' He cackled with laughter, feeling a lightness he'd never felt before. 'Holy *shit*. How much *does* come weigh? I feel about a stone lighter.' They giggled together for twenty minutes, Sel rambling about what he'd seen and thought, aside from Faye. Olivia thought it hilarious.

'Oh man,' he said. 'Let's do that again. I *totally* get it now.'

It was a few days before Christmas when he finally got up the courage to tell Faye, at her home. They sat across the sitting room from one another, she on the couch, he in an armchair, legs crossed, staring at the coffee table between them.

'Well, that was obvious.'

'Mm.'

'You should have told me, Sel. I'm *happy* for you. Did you think I wouldn't be?'

'I thought … I dunno. That I'd be hurting you.'

'Ahh, *no*. I'm not *hurt*. I just *miss* you. That's all.' She gave him a pained smile.

'I'm sorry.'

'Oh, *don't* be. *Really*. It's …' A tear fell, then another. Then she gave into her sadness. 'I … part of me wishes I … could have been *normal* for you. You're *so* lovely.' She sobbed quietly. Sel squirmed, the self-loathing writhing inside. He pulled and twisted his fingers.

'I *knew* it would be like this. You crying, me feeling like a shit.' She didn't answer, just shook her head, face buried in her hands. 'I don't know what to *do*. I don't want to see you like *this*.' His foot began tapping rapidly, he bit his lower lip, he could not bring himself to look at her.

'I think …' she said, taking a few breaths and slowing the sobs. 'I think that this was *always* how it was going to end. And I knew that.' She wiped more tears away, and looked at him, hands in her lap, meek and naked. 'If you love someone, set them free. That's the received wisdom on this. Isn't it?'

'I didn't *plan* this, Faye.'

'Of *course* not. You're just a *normal* young man, despite what you might think. You're giving your*self* a hard time. You just don't want to see me upset. Of course I could get angry, throw things, accuse you of all kinds of … *bull*shit … but this is the *reality*. We had no *agreement* … that you'd never fall in love, never look at another woman. We're *friends* Sel. I'm your *friend*, and I want you to be *happy*. Don't you *know* that?'

'I feel the *same*, but I'm looking at you in floods of tears.' He gestured weakly, looking defeated.

'Look.' She sighed, carefully wiping more tears away and sniffing. 'All this will make sense to you over time. I could beat myself up too ... plenty of people'd say I should have sorted myself out, been able to fuck you, keep you interested. Have a toy boy. Well, I *assume* they would. I've seen enough TV shows where everyone's dysfunctional, morally ... *weird*, to know that our culture seems to think that *any* sex is better than none at all. And I don't understand that.' She leaned back in her chair, taking a few more long, deep breaths, looking thoughtful. 'This is just what happens. This is our story. And now *this* part of it is over.' She looked at him without expression, and it was his turn to burst into tears.

VII

Ten years passed. He found an email in his inbox one morning, and made a decision.

London, the spring of 2012. Sel walked up the red carpeted steps of the gallery of modern art with a box under one arm, and a tall, dark, slender woman on the other. He was dressed in black tie and Homburg, and she in a long black strapless dress and black heels. It was approaching dusk, and the entrance was lit with flickering candles. He gave his invite to the broad, sharp-dressed, dead-eyed man at the door, and entered.

The room was high and wide, but the placing of partitions throughout created an intimate space for viewing the paintings. A soft, undulating soundscape played from hidden speakers, and wine was being taken from trays by the dozens of exquisitely attired guests also arriving. Many of them were already mingling. There were shrieks of recognition, dainty air kisses, laughter. Sel and his partner took a glass of wine each and began to circulate. They moved slowly through the exhibition. He looked at the paintings, recognising only a little of the style. He did not stop for long at each. His nervousness was picked up by his partner; she squeezed his arm, and whispered soothingly to him.

'*Stefania!*' They turned to see a tall, dark good-looking man in his forties coming over. 'Greetings! Wonderful to see you here. I'm Jack.' Air kisses and a handshake.

'Oh, *Jack*. Is good to meet you. This my husband, *Gregory*.'

'Of whom I've heard so much. A pleasure. So glad you could both make it. How was the journey?'

'Was fine, thank you.'

'Well, great. Let me grab the star of the show. I'd love to introduce you.' Sel and Stefania looked at each other, and she stroked his back and smiled. He smiled back, then stiffened. It was her. She was in conversation with three people, and seemed to know them well. A moment later Jack pulled her away with jovial apologies, pointed … and she saw him. She and he heard nothing, the sound fading out as she walked towards him, squinting, knowing it was him but not quite able to believe it. She wore a long black evening dress, and walked with an ease he did not remember her having. Sel didn't hear what Jack, Stefania and Faye were saying to one another as she joined them. He was examining Faye, trying to process all the similarities and differences. She had more presence, he thought, was brighter, more comfortable, sort of *unfurled*. She looked at him, and her hand went to her mouth to cover a smile, just as it did the first time they spoke. Their faces broke into grins, she looked him up and down, shaking her head.

'The beard …' she said, and reached a hand to it.

'Yeah. Why not? Makes me feel … *older*.'

'You *are* older.'

'Yeah. You're right there. And *you* …' he took a half step back and looked her up and down. 'You scrub up pretty well.'

'*Ha!* Yes. I've been practicing.'

'Right. This all looks …' he shrugged, gesturing to the paintings. 'A whole lot different. Tender, by comparison.'

'Yes. This has been happening for a while now.' She went quiet for a moment, and then said to Jack and Stefania, 'Well, why don't you two get acquainted, while I have a catch-up with my old friend?' They nodded agreeably, and Faye lead Sel away by the hand. She took him out the back and to an elevator. He gave her a quizzical look, but she just raised an eyebrow and smirked knowingly. In the lift they took turns coughing, scuffing the floor with their toes, feigning discomfort. Moments later she was leading him out of a door and onto the roof terrace. It was cool in the night air but she stood near a warm vent and wrapped her arms around herself.

'*You've* been up here before,' he said.

'You betcha.'

'Nice.' He walked around the edge, looking over the nearby streets, busy with traffic and pedestrians. He nodded, impressed, then went to stand with her by the vent. 'You hang out at these places a fair bit these days?'

'I do. Seem to have the social phobia licked.'

'Wow. Well. You look *amazing*. Hardly aged a day.'

'That's the foundation. Covers a multitude of sins.'

'Mm. Jack seems nice.'

'Yeah, he's a painter too. I never realised how self-indulgent artists were until I met him. And Stefania's lovely. She looks like a dancer.'

'Good guess. She teaches at La Scala.'

'Good *Lord*. You've come a long way, baby. Your mum must be beyond proud.'

'Yep. I did okay.'

'You *did* do okay. Bravo. And what do you do now? The pot plants at La Scala?'

'This.' He handed her the box. She took the heavy cardboard lid off and gasped.

'Oh … oh *my*. You *didn't* make these?' She drew out a pair of sleek black heels with scarlet trim and buckle.

'I designed them. But I can make them too. Sort of took to it.'

'Oh my *gosh*. And *this?*' she reached into the box again. Underneath the shoes was a hardback book. She handed Sel the shoes and looked at the cover. She clapped a hand over her heart. 'Faye, and Other Poems, by Gregory Selby.' Her hands were visibly shaking as she opened it. She bit her top lip. 'For Faye, an inspiration, a most treasured friend. Oh *Sel*. This is … *too* much.' Then she said quietly, 'I wondered if you'd forgotten.'

'*Really?*' He looked stunned. 'How *could* I? You were my first real *friend*! I know it was … short, but … you've *never* left me … not for a *day*.'

'But you left me for ten *years*.' She looked half serious.

'What can I say?' He stared up at the clear night sky, at the few stars bright enough to shine through the light pollution. 'It was so *intense*. I didn't know how to handle it. I thought that I must be screwed up somehow … that I could only get close to someone who also hid from the world. I don't know. I can't necessarily explain it very well.' He looked down. 'It's all there in the poems. Sometimes it's just images, sensations that I tried to get down in a way that others … *might* understand. Sometimes I just wanted to preserve you in that perfect way, like when we first met. How it was. That was so … well it was *unique*. It was our thing. I suppose I wanted to grow up, to … I felt like I upset you so much when I met Olivia. I suppose I didn't want to repeat that.' He stuck his hands in his pockets and looked at Faye, then at his shoes. 'I rehearsed this so many times and now it just won't come out straight. Well. Maybe it makes *some* sense.'

'Yes. It does. *Every*thing you've said ... *has* passed through my mind at *some* point. I've thought about it, I've painted it ... but in the end I just held you, very fondly, in my heart. There was nothing else like us. And I choose to celebrate it.'

'That's true. And I guess it came out of me in many ways. You've been my muse.'

'I don't know what to say.' She looked at the shoes and the book. She looked at him with eyes that said what he needed to hear. That she was grateful, that she was touched, that she still had love for him.

'I just ... needed to *be* here tonight. I wanted you to know how much you mean to me. How much you've meant. If I hadn't met *you* ... I just don't know. You changed my life. I got interested in art ... in other *people*. You made me want to *live*. To leave my room. And I really did. I travelled a lot, I met *all* kinds of people, all over. I learned how to mend shoes in India and then ended up in Italy learning how to make them. Started going to all sorts of art and design things around the country ... made a pair of shoes for a friend of Stefania's. She wanted to meet the man who made them and, a year later we'd made a baby.' He laughed. 'It sounds *nuts* when I say it all out loud.'

'You're ... a *father?*' She looked like she was about to well up. She stepped closer and embraced him. 'That's wonderful.'

'Yeah,' he said, patting her back softly. 'Sandrine. She's ... well, you'd love her. *She* paints. And never stops talking. Mostly asking questions.'

'Ha! I'd *love* to see her work.' They pulled back, gave each other a look that said they were all square.

'I'm sure it can be arranged. Anyway, how's it going with Jack? Children?'

'Well, no. Jack's sister has twins, and we see them every month. That's kind of enough for me. We, er, worked out ... that *other* thing.'

'*Other* ... oh ... *Oh! Well*. Congratulations! *Nice* one.'

'Yeah. It was kind of a big deal. But ... we got there. So yeah. Hm. Made me feel like a whole person. I never thought I'd know what that felt like. So ... obviously you didn't stay with Olivia.'

'Oh, yeah. Well. She was good for me, for a while. But, I can't say we really *connected*. You sort of spoiled me in that way. Well, ships in the night, more or less. Good laugh and all that. But off on her own trip. Very much. And I guess she helped me go off on *my* own trip. Yeah. Without the two of you ... who knows?'

'*Who* knows. Indeed.' She shivered. '*Ooh!* Cold.'

'Yeah. Well, let's get back inside.'

'Before we do … let's keep in touch this time. Okay? I'd *really* like that.' She looked more beautiful to him, in that moment, than at any other. It was her sincerity, somehow. He felt fuller, being the subject of that look, that sentiment.

'Me too. And Stefania *loves* your painting. She's desperate to buy one.'

'See? She *has* got good taste.' She smiled at Sel, stroked his beard, and laughed. '*This* will take some getting used to.'

As they left, arm in arm, Stefania asked Sel, 'So, the *thingy?*'

'Yeah, they worked that out.'

'Oh, that's good. That's good.'

That night, after Faye and Jack had got home, she took Sel's book of poetry with her while she took a bath before bed. She turned to the first poem.

Faye

In, without knocking
through a new door
the sign above it says
Faye
In quietly, and with time let me know
that I was to her as she was to me
but
every instinct delivers a bill
and the expectation that follows us
 the thought between every other thought
And yet
 none would tell the truth of it any more than
 admit they share it
The doors that open
by whatever degree
remain open
the sign too
and wherever the body may go
 the old footprints in dust never swept
 always

Janie

A candle-lit room, of dark corners, purple velvet, black lace, incense curling up in air moving in gentle music: saxophone, smooth, full and throaty; sonorous double bass; soft, brushed drums; piano speaking jazz, slowly. In a leaded, arched mirror, her face. It bobs to and fro, coming close to peer carefully at itself, slow strokes and dabs of colour, arcing with the curves and swells of her features; eyes, a darker blue than in the shallows of her youth, serious, steady, at once full and empty; cheeks, soft, tiny red fractures, the taught sheen gone twenty years before; lips, full, wide, still an object of desire daily, wherever they are seen. Lipstick flows over them, a practised hand. In warm hazy scented gloom by slow music, her face, glorified, melodramatic, made ready for the night. Thousands of times the ritual, back on through years, and years, and still the magic of transformation. Tonight, men of all ages will feel the heat when she is near, gentle flames licking thighs, groin, belly. The only thing that can quench this special fire is her wetness. For the want of it, men have fought like beasts, as if their lives depended upon it.

She moves around the room, hand-cupped candle-flames expiring in the little streams of her breath, she lets the night in by degrees. The window she sets ajar, letting the scent of the cooling city drift in. She stoops to blow the life from the last candle, the curve of supple buttocks in tight black in shadows, then darkness. The music plays on, alone.

In the benighted streets, under gentle misty rain, sharp, quick echoes of boots striking the pavement: she walks, slender from toe to forelock, then a mane, thick, jet, flows and waves as she heads back, out, to where she feels *most* like her, in hot, dark, loud places, shining in the eyes of men. Only there can she see herself clearly.

This night she makes for a favoured haunt, setting herself for a moment, then entering, confident, her tiny frame dwarfed by her stature. She moves slowly into the densely packed, small modern wine bar. It is all sleek lines, low lights and square furniture. The walls are a rich purple with minimalist gold floral detailing, but both the walls and the hardwood floor are obscured by the hundred or so people filling the space, mostly standing with their drinks, shrieking and barking laughter into friends' faces. The clientele are comfortably middle and upper middle class, mostly dressed to look slightly younger than they are. The bar runs along the back wall, where in a multitude of alcoves, wines from around the world are nested, colourfully illuminated with tiny LEDs.

By the time Janie reaches it, hailing and embracing her friend, her partner for the evening, more than a dozen men have seen her, and the chemical reactions take place. Some try to look away, back at friends, at girlfriends, but she is compelling. Her laugh, a huge, expansive, hearty and contagious thing, finishes the work of attraction that her appearance begins. When she laughs her head tilts back, eyes closed, mouth wide, and the whole of her upper body shudders with pleasure. It is a too-loud laugh for some. Women can be seen bunching together in barbed, whispered commentary. She is a Threat to them; their eyes see a woman too open, confident, sensual, and too single. She dresses too young, too provocatively, and they know that every straight man in the room wants to know what it is like to bed her.

A group of three men are drinking together, now into their fourth hour. The bar is hot, busy, and in the three hour peak where the night is still a high, buoyant, rollicking thing, not yet in the darker, final phase where anything can happen to anyone, suddenly. The first to catch her eye tilts his pint glass in her direction, saying to the others that *there* is a *real* woman. Another says she is the kind of woman who would fuck *you*. The alpha of the group says she would have a finger up your arse before she's even kissed you.

Another man, early thirties, is nodding with blank eyes, agreeing with his girlfriend that the woman is making a show of herself, that she obviously has issues with self-esteem. He is thinking that she looks fantastic for her age, and wishes his girlfriend had an ass that small.

The bartender, Dan, knows her, he says hi Janie. She gives him a look which blends mock-innocent with mock-sultry, and he goes automatically to pour her a large glass of pinot noir, ignoring other customers who were ahead of her. The first night she came to the bar they drank together for two hours after closing time, and he has wanted her ever since, though she has never allowed him close. He is now a kind of willing, supplicant plaything, and gives her free drinks whenever he can, particularly at the end of the night.

Some of the other customers have drunk with her in the past. One of them, Louie, has known her for over twenty years. He sees her tonight, for the first time in months, and reflects that she has barely changed in all that time. He says this to his lover, another man, who says she looks the perfect fag hag. Louie says she pretty much is. She is a sweet, sometimes rowdy drunk, a lively dancer, often the focus of melodrama, almost permanently single – aside from brief, hilariously disastrous affairs, usually with married men, has the occasional sexual episode with another woman, and is a good listener.

Janie's friend and drinking partner for the night is Heather, cast from a similar mould, if not physically. She is taller, with a much bigger, pear-shaped frame; she has curly brown hair past her shoulders, a full double E chest in a low-cut top, and a curvaceous ass that appears increasingly inviting to men through any given evening in a bar. Her third husband just died of old age, as the previous two had. She literally fucked them to death. It is sometimes assumed that this is pure exploitation, a kind of prostitution, verging on criminal behaviour, but each of them thanked her every time she shared herself with them physically. She was never repulsed by their age, not even mildly put off. Her spirit is one of generosity. She is a bon viveur, and consumes life with gusto. Picture her in a Beryl Cook painting. To her, men are playmates, to be brought no closer. They are equals, but none have ever got deeply into her. She lives between mind and body, specifically her gut and her erogenous zones. Her heart is the only virginal part of her body.

Janie loves her for this, though she has tried to find an idea of love all her life. The Catholicism of her Italian parents infused her ideas of sexuality and romance, and she has transposed the personal guilt and shame into dysfunctionality in love. What she thinks of as love is drawn from film and song more than anything: the idea that happy endings are inevitable, that true love conquers all. She has never been equipped for struggle, and sees any difficulty in relationships as a sign that she has not yet found true love – *the one*. She believes he will appear one day, and it will be immediate, effortless and permanent. Her penchant for picking unavailable or otherwise unsuitable men, however, has kept the possibility at bay for over thirty years.

The first hour swims by. Janie and Heather field the usual inept enquiries, and accept a few drinks from eager, often nervy patrons.

Heather allows herself to be drawn into conversation with a man in his late sixties. His beard and dress are from almost a century ago, and he screams *widower*. He looks as though he has just walked out of a painting of old Bristol merchants.

She and Janie stand back to back at the bar. Janie is now listening to Greg, the alpha male previously mentioned. He stands taller and broader than his buddies, and is of square jaw and heavy set. He boasts loudly about his business, his staff, his money, his cars and his holidays – in the guise of telling *funny stories*. Janie lets him scale the heights of pomposity, nodding and smiling in all the right places, and just as he peaks, and picks his moment to begin complimenting her, the very instant his body language shifts, his tone, his eyes, the second he says *you*, she looks over his shoulder and folds an arm across her chest, the smile falling from her face. He sputters into silence, confused, momentum tripping him up; he takes a deep gulp of lager and sweats slightly. Janie turns without another word to Heather and tells her she is going to the bathroom. She excuses herself from the men with a false smile calculated to turn the knife. Greg waits for her to leave and mutters to his friends that she is a fucking cock-teasing old hag.

On the way to the bathroom she passes a group of teenagers squashed onto a table next to the door. There are two boys and a girl. There is a couple, and a gooseberry: the single, bored friend. He looks just old enough to be in the pub, and gives the immediate impression of just barely enjoying the evening.

When she returns to the bar, Heather is being notably tactile with her new friend, laughing and gripping his arm. The rest of the evening is almost certainly set in stone for them. Janie knows what lays in store for this man better than he does.

She stands alone, facing the bar, waiting for the next in line. It does not take long. A pair of men this time: players. They have the look of those who know the game but think that they successfully conceal this. It will normally take her mere moments to discern which type of man is presenting himself. These men are slick, she observes, quite the double act, and probably very successful with this approach. They play off one another, keeping it light, again pointing to one another's successes, their fun-loving nature, and ability to share this with others. They even touch on their mothers and daughters, switching the tone to quiet dignity with regard to the sainted women in their life … then moving colourfully back into party mode, talking of a trip they are toying with, to a resort on Mexico's gulf coast.

Janie lets her eyes glimmer with enthusiasm, ignoring the glances from the previous unsuccessful group. These men look as though they can handle themselves, and this impression may be tested. Greg's body language says his shaming, and now supplanting by these two, is whipping up a fury in him. He turns to look at them, again and again. His shakes his head minutely each time, mouth tight. She notes this, and gets the crawling feeling in her belly, the loathing of violent and egotistical men. In her youth it was a thrill, then later frightening, then boring, then despicable. Just then Heather lets out a great hoot of laughter and bumps into Janie, who spills her wine on herself. One of the men – Craig, she thinks – immediately grabs a bar cloth and dabs at her breast, a concerned look on his flushed face. From the corner of her eye she sees Greg lurching towards them, and quickly steps into his path before he can reach the man.

'Problem?' she says, staring up at his face, which is suffused with barely controlled rage, his teeth gritted.

'What the fuck's he think he's doin', hands all over your tits in a pub?'

'It's not *your* business, *is* it? She steps toward him, glaring, standing nearly a foot shorter than he. The bar is almost silent. Heather turns around slowly and steps around Janie to stand toe to toe with Greg. She is still a few inches shorter than him, but her eyes are on fire. She pushes her shoulders back and her jaw forward.

'You turn around, and *fuck off* back to your mates, or I'm gonna put *your* head through *that* window.' She says it quietly, but looks crazier by the second. 'Try me, you big twat. *Try* me.'

'Alright, ladies and gents, let's relax ourselves.' Dan has come around from behind the bar to stand beside Heather. He smiles at Greg who looks to be weighing his options, and at his buddies, whose hearts are not in it. 'Sir, best you and your friends move on for tonight, yes?' Greg looks around the bar, snorts and shakes his head.

'*You* fucking lot. All tryin' it on with this cock-tease? She's fucking late fifties if she's a day, and every dick'ead in 'ere tryin' to crawl up it! You're fuckin' *welcome* to it.'

'Alright sir, that's enough. That language-'

'*Stick* it up your arse, faggot,' says Greg, who turns and barges through the crowd to the exit. His friends, heads bowed, follow.

'Sir? You forgot your jacket, sir,' calls Dan. Then, 'What a *nice* man. I hope he comes back.'

There is a profusion of apologies, thanks, explanations between the women and the men. Janie smiles through it all, but she knows that most of the people know that she caused it, and has done so before. Suddenly she has had enough of the bar, the night, but Heather has already turned back to her new friend and is cackling with laughter again. Janie's companions have cooled their interest; she feels the energy drain from her, the years asserting themselves, sucking the moisture from her face, the foundation cracking; her eyelids gain weight, facial muscles slump. Even Dan is now too busy to make eye contact. She pinches her wine glass and twirls the stem, feeling both ignored and studied by the other customers.

She goes to the bathroom again, for something to do. Sitting in the stall she pees, wipes herself and makes a decision. After washing her hands in the wide granite sink she stares at herself for thirty seconds in the mirror. She nods.

As though about to take to the stage she breathes, readies herself, then takes a winning smile into the bar. She immediately picks on the gooseberry, saying hi. His eyes bulge, then begin darting around, colour rises to his cheeks; his young friends, holding hands across the table, gawp. He clears his throat, hand darting to his drink then back again. She laughs, and says come on, you look bored, let's go and have a drink somewhere quieter. She leads him out by the hand, then he dashes back for his coat and scuttles along behind her, head down.

'How's your evening going?' she asks.

'Alright. Yours?' he has his hands in his pockets, walking next to her, eyes on the pavement. He looks back over his shoulder.

'It's okay. I had enough of that place though.'

'Understandably,' he mutters.

'Yeah? Why's that?'

'Well. All that … mayhem.'

'Yeah. What's new?'

'Happens to you a lot?'

'It's not the first time, let's put it that way.'

'But you still go?'

'Why not? Can't let men decide what I do and don't do.'

'Fair enough. Where are we going?'

'We can have a drink at my place.'

'I don't really drink.'

'Oh?'

'No. I smoke. If you know what I mean.'

'I'm sure I do. That's okay too. Come on.'

Five minutes later they climb the last of the stairs to her flat. Inside, he looks around, agog.

'You've never seen a woman's flat before?' she asks, lighting candles.

'Not like this.'

'Okay. I'll take that as a compliment. You want a tea?'

'Milk and two. Thanks.'

'You're quite welcome. You know what? I'm going to join you. I think I've had enough to drink tonight.' He follows her to the small kitchen and leans against the doorway while she gets the kettle on and makes the tea.

'Your friend's fierce.'

'I'll tell you something, she would've mopped the floor with that guy. Seen her do it. She's kneed more men in the groin than you've had hot dinners. She could give lessons.'

'Ouch.'

They make more small talk, and she finds out his name is Lonnie, short for Alonzo. She asks if he is of Spanish descent, he says no. She says she's of Italian descent. He says he can tell. By her eyes, and her nose. And the fact that she wears black all the time. No offence. She absorbs all of this with a look of mild amusement. He is less nervous now. She pours the tea and invites him to sit on the couch, then joins him. He rolls a joint of Afghan hashish on the coffee table with great care and attention. She gets an ashtray.

'It's clean. You don't smoke?'

'Only sometimes.'

'You sure it's okay?'

'Course it is. I'm not your mother.'

'You're right there. She'd find you ... baffling, I think.'

'Yeah, I baffle a *lot* of people,' she says with emphasis, and puts her feet up.

'Mm.' He lights the joint, blows a thin stream of smoke up towards the ceiling, and almost immediately feels the melting sensation in his back muscles, flowing down his legs. '*Man.* That's better.'

'Good. It's good to see you relax.'

'Yeah. *Long* week.'

'College?'

'University. And I do other stuff.' He takes another puff and passes it to her. 'Community stuff.'

'Hm?' she says, holding the smoke in.

'Oh ... you don't want to hear about that. Friday night's for ... well ...'

'This?'

'Er. I suppose.'

'You mind if I ask you something?'

'No.' But his eyes say he might.

'You make a habit of this?'

'*This?*' He looks around, then towards his crotch then at her. 'What?'

'*What.*' She looks at him with mock disapproval. 'Going home with strange older women.'

'Oh, *that* this. Then no.'

'I didn't think so.'

'And now I feel faintly ridiculous.'

'Why?' She looks surprised.

'Well. I watched … all that per*for*mance tonight. Those guys.'

'And what? You think I prefer *their* type?' Aghast.

'It's not *that*. But … look at me. Skinny … *kid*. What am *I?* I feel like the wooden spoon.'

'You're more interesting than all of them put together.'

'Right.'

'What do you want me to say? That I picked you as the stud of the bunch? Good marriage material? For your money? Come on.' She laughs, passes him back the joint. 'How can I make you understand?'

'Don't worry about it.' He takes a few puffs, holds it down, then sends a huge cloud of smoke toward the ceiling.

'You have a girlfriend?'

'I *did.*'

'What happened?'

'She graduated, left the city.'

'Oh. Sorry.'

'Pff. Nothing to be sorry for. She didn't really like me anyway.'

'Oh?' She gets up to go to her CDs on a black wall unit, begins flipping through them. 'Why was that?'

'Too young.'

'That's it?'

'Well. She was always going on about some older guy she'd been with. What a genius in bed he was.'

'She sounds like a bitch.'

'*Well*, you're not the first person to offer this perspective.'

'Okay, I have it. Jah Wobble.'

'*You* like Jah Wobble?'

'I've been listening to him since … probably before you were born.' She puts the CD on, and the ambient dub rises up from small floor speakers.

'Figures.'

'Anyway, women are complex. They often want what they don't have, and vice versa. Men are the same.'

'So men *and* women are complex?'

'No. Just women. Men are boringly obvious. Women are … well. You'll never *really* know what they're thinking.'

'Okay.' He looks studious. 'So you're saying that you know what I'm thinking, but I don't know what you're thinking. As a for instance.'

'I could guess.'

'Well, *I* could guess. But you're saying that men are obvious.'

'Maybe I asked you here tonight because I thought you wouldn't be obvious.'

'Well, fine, but I'm trying to understand this. I mean, it seems important. What's your evidence? Experience?' He sits up, takes another puff.

'What else? *Being* a woman.'

'And knowing … *enough* men … to make an educated guess?' She sighs.

'I suppose so.'

'Right. *So*. You think that you would have a reasonable insight into what I'm thinking? And I *wouldn't* know what *you're* thinking?'

'Where's the mystery, if we talk about it all?'

'I'm the curious type. Indulge me.'

'Okay. Let me see.' She looks at him, fixes him with a studious look. 'I think you came out of curiosity. And let's face it, you were a third wheel. You thought that even if it was hell with me, the barroom slut, you'd have a story. And a funny story would be better than nothing. Your friends would have their usual happy-happy cutesy teenage couple story. Maybe throw themselves around in a club for a while then ditch the place as it's full of saddos trying to get laid. Maybe later the sophistication of drinking a bottle of wine with their spaghetti Bolognese. So, what choice did you have? It was this or nothing.'

'Huh. Well, I'll concede *some* of your account has resonance, but believe it or not, I have *plenty* to do when I'm not here.'

'Oh yes?' she looks amused.

'Sure. But enough about me. If you ask me to read *your* intentions, I can only go on what you've told me. That you pulled me out of there for the same reason you think I agreed. You were curious. Bored of *that* lot, and prefer some possibly non-obvious company to none at all.'

'That's about right. *Mm.* This hash is *nice.*' She takes a hit and leans across to place her lips near to his. She blows gently and he inhales, pauses, then blows it out with a soft whistle.

'Haven't done that in a while.'

'Me neither,' she says, tapping her lips and looking thoughtful. 'I haven't done this in a while either.' She sits up and stretches a knee across his lap, facing him. 'I'm Janie, by the way.'

It is nearly dawn when he climaxes inside her for the third time. The bed is a mess, the sheets are soaked in sweat, and the incense mingles with the smell of their sex. Her hair is matted and tangled, his blond hair is slicked to his scalp. He withdraws, winces at the sensitivity as he pulls the condom off. He takes a brief look at it in the candlelight.

'Thought so. I'm just about shooting fresh air at this point.' He throws it into a tiny wastebasket by the bed. '*Man,*' he says, and collapses onto his back next to her.

'Do you *feel* like a man? After all that?' she asks earnestly.

'I wouldn't know *what* a man feels like.'

'You ever sleep with a man?'

'Guess.'

'Hm. Let's see.' She looks him up and down. 'I think maybe you *have.*'

'Covering all your bases, eh? Well, I can tell you that I have.'

'Thought so.'

'You said you thought *maybe.*'

'I also said women are *complex.*'

'So you did. My mistake.'

'So? You do it often?'

'What, with men? No. In first year. Drunk. I only remember him going on about what a *magnificent prick* I have. That stuck with me.'

'Well, he was quite correct. But seriously, you don't remember anything else? What you did with that equipment of yours.'

'Honestly? No. I mean, sure, rolling around in the bed. Him … *you know* … fel*lating* me, I believe is the term the kids use. But *fucking?* No. We never discussed it again.' He looked pensive. 'But everyone else did, of course.'

'So, you're bi?'

'Pff. No idea. Not *really.* You?'

'Sure.'

'You and …'

'Heather? God yes. Wouldn't *you*?'

'Hm. I think I'm *probably* not her type.'

'Oh, she'd eat you alive. If I tell her about you she'll be desperate to meet you.'

'Sleep with me, you mean.'

'Fuck you silly, I mean.'

'I see.'

'And what about you?'

'What?'

'Oh yes. Forgive me. That was a rather vague question. *You know.* You and relationships. You and men. No boyfriend?'

'Okay, let's do this the easy way. This is the first time I've had sex for … nearly a year. I don't tend to be in relationships that last. Given that you're the curious type, I suppose you're curious why.'

'Well, you don't really seem to *like* men very much. My friend would say you're carrying around a lot of anger towards men. She'd suggest it has something to do with your father, and other significant males. That sort of thing.'

'And what does she say about you?'

'That I'm carrying around a lot of anger towards men. She says that about everyone, sooner or later.'

'Right.'

'Yeah. She's a great example of the saying, that if all you have is a hammer, the whole world looks like a bunch of nails.'

'She's doing psychology?'

'First year.'

She leans her head down to his penis and runs her lips along its length, which almost immediately begins to increase. He tries to protest, but she pushes his hands away and closes her mouth over the tip.

'Are you sure? I'm getting a little sore,' he winces, as if to make the point. She stops sucking for a few moments.

'Then you'll have to get me *really* wet.' She continues, then murmurs. 'I don't want to talk any more.'

Tales from the Dungeon

A friend used to beat men for a living. Let's call her D. She was approached by a couple of shady characters at a gig that she had blagged her way into. She was pretending to be a photographer looking for live shots of the band, and was dressed in some kind of S&M gear. These guys assured her that she had what it took to work as a dominatrix. Now the journey is not the point of the story. Suffice it to say, D took to it, and did seven years behind the whip. She is the funniest storyteller I have ever met, able to find the humour in any situation, and has a seemingly endless supply of dungeon tales. So one day over tea I asked her for some of her craziest stories. Here are a few. If you are of a nervous disposition or easily offended, I strongly advise that you read no further.

The Rabbit Guy

This guy calls up asking, in a broad West Country accent, would she stomp a rabbit to death wearing a pair of high heels and feed it to him while he is tied to a chair.
'No. Absolutely not. I like rabbits.'
'How about a mouse?'
'Sir, I wear six-inch heels. I can just about walk in them, let alone manage to tread on a mouse hurtling around the dungeon floor.'
'You could put in a plastic bag.'
'Not happening, not possible. And besides, I like small furry animals.'
'Well … what about a fish?'
'A fish? Well … *maybe?*'
'Would you supply it, or would I have to bring my own?'
'What do you think? This is a dungeon, not a fucking pet shop.'

145

Houdini

This guy wants to know, would she be prepared to tie him up, as securely as she can manage, and leave him hanging suspended for a while. Sure, why not. So he comes around, and they get to it. She has a metal table suspended from the ceiling. He is strapped to it, chained, spread-eagled, and left to hang. The door is locked from the outside, and she goes to have a cup of tea.

The staff room is around the corner from the door to the dungeon. As she boils the kettle, she hears what she describes as 'a fuck-load of rattling, which goes on and on and on.' It continues while the Mistress chuckles darkly in the staff room, with her tea and crossword. She expects him to quit after ten minutes at the most, imagines she'll walk in to find him hanging, spent, in his chains. But no. It takes another fifteen minutes for him to fall silent. Feeling it important to ensure some level of suffering – as that's what these people pay good money for – she takes her time finishing her tea before going back to the dungeon.

She unlocks the door and enters to find the table bare, the chains neatly coiled beneath it, and the guy's clothes still folded on a chest in the corner. Her jaw drops. She looks from the table to the chains and back again, to his clothes, and back to the table. Shakes her head. Then catches a movement out the corner of her eye. He's naked, hiding under the bed. Quick as lightning she grabs a length of chain and whacks him with it, asserting her Authority, scolding him for daring to undo Mistress's work. Well, it turns out that the guy is in fact a professional escapologist, and he practices by going around the country to dungeons. He never tells them this up front, but gets them to try their best to restrain him so he can't get out. She had never seen anyone get out of her chains before, and none since.

The Guy Who Wanted to Die

The strangest tale, to me, was of the guy who wanted to die. He wanted her to film herself tying him up and killing him.

'Oh yes? And what are you going to pay me for this?'

'Well … five grand?'

'Five grand. For a life sentence in prison.'

'You won't get caught.'

'*I won't get caught*. Of *course* I will.'

'Look, I'm serious.'

'Yeah right.'

'I'll prove it to you. I'll meet you at a motorway service station near you, and I'll eat a bag of your shit.'

'I see. So let's say I, or anyone else, does this. How are you going to *watch* it?'

'You put it on the necromantics website.'

'Mm. And what am I going to do with your body?'

'There's plenty of ways to get rid of a body. I'll find out.'

'No. Try looking under M for Mafia in the phone book.' Clunk.

Well, he didn't quit for some time, but pestered her with text messages and letters, assuring her of his sincerity, and offering more money. It is not known whether anyone else fulfilled his request.

The line between fantasy and reality came up numerous times in her stories. She spoke of the swinging parties she 'dommed,' where she would wander around among the copulating middle class, middle-aged folks, whipping the occasional backside.

'There are very few *real* swingers at these parties,' she said. 'Less than ten percent. Mostly it's the case that men have dragged their wives along, and the wives get more into than they do. As soon as they see a bloke or two all over their wife they hit the roof. Lot of fights break out. That's why good places always have a bouncer.'

Another classic story on the *line* concerns a punter who telephoned, then wrote, describing the heavyweight hardcore S&M he wished to experience. It would be his first time, but he wanted it *serious*. So, she's stood behind the door of the dungeon waiting, and immediately his head appears she smacks him in the face as hard as she can. The guy goes down like a sack of potatoes, and after a few moments he crawls to the bed, where he proceeds to sob like a child.

'You're a … really *horrible* woman,' he blubs.

'And you're a *very stupid* man.' Well, she made him pay up, then got changed and took him across the road for a drink, to explain about this fantasy/ reality line, and how it must be approached with extreme caution.

Apparently there are many who would get their thrill from discussing their fantasies with a dominatrix by phone, but save themselves the time, money and actual pain of going through with it. They stayed *this* side of the line.

It was amazing to hear these stories, particularly of the lengths men would have to go to in order to get an erection. One guy could only achieve it through having his scrotum stretched out and nailed flat as a pancake to a wooden board. Another had to be suspended upside-down by the ankles, legs akimbo, and have a large plastic bottle (filled with warm water) inserted in him. Others needed to be electrocuted, burned or stapled, not to mention the usual whipping, spanking and so on. Her first client was a neurosurgeon who was an olfactophile – turned on by smells. The details are too stomach-churning to relate.

Another, a wealthy, powerful individual, loved to be chained up in a French maid's outfit and be ordered to spend hours scrubbing her bathroom. He had to go in the end, as others in the house were sick of having to use the downstairs bathroom to avoid him.

The lesson of these stories may simply be that some people are crazy. That the wiring gets twisted up inside. You can ask how, and why all of this happens, and surely it makes for fascinating study. Childhood stuff in the main, according to D. Something becomes associated with sexual pleasure, and sometimes it's not something that can be discussed in polite society, and often is not something that any 'normal' lover would countenance. Perhaps a traditional prostitute can provide, but if not, if specialist pain or humiliation is the thing, the dominatrix provides. Because most importantly, it requires skill, presentation, performance. The setting, the costumes, the actor, the tools of the trade – all aspects of the mise-en-scène must be Right. But most of all, it is the charisma, the presence, the ability to command and to convince.

But the mask *has* slipped. On one occasion she had a man tied over a table, and was in the process of spanking him. She made some quiet aside as she worked – a pun or inside joke that she cannot recall the details of – but apparently he got it, and started to giggle. She immediately bellowed with steely authority, 'Do I hear *laughter* in my dungeon?' at which point he *cracked* up, and set her off too. Sexual frisson can dissolve in the harsh light of reality, and it is vitally important to remain in character in the mutual act of S&M. Both parties need to be fully immersed in order to make the fantasy real in an effective way. Again, she had to call a halt to the proceedings, but did not charge him, as in this case *she* had broken character.

I know her as a kind, generous and warm-hearted person, but I am aware that a whole other side to her exists. And what of the rest of us? What capacity for cruelty do we possess? One might argue that she did this primarily because she was paid handsomely to do it, but perhaps she got more than just money from the experience. However, she could not do it eternally. She said she had to quit before she went crazy herself. Being around perverted, depraved people for a living wears away at the soul, and distorts one's image of individuals, and the society which they make up. Something similar is admitted by police officers, who routinely deal with some of the worst aspects of humanity.

She says she has always been fascinated by human behaviour, and her work took her into the realms of psychiatric disorder in the most applied manner. What therapy it may have provided for either party is debatable, but the purveyance of rare, dark pleasures is something that a surprisingly large number of people feel the need for. Does it prevent them from inflicting it on others, if they can pay for it, safely, in a private space? An open question.

A window into this world can provide some useful perspective on one's own inclinations. Most would recoil. Many would find themselves downgraded from pervert to mildly kinky at best. Some may be tempted to venture forth. This glimpse also demonstrates that you just never know what goes on beneath the exterior – of buildings and of individuals. Who knows what curious desires dwell within the people you meet? How much of it exists within our society? Is it in fact more 'normal' than we realise, or care to admit? How scared of our desires are we?

They are relatively few, those that cross the line, and I am tempted to feel some sympathy, as it is easy to imagine that they are suffering, being in the grip of a need that, were they to confess it publicly, would cost them dearly. No one wishes to be the object of scorn, shame and all manner of criticism, or worse. Their desires blur the line between pain and pleasure in a way that would make most people think them mad – perhaps because we are told that nature designed us around avoiding pain and seeking pleasure. Most people would concur, and conflating the two seems genuinely perverse. In the end, whether it is braver of them to submit to their desires, or resist them, I do not know.

Letter to an Ass Kicker

It's about time I wrote this – *for* myself, as much as *to* you. I don't know who you are, or even if you're another woman. I doubt it, for some reason. You put me through *so* much. You changed my life. I don't believe you meant to. I know nothing about you, except that you were at the same event I was, almost two years ago now. The *Waypoints* seminar, helping confused young people find a direction in a broken economy. I added that last part. It was a well-meaning event, with lots of advisors smiling as though their job depended on it. There's a particular energy around those whose job it is to find jobs for other people, don't you think?

Anyway. I was there because my parents told me to go. If you're my age, I assume the same about you. I was sat in the middle for the afternoon talks. Right in the middle, the last seat left, as I was late, having had a bathroom mishap. You might remember me, bumbling and apologising my way along the row, while the introductions were in full flow. I was bright red, sweating, feeling like crap. I remember trying to quietly get my pad and pen out and make some notes. I ended up mostly doodling. I remember there was to be someone come up and talk later about what they'd done since A levels. Now a designer for a car company. A Japanese one, I seem to think.

There was a woman up there talking when it happened. I still have that notepad. What I *can* read from that day doesn't make any sense. That's the thing with notes – it's an art, isn't it? In fact that pad's *full* of notes that I do *not* remember writing. It's my writing, but I don't know what any of it means. I don't suppose it's that uncommon.

But this isn't about notes.

It's about you, kicking me in the ass.

And me farting loudly, and having to leave the room, to the kind of laughter that any stand-up comedian would sell his mother for.

And I want to say a few things about it.

1. I don't know if you did it on purpose or not, and I've wondered that too many times to mention.
2. It sent me on a path that I would not otherwise have taken.
3. The following is what happened to me afterwards.

Immediately afterwards, I left there in tears. I cried on the bus, with all the dignity and grace I could muster. I went home and cried. I woke up and cried. My parents wouldn't believe me – they thought I was pregnant, or had been raped, or both. My dad couldn't see why I would get so upset over something like that. He said I should just laugh it off, that one day I'd realise that it was actually pretty funny. Obviously *he'd* never been publicly shamed like that. My mum was a bit better about it. Or at least, more understanding, when I finally convinced her I really wasn't pregnant. I was still a virgin for God's sake. My mum thought I should talk to someone about it. So that's what I did. I went on a load of web forums, and here is a typical exchange:

JS: Find out who kicked u n kick m in d nuts lol
PJ: What makes you think it was a bloke?
JS: Blokes are like that
Me: I think it was a guy
JS: y?
PJ: Y?
Me: It felt like a man's boot
Me: Or shoe
JS: ????
Me: It was rounded
JS: ????
Me: Not pointed, like women's shoes, or boots
PJ: o, i c
OM: I think you should get over it – yo have to leave that shit in the past girl – move on with your life
JS: Women cn wear boots to lol
Me: It just made me feel like a big fat joke
JS: u cn just write jk
OM: You have an opportunity here – either you let this beat you down, or you get up and take charge
OM: You said it was about your future, right?
OM: So get out there and make your future what you want it to be

PJ: Yea, just do what makes you happy

Me: But I don't know what any of that is …

OM: You gotta find out

Me: How?

OM: What makes you happy?

Me: idk – that's the problem

OM: Then you gotta try some things out girl – do some volunteering in your community, help out people having a hard time, learn sth about yourself

OM: You'll figure it out – Ask, and it shall be given you; seek, and ye shall find; knock, and it shall be opened unto you. Matthew 7:7

JS: Yea, ask Jesus lol

JS: Cos hes a real person lol

Me: Thanks

JS: np

Well, somewhere in there, I got the feeling that there was wisdom. I did get into voluntary work, and found myself wanting to help out younger women – young teenagers. At least I knew a bit more than they did, and could see that they were at the same place I'd been a few years before. I was 19 by that point, and they thought I was an old woman. It was strange.

In a spirit of helpfulness, my dad took to farting in public when we were out together, and after the first couple of times, when I went off in a rage, it *was* actually quite funny. He'd even stand at a counter, being served, and do it. Just squeak or trump one out, and apologise without batting an eyelid. Though he did it one time and I think by the way he went pale and went off to the bathroom, I think he sharted. He said he hadn't, but I noticed he stopped doing it after that. But I have to say, he was trying to help in his own way. He wasn't an agony uncle, he was too old school blokey for that. He's a working class guy who's done well, and married well. My mum's from a comfortable middle class background, and doesn't like to talk about intimate problems very much, but she will at a push. Like most people, she's fine in a crisis, but rubbish in a drama.

I ended up going to counselling, and maybe if my dad hadn't played the buffoon so well, it would have been harder. I've had an amazing counsellor. I won't use her real name, so I'll use Jill. Jill has the look of someone who's been through it herself. You never doubt her sincerity for a moment. It's in her eyes. Her body too, but her eyes have that look, and when she fixes you with them, you stay fixed. She sort of holds you in this gaze and it's as though she can see it all anyway, so you may as well be honest and just let it all out.

She got me to talk about my weight, and my relationship with my body. She has a way of talking with you about things so that you find yourself doing the thinking, and the talking. You can really get somewhere each week. And whatever you talk about, it stays with you, and you keep remembering it. I started to realise that I had seen my fat as a kind of insulation against the world. Something that I thought hid me. Before I put on the weight I used to hide behind my hair. It was so long, and always in front of my face. I hated cycling with my parents when I was around 14 because I had to have my hair jammed out the way under a helmet. I got a kind of militant thing going after a while, and ate because my parents told me not to. My dad said I was so pretty, why did I want to do that to myself. He kept on about diabetes and a load of other health problems. But when I got scared, I ate. I wasn't massive, but I was pretty heavy. Jill is one of those middle-aged women who looks better than most women half her age. She's always doing yoga, pilates, swimming or something. She got me to try swimming, and that was it. I was soon going every day, pretty much. I hardly even remember the change in diet. I just ate what would give me the right kind of natural energy for swimming, and avoided things that would give me sugar highs.

It was a year since the ass-kicking, and things were already *totally* different. I'd started working three days a week for a little online business, learning a lot, from processing orders to marketing and customer service – and how to deal with other people! It's a small team and we all get along really well. There's the occasional bit of friction if we have a lot to get out, and all have to muck in and work like crazy to make the post on time. But mostly, it's a good laugh. We sell a range of designer kitchen ware, and it seems to be recession-proof.

But the other days I was doing my volunteering, and made the decision one day I was going to go for it. There was one young girl who came in to the centre about six months ago, she was 15 and pregnant, and hadn't a clue what to do, or even what she *could* do. There was no one else available in the centre at the time, they were all in a meeting, so I just chatted with her in one of the rooms until the meeting finished. She was in floods of tears, kept telling me she didn't know how it happened. After a while I was nearly in tears too. I suppose a lot of people encounter this in their time – teenage pregnancy – but when it's right in front of you, and it's someone who is so innocent and helpless, it really affects you. It was so hard to hear. She had someone she called a boyfriend, but it sounded as though he was only her boyfriend when he wanted sex. She said that he and his friend would both take turns. It was at that moment that I decided what I was going to do next. I start a university course in September, and can't wait. It's on Applied Community and Youth Work. I don't know what I think I can really do about these things, but I know I want to try to help people you need help. I don't have a great deal of experience myself. I've never had what you'd call a relationship, and I still live with my mum and dad, but all that's going to change.

Oh my God. The strangest thing *ever* just happened. I'd not written any more of this letter in ages, and ... well. Here's what happened. I got an invite to that same youth event through a mailing list. It was for people who'd been to the Waypoints event, to see what they'd done since, and they also welcomed speakers who would share their story. I said I would. The idea was to inspire other young people trying to pick a direction. I was so nervous it was unbelievable. Jill urged me to go, to assert myself as the *me* I am *now*. She's very persuasive. And I thought, no one will recognise me, minus almost two stone.

So anyway, I went, and I'm on the little stage, next to a couple of other young people, on this panel. There's maybe 150 kids in the audience, and quite a few adults. When I got up there it was really alright. Then this guy, Rich, gets up and starts talking about his experience. He says that at the same event two years before, he'd accidentally kicked someone in the backside and embarrassed them. Clearly he didn't recognise me. It made my head spin. I couldn't believe my ears. But he spoke so gently. He said it made him so conscious of how easy it is to upset people and cause offence that he had started a degree in psychology, as well as becoming involved in Buddhism. I thought of all the comments I had on web forums, the ideas people had about him. And the ideas I had. I thought about the letter I started writing him or her. I thought about telling the audience my side of the story but couldn't get my head around it. So I just told them about the voluntary work and the university course. I wanted to be inspiring, but was totally thrown. Still got nice polite applause though. Afterwards there was a little gathering of the speakers and organisers over tea, and after a little speech to thank us, people were sort of mingling, so I went up to him.

'Hi, Rich?'

'Hi. *Jody*, yeah? Really interesting ... your story. Nice one.' Up close, his eyes really were quite nice. Sincere.

'Yeah. Yours too. This is going to weird you out probably, but it was *my* butt you kicked.' The look on his face was priceless. His jaw literally dropped. He stepped backwards and looked me up and down, like he was seeing a ghost. I started giggling. It was really comical. He had a hand over his mouth, and it was as though the words were all queuing up on the tip of his tongue like paratroopers in movies, but instead of jumping they were all trying not to. 'Look. It's okay. I didn't say anything about it, up there … but it changed *my* life too.'

'I … I honestly don't know what to say.' I laughed.

'*Really*, don't worry about it. It changed my life for the *better*. Character building.' I even patted him on the arm.

'Well … I'm just … *stunned*.' He looked it. Kept scratching his head and was making these 'pff' noises.

'It's okay, Rich. *Really*. Have some tea. Relax. There's no judgement here.' I could hear Jill. 'In fact, looking back it *was* kinda funny.' I could hear my dad. 'But I *have* always wondered, *why* it happened.'

'Oh man, it's ri-*diculous*.' He stood there shaking his head for a few moments. 'I was sat there fuming, about my dad telling me I needed a kick up the arse, as he had a *million* times, and … it was like a kind of *nerve* impulse. I was picturing myself kicking my *dad* up the arse, and I had my legs crossed. You know …' He went and sat on a nearby chair and crossed one leg over his knee, with the right foot forward. *That's* the foot, I thought. Never thought I'd actually see it. It was kind of like seeing a minor celeb. 'And then … it just kind of *flicked* up. I hardly felt it, except when it hit your … you know.'

'Yeah. I know. It *wasn't* hard. So weird how such a small thing … it affected both of us so much.'

'Yeah. You're tellin' me.' He was looking a little better. In fact he looked great. I suppose I was feeling such a mix of relief, and I think, forgiveness. It was strangely powerful, and reminded me afterwards of stories about prisoners of war forgiving their captors and staying in touch. Well, we've swapped numbers, and we're going to have a coffee next week. I haven't seen Jill yet. That's in a couple of days. But, I think she'll be … well I don't know. I want to see if this catches her out. Probably not. It's like she was in 'Nam or something, nothing seems to throw her. Anyway. I wonder if Rich has a therapist. I wonder if it'll be … well, I suppose it's best to just let it be whatever it is. I'm sure it'll be something to draw on in my studies though. Should I show him this letter after all? We'll see.

Snowbound at the World's End

She stands at the large upstairs window in the gloom, arms folded, her right hand squeezes her left bicep with a slow rhythm. She grows tense, gazing out over the frozen landscape, its features absorbed by the thick white blanket, driven across it by an angry wind. The snowflakes dash and thud against the glass; the drifts are getting deeper even as she watches. Seven winters high up in Snowdonia, and she has never seen it like this. The speed of it, the sheer volume of it, it seems like wrath.

The tension has been growing in her since her mother, Sue, made the decision to stay the night instead of heading back to her flat in Manchester. This is more vexing than the endless babble on the radio about the Mayan apocalypse. They are counting down to Armageddon, timed for 11.11 am GMT the following morning. Less than 24 hours. She doesn't believe it at all. She feels that the Earth is somehow just too *old* to be destroyed, and at the same time has too many stories left to tell. In a pub that has stood nearly four centuries, it is easy to believe that the Earth can handle itself. But, there has been nervous laughter about it among the staff in the kitchen, and among the customers in the bar.

Armageddon or not, the world seems to be crowding in on her. Downstairs, Kenny, the Malaysian barman, is holding the fort, looking after the few souls trapped by the blizzard. and she lets the moments drift, like the snowflakes when the wind drops between breaths. She wants to take every moment she can, before she has to get back into character.

After some time, she focuses on her reflection. Dark eyes stare unblinking from within the pale visage, which is framed with long black hair, dyed these days. She sighs, takes a couple of long, slow breaths and descends the stairs, metamorphosing, becoming once more

Anna the landlady. In Charge. The strong, silent type. Almost mystical in her aloofness, her opinions buried secrets, her laugh a collector's item. Passing through the door to the bar she grows, fills out, meets Kenny's eye, to read there any messages concerning the status of her bar and its customers. He nods warmly, looking relaxed. All is well, almost certainly.

It is an old pub of modest size, its oak beams are decorated with antique copper and brass cooking and farming implements. The bar is at the top end, opposite the front door and has a snug and a large fireplace to its left, and the staircase to the guest rooms to its right. Next to the stairs there is a door leading out to the kitchen, the bathrooms and the beer garden. The floorboards are bare, the walls are of local stone, and the room has been almost unchanged since it was built, save for minor refurbishments. Buildings of significant age tend, like this one, to have relaxed atmospheres, as though their souls have now seen enough to take every day in their stride. Anna feels the same, and finds little riles her these days. She and Kenny make a little small talk, then she glides about, assessing stocks of drinks and snacks, mainly for the sake of something to do. The kitchen staff have departed for the day, and there will not be anyone in through the door now, besides some emergency. The weather is too foul for fun, it is now officially hazardous to human life. She talks quietly with Kenny, serving another couple of rounds while outside, night falls with a gentle thump.

The bar will take over 150 people when full, but now has just a handful. More guests were booked but didn't make it through the weather. Those that remain are mostly booked to stay at least one night. Maggie and Arthur, in their mid-eighties, try to make it every year, for their wedding anniversary. They sit on a sofa near the fire and find things to joke about, sipping port. They give Anna hope.

There is a balding, barrel-chested forester from Yorkshire called Al, who has his 19 year old son Dan with him, who is visiting for a few days before going back home to be with his mum for Christmas. He is a university student with floppy dark hair, and wears jeans, a hoody and skate shoes. He seems to blend a quiet intensity with modesty, and some insecurity. Al is working locally, doing contract work in the national park. For the time being then, he is a regular, and is a jovial, playful sort. He and Dan are playing cards, and he is losing noisily.

A man she does not know the name of, a tall, greying late-fifties or early sixties well-to-do Tory type, is with his daughter, who may be late teens or early twenties. It gets hard to tell, thinks Anna. She is beautifully attired, in a designer dress of dark floral greens and purples with gold stitching. Her outfit is finished with high brown leather boots. Her skin is light brown, her features smooth, her brown eyes are soulful, slightly sad, thinks Anna. Her father seems to be calling her Stefanie. He looks agitated, grumbling into his phone about what is apparently a business matter.

Another man, somewhere in his sixties, drinks alone in the snug, nursing pints until they are warm, and pretending to read a dog-eared novel. He has an academic appearance, with his high forehead, bushy whitening hair and beard, and thick-rimmed glasses. She has caught his eye once or twice and he just nodded amiably. He has asked for a room for the night.

The landlady sits down at a table near the bar to read the paper and do the puzzles, and finds herself reading a few articles on doomsday. It is December 21st 2012, and around the world many are taking seriously the suggestion that the Mayans predicted that this date would see the end of the world as we know it. Another article explains that the Mayans actually meant that it was the end of one age and the beginning of another, not the apocalypse. Perhaps a more enlightened time, if anything. She raises one elegant eyebrow at this suggestion, sandwiched as it is between stories of fresh atrocities of all kinds, including another school gun massacre in America, the horrors of the uprising in Syria, and religious murder across Africa and the Middle East. Add to this the endless anti-austerity protests in Europe, financial/ political turmoil in Washington D.C. and the froth of consumerist mania, rising in intensity toward the final frantic few days before the orgasm of Christmas. Apparently numerous high street chains are desperate for an infusion of income to prop up their year, lest they drop dead at the feet of their creditors.

She glazes over with a listless sigh, and goes back to the 2012 stories. There are tales of 'preppers' in the U.S. stockpiling guns and supplies in underground shelters, a Christian doomsday cult in China whose members have been rounded up by the authorities to meet who knows what fate, and a $1,000-a-ticket 24-hour party at a Soviet-era bunker, 56 metres under Moscow's streets. She mutters 'uh-*huh*' to herself, and decides to give up on humanity's antics and go back to the crossword instead. The world seems more a riot of madness than ever, somehow. Maybe an end would be no bad thing, she muses; the universe could just write us off as a failed attempt to work towards higher consciousness in animals. She taps the pencil and reads through the clues again. The world closes down to a few square inches of black and white.

The lone drinker in the snug leans forward so he can see her. She has her back to him, but he can see part of her profile. He scratches thoughtfully at his bottom lip with a thumbnail, then smoothes a hand across his densely bearded jaw. He takes another sip of his beer and feels the momentary rush of nerves as he goes to stand, then is beaten back down by doubt. Not *right* now. But if not *now*, then when? He has been pretending to read the same two pages for twenty minutes, save for his brief business with Anna to ask for a room. It gave him the sweats. He has been making ready for the last hour to speak to her, properly. He gives himself sixty seconds on the watch. His heart rate leaps up and his chest thumps in a way that would have his G.P. nervous. So: not just now, then. The moment may have to choose itself, he thinks.

At another table the man and his daughter are quarrelling. She is entreating him not to leave, not in this weather. They can stay the night – better alive and late than the alternative. He grumbles at her about the urgency of getting back to London, then tries gentle persuasion again. She shakes her head, looking fearfully towards the door. Al and Dan sit within earshot, two tables over, nearer the door. Dan is biting the inside of his mouth and glancing across. Al just shakes his head, puts his cards down and takes a sip of beer. The daughter looks scared, on the verge of tears. Her father stands, putting on his coat and snapping at her to do likewise. She sniffs and shakes her head quietly. Al puts down his drink and quietly slides his chair backwards, not taking his eye off the man. Maggie and Arthur are watching from the fire, her arm suddenly on his. Kenny stops wiping a glass and Anna feels the vibe, turns to assess the situation. The pub seems suddenly smaller.

'No, this can *not* wait,' says the father between gritted teeth. 'You don't understand the ways of the world, young lady. This *matters*.'

'You'll go nowhere tonight,' says Al, gently but firmly. The other man turns around as though slapped.

'I *beg* your pardon?' he says, as if to a rude child. Al remains seated, and folds his hands in his lap. He takes a deep breath and inflates his chest with an easy smile.

'You heard me. Best settle in. Nature has the best of us tonight.'

'My *Range Rover* will have the last word, not a bit of *snow*. That's what these cars are *made* for,' he says, jabbing a thumb at the front door. His anger is growing. Al seems to get more relaxed as it does.

'*You* can leave then, if you fancy your chances, but I'll not have you risk your daughter's life too.'

'Sephone. Put *on* your coat,' says her father between gritted teeth.

'Young lady, you stay sat. My good man, do *not* make me stand up.' Al's eye is unwavering. Dan's are wide, darting from one player in this drama to the next and back again. He's seen his father in action before. 'Sephone bites a fingernail. Anna pushes the newspaper away and goes to the edge of the bar, folding her arms and looking icily at the father. As though he felt her gaze, he turns to look at her.

'I have a room each for you and your daughter,' says Anna. '*No one* is leaving in this weather. A blizzard onto wet roads means only one thing. The roads are death.' Her words settle upon each of the customers. The man looks down, holds his breath for a few moments, then snorts.

'Well, how *can* I refuse your hospitality?' he says acidly.

'You can't,' says Al companionably. 'You don't say no to Miss Anna. Come on then, what'll I get you?' He stands, one hand in his pocket. The father subsides.

'*Well.* A gin and tonic, if you would.' The fury is boiling away.

'And for the young lady?' She looks at her father, but there is no command either way.

'A rum and coke please.'

'Right you are.' Al heads for the bar, and the man gets his phone out again. He goes through the address book slowly, not keen to get to the right name. He shoots a withering glance at 'Sephone, then dials.

'Much obliged,' says Al with a wink.

'*Likewise,*' says Anna, shaking her head and smirking. They share a chuckle. 'Haven't had a bar fight in here this year. I think. The English don't do a lot of it, eh?'

'And Canadians do?'

'Well, the bars I worked in growing up, yah. Every frickin' night some asshole'd square up to some other asshole.'

'National sport is it?'

'Huh?'

'You go to the wrong pub anywhere and you'll get shite.'

'I guess *so.*'

'You alright, love? You look paler than usual.'

'Ah, it's my mom. She's staying another few days by the looks of it.'

'Well, you only get one of 'em. Remember that.'

'I know dude, but you know how it is with mothers and daughters.'

'Fight like cats in a bag do ya?'

'She just … y'know. Tells me how to do *everything*. Like I don't know.'

'*My* lad, I just leave him to it. Whenever I give 'im a talkin' to, I find out he knows what he's doin' really. But they're young, and they haven't 'ad time to work it all out. Did you leave the nest young by any chance?'

'Me? I was *outta* there.'

'Well, maybe she never saw you growin' up, lookin' after yourself. She probably worried all the time, bless 'er. She does it because she cares. Let her make a fuss. You're doin' her a favour.'

'Huh. Maybe you're right. You're one smart dude, you know that? What are you doin' cuttin' down trees for a living?'

'Well, I'm takin' a break from me research in nuclear brain surgery, you know how it is. Got bored of it to be honest. Thought I'd study whether or not falling trees make a sound or not. Applied philosophy, like.'

'Cool. How's that workin' out for ya?'

'Oh, you know. It's alright, like … but next time I'm gonna research summat wi' more women.'

'Right on. Can't say I blame you for that. Okay, you're good to go. On the house.'

'You're an angel. Let's hope he takes it easy for the rest of the night.'

'I'll start hitting him with glasses of gratis red wine in a bit. If that doesn't knock his ass out I'll have to start diggin' through my mom's meds.'

'You've done this before.'

'Like I said, I worked in some rough joints.'

At 10 pm, Anna's mother makes her entrance. She walks around the bar and takes a stool, nodding cheerfully at Kenny, who approaches. The man in the snug sees her and his heart simultaneously leaps and sinks. He is now softened up by alcohol perhaps too much for this. But, somehow it makes sense to him to forego further consideration and instead move unsteadily across the bar and plonk himself down beside the lady.

'This will be *my* pleasure,' he says to Kenny who is pouring a glass of wine for Sue. She turns with a trace of recognition forming around the corners of her mouth and eyes, which blooms immediately as she studies his face. He watches fuzzily as her face is swept by various expressions. Finally, she settles on a kind of low-key fascinated distaste.

'Well,' she says, looking him up and down. 'Older … drunker.'

'Otherwise, much as you left me.'

'Hm. I suppose this is no coincidence?'

At this moment, Anna walks around the bar and takes in the expressions of her mother and the man as they turn to look at her. She sees in their eyes a story, and knows that she has a starring role. She shrugs.

'Okay, what?'

'*Well*. You first,' Sue says to the man, inviting him to address Anna with a wave of her hand.

He takes a moment to focus on her, then takes a breath, goes to speak … Anna feels the uneasiness creeping up her spine. She can almost pick the words out of his eyes. And gets there precisely as he shrugs and says, 'Anna? I'm Colin. I'm a dad. *Yours*, dad.' He wags a finger at her. She watches it, noting every minute detail of its movement, and its contours, the shape of its nail. What feels like roughly a minute later, though it is almost instantaneous, she tries to respond, but nothing happens.

She glances around the bar, checking that the other customers are all absorbed in their own affairs. Maggie and Arthur have their heads leant together, facing the fire, almost motionless. Al and the other man – who's name is obviously Stuart, as Al keeps using it – are now sharing a table, locked in animated political discussion. Their children sit at an adjacent table talking quietly but intently.

She tries again to find something to say, but she feels numb, her mind is empty. She tries to access any feelings she may have carried with her, however deeply hidden, concerning her real father, but they are now so long buried that she can find nothing easily. When her mother split from Henry, her second husband, she had told Anna that he was not in fact her real father. Her father was actually an eccentric hippy chemist who had vanished overseas fifteen years previously. After a week she decided it belonged to the past, and thus established her habit of never looking back once she has moved on.

She now realises that she has not consciously thought about the matter for years. Then she feels anger begin to awaken, an anger at feeling like the subject of an ambush. She lets a breath out slowly, trying to release the tension. It is not in her nature to blow up, and she breathes steadily, observing her emotions, trying to ride the waves all the way into the beach without wiping out. Her parents exchange a complex look, and wait in silence.

Kenny serves the few orders over the next hour as Anna talks things over with her parents.

'Why *now?*' she asks Colin, shrugging and tossing her head, as if to say it doesn't really make any difference, she's just interested on a purely academic basis.

'Well. It may sound somewhat ridiculous ...' he answers, taking another sip of black coffee. His mind is clearing, and beginning to thump.

'*Obviously,*' she says with mild sarcasm.

'I suppose I felt ... that I'd be intruding. As silly as that may sound. I felt that I ... perhaps wasn't worthy ...' He clears his throat then taps at his lower lip with a thumb. 'It seemed to me that fatherhood was too important to get so badly wrong.' He gives her a brave smile. 'But Sarah, my partner for the last three years, found out about you.' He takes a deep breath. Then another. 'To tell you the truth ... I had a cancer scare earlier this year ... and I told Sarah about you when I was in the hospital. She found you on Facebook that night, and came in the next day with photos of you she'd printed out ... and she insisted I buy a ticket over here when I was well enough. Those pictures ... I was over*joyed* to see you. I wasn't sure you'd welcome me ... but when I read this stuff about doomsday prophecies ... somehow I felt compelled to introduce myself. When you get to my age, you look at your life, and you look for some meaning to it all. What does it add up to? You think about your legacy, what you want to leave behind, and what is still undone. And I thought about it ... and I didn't want a black hole left behind me. I thought that you should know who I am, regardless of what you *do* with the information. I don't expect ...' he shrugs, looking towards the teenagers, 'a fully-fledged daughter ... to be *mine*. I had to give that up long ago.' His eyes are sincere. 'And naturally I've always wondered what became of you. But time passes so quickly, doesn't it? One minute I'm toasting your tenth birthday, the next it's your fortieth, and hardly a day seems to have passed in between.'

'Okay ... I get it ... but why didn't you contact me *before?*' He frowns, looks at Sue, takes a moment to choose his words.

'When your mother and I separated you were less than a year old. She didn't think me much use as a father, and I suppose I *was* rather preoccupied.'

'What *with?*' asks Anna, looking faintly horrified.

'I was a materials scientist, working on eco-friendly packaging. It was pioneering research, and I was at the lab 18 hours a day at that time.' Anna looks at Sue, who nods regretfully. 'And ... after a while, your mother lost patience, and asked me to leave.' Anna wants to ask her mother's side of the story, but doesn't trust herself to keep her emotions in check.

'*Right*. And then?' says Anna.

'And then, your mother met Henry, and soon after, I met Valerie. She's a Kiwi, and after you all left for Canada, I went to New Zealand with Val. I've been there ever since. As I said, I think I simply felt unworthy of you. The more time that passes, the more that feeling grows. But when you feel you are facing death, your perspective changes. *Dramatically.*' He takes his glasses off and rubs his eyes, then squints at her with a smile that is absolutely real.

She nods, and finds herself thinking about her life in fast-forward; she has no memories of West London or Colin. Nor of leaving with her mum and Henry, the huge, square-jawed man with the exotic accent, who took them from the browns and greys of London in the early 1970s to that wonderful clapboard house in that enormous new land. Growing up in Toronto, her friends and their parents – and many of the boys – crowed over her accent, a thing of wonder and delight. The power of her voice surprised her. She found strength in using it, and loved the way it captured the room. But, it became watered down over time, and it became increasingly common. As the cost of international air travel fell, she became just another 'British' accent. As its value diminished, so did her attachment to it, and after a few years she could barely recall what her old accent had sounded like. When she heard English accents on film they sounded almost comical. She became a citizen, and by the age of sixteen had left Britain far behind, except for its music. Some things were eerily similar, and some things were very different, leading her to a life-long interest in the concept of parallel universes.

The next year, Sue divorced Henry, who had developed a penchant for younger women. Not that Anna knew much about this at the time. Her mother begged her to go back to London with her, but Anna thought her mad. She finished school and studied hotel management in college, then left Toronto to work in the Caribbean for a few years. A fling with an American financier took her to Florida for a while, but she could not settle in the U.S., finding it too politically and racially divided for her tastes, and too religious. She drifted through a number of European capitals as various relationships nudged her progress through life. By her mid-thirties she had had enough of moving, and found herself running a pub in the Highlands of Scotland, before a punter suggested she take a look at Snowdonia. When she made her way over she was smitten, and took on the lease of this pub, with its dramatic view of the mountain, and the steady stream of people from across the world who came to marvel at it. She could finally stay put, and let the world come to her.

It flashes by her in moments, and she searches for a blank spot where her father should have been. Was she looking for *him* in all those men, all those places? *Was* it a search for him, on some level? Or was she moving so that those thoughts and feelings, perhaps also the reproductive expectations of her as a woman, would not catch up with her? Looking at Colin, with his mad professor hair and beard, those strangely innocent eyes behind those glasses ... she cannot see a father. He is just a man. She looks at her mother, whose expression blends matriarchal assurance with a hint of regret. Anna glances at the table in front of her, then up at the customers, and wonders what kind of dramas are playing out in their lives.

The teenagers have been talking about A levels, about their friends, about music, and they have been talking at least as much about how awkward their fathers make them feel; not with words, but through a profusion of subtle gestures, shifts of the shoulders, inflections and dances of the eye. The two men have been locked in political discussion for an hour and seem deadlocked. It is a war of ideology, right versus left, one seemingly unable to accommodate the worldview of the other. Their children have heard their views expounded almost daily for as long as they can remember. 'Sephone and Dan have held a peaceful protest on the sidelines, holding up banners which, if they turned to read them, would tell their fathers that they demand a resolution to the impasse, a détente, and a change of subject. But, they both know well that this will not come. Anna reads this in moments, and knows too that there is little hope of such entrenched views shifting, especially when so long and dearly held. And, once men have had their blood up in public, backing down becomes unthinkable.

She considers her situation for a moment in light of this. Is the onus on her to get to a place that the two men cannot, and make the peace? Does the matter, and the moment, require that she tell them that all is well, that they are both forgiven, released from any guilt they may have dragged around for the last four decades? She sees in their eyes that they *need* it.

A glance at Maggie and Arthur tells her that, whatever they have been confronted with, they have found a way through it. It passes through her mind that she is at a kind of midpoint between the teens and her parents, looking up and down the tracks … and all of them still face significant challenges. Age and experience are little defence against the problems of life, which assail each of us year in, year out. Anna has steadied her ship however. She pictures a square rigger at anchor in a harbour under warm blue skies, its sails folded, gentle movement only, an elegant, sturdy vessel taking a break from the high seas. Her parents look as though they have been forced to set sail in heavy weather, and are finding it a battle to keep to their intended course. She takes a breath.

'Well, I'm sure I won't hold it against you,' she says to Colin, whose eyes redden and fill. He looks at Sue, who reaches a hand across to his. He looks like he has much more to say, but this is not the moment.

'Don't be so *daft!*' says Stuart testily.

'I'm just *saying*,' says 'Sephone, holding her hands up, mock defensively. 'Don't shoot the messenger.'

'But what if it *were*,' says Al, making a hypothetical face. 'What would you want to do with your last night on earth?' Stuart looks around the room with a cynical expression.

'Well, I can think of other places I might like to spend it.' Al looks at 'Sephone. 'Though naturally I'm happy to be with my daughter. And what about you?' he says, looking slightly smug.

'Some ways, it don't matter where I am, or wi' who. My loved ones *know* I love 'em. Right boy?'

'Mm-hm,' murmurs Dan, reaching reflexively for his Coke and reddening slightly.

'Right,' says Al. 'Any road, this wouldn't be a bad place in which to shuffle off this mortal coil. And what about yourselves, Maggie and Arthur?' They are only a few feet away. They turn slowly, then turn to each other.

'We've lived through a great deal,' says Maggie. 'A few times … there's been a threat that seemingly might be the end of it all. But,' she smiles at Arthur, 'we're still here.' She pats his arm. 'Aren't we?' He nods, and smiles. 'Sephone can see his blue eyes, and they sparkle in the firelight. Al smiles, and cannot find the right response. He nods humbly and takes a sip of beer instead. Kenny comes over to ask if anyone would like another drink, and Al asks him what he thinks about this perhaps being his last night on earth.

'Well you know, I almos' died two year ago,' he says seriously. Anna gets up to go and busy herself behind the bar, as she knows this could take a minute. Kenny sits at the empty table between the old folks and the dads. He begins slowly, looking at each of the listeners in turn. 'I had a collapse lung. I was drinking with friends, then I go home. Some hour later, I thought I would die. I could not breathe. I couldn't move an inch. I *couldn't* breathe. I was alone in my room. Just as I thought I was gonna lost my last breath, I forced myself up, with utter pain on my chest. I went to the kitchen ... drank water ... tried to breathe ... I stood there for more than two hours, because I was afraid if I lie down I will go unconscious. I didn't know what was happened, I kept drinking water until my bladder was full ... and I lost control ... urine came out everywhere and I black out for a minute. But I kept standing until I could catch my breath again. I called the ambulance ... they finally came when the sun rise ... the morning never been so different and meaningful until that day. The thing is ... I made a choice. I want to live. On that very last moment.' Kenny looks up and sees a row of faces, stunned, silent, waiting for him to continue. He looks at Maggie and Arthur, but can't find the words he wants. His limited English frustrates him. He looks at the teenagers. 'All these people, older than you ... they know something about health ... they know the things not to do. *Mostly*. They know that something happen to everyone ... you don't know what until it happen. *You* guys ... your family love you, you know? You gotta look after yourself. You never know if your last day already come.' There's a moment as everyone lets the story sink in.

'Why aren't you with your family?' asks Dan.

'Ah,' says Kenny with a grin. 'Too many crazy stories. *Too* many! This how I know your family love you. Now, in case the sun won't come up, is the end of the world, who wants a drink? I buy for everyone.'

Anna observes the brightening scene, the smiles, the warmth that oozes out of everyone once someone leads. She catches her mother's eye, and makes a 'go on, go and join them' gesture. Sue makes the suggestion to Colin and they take their drinks over. A little rearranging of the furniture in a semi-circle allows them all to see one another, and share the fire. Sue and Colin sit on the far left, Maggie and Arthur in the middle on the couch, then Stuart and Al, Dan and 'Sephone. Kenny sits beside the fire on the far right. Anna sits on a chair behind Maggie and Arthur, keeping all in her sight. In response to another question, Kenny launches into the story of how he got to England, being a kind of Chinese-Malaysian gay mail order bride for an Englishman.

'He was 44, I was 24. His parents are like 70 or something, and they think me and him are just *friends*. He didn't tell me he have old parents he still live with. It was *horrible* I tell you! They don't like me at *all*. Most of the days we drive two hours to his work, in optician outside London. Some days I sleep in the store room. Then two hours home to people who hate me. One morning his mother find me in his bed, the other single bed not made.' He sits back and acts out the shock and horror. 'She go *crazy!* Kick me out of the house! I all alone, walk the streets by myself, call him, he tell me it all *my* fault! I should have make the bed. Well.' He waves his hands in a 'that's all in the past' gesture. 'I leave, I travel. I go all over the place, meet nice people, one day I meet Anna in Scotland, another day she invite me here for job. And I stay. Happy now!' He claps his hands with joy, and with a theatrical, lanky run, goes to give her a hug, which she accepts with a magnanimous grin.

'I'll bet *you* can top that,' Al says to Arthur with a smirk. Arthur mutters modestly. But, his wife gives him a look, and he gives in.

'Well, I flew Hurricanes in the war. For a little while at least.' He chuckles endearingly. His voice is fragile, dry as paper, but it reaches everyone sharp and clear. 'Egypt, November 4th 1942. Shot down during a dogfight. Cockpit was in flames, got shrapnel in my left eye, could hardly see a thing … my wingman helped me get her down, keeping Jerry off my back so I had half a chance. Well, I brought her down in what turned out to be a *mine*field!' He chuckles again, shaking his head, as though he still can't quite believe it. 'There I was, trying to get out, the desert sun baking the sweat and the blood on me. *Ooh* it *was* painful! Good *Lord.* I managed to crawl out, flop over the side like a fish, and lie in the shade. Bloomin' good thing the fuel tanks didn't decide to go up and take me with 'em. Germans didn't get back to finish me off either. Anyways, after half an hour I hear an engine, and it's the Sergeant from the base, in his old jeep. I might not look it now, but I was a strapping lad back then, six four and a lot of me. I couldn't see … I collapsed in the passenger seat … and God rest his soul I sat on the Sarge's Jack Russell. Killed the poor little bugger.' He takes a moment, a little shake of the head. 'Cor. What a day. We got back through the mines in one piece, don't ask me how. I had months in hospital in Egypt, then got sent from pillar to post in West Africa, and finally they packed me off home. Combat flying days over o' course. Ended up training pilots to bomb … stationed on the south coast. That's where I met a lovely young lady in the WAAF.' He touches Maggie's arm and smiles again. She reciprocates and says *yes* quietly. 'It was at a dance in Chichester. Glen Miller was playing, our first dance. In the Mood. That's our song. February '44 that was. Married 68 years today.' Maggie lets out a sigh, her eyes red. She nods, wipes a tear, as the others clap and wish them a happy anniversary.

'Lovely. That's lovely to 'ear that is. Congratulations. You won't be 'earin' too many more stories like that, young'uns,' says Al to the kids. 'And what about you Stuart? You got a war story, or a love story?'

'Not one anyone'd want to hear. I wouldn't wish to ruin the mood.'

'We're all adults here,' insists Al. 'Aren't we?' he says to their children with a wink.

'Very well,' says Stuart. 'I could tell you a few. Served in the Falklands. Not a day goes by-' He stops abruptly as the words catch in his throat. He takes a sip of gin and tonic, clears his throat. His voice is tight as he continues. '*Ahem*. Yes. Well … *ahem!* You know … the thing that stays in *my* mind, more than anything else … it was the end of one of the worst scraps, there's been plenty on the television about it this year … thirty years ago … *already*. Well, we finally overran the Argentine positions above Stanley … and we found a bunch of teenagers, cowering in the trenches, their bloody feet shot through by their own lot. The rest of them had plugged the feet of these kids … then cleared off, leaving these poor buggers to keep us at bay while they made their escape.' He looks around the group. 'I'm sorry to say it, but there it is. Men can be such beasts to one another.'

'Why?' asks Dan. Everyone turns to look at him, and like a snail he physically pulls his neck in.

'*Why* are men like that?' asks Stuart. 'Because we're animals, under these clothes.' His brown eyes are fogged with emotion. It is discomfiting, delivered as it is in clipped, public school pronunciation. 'Whatever you may wish to believe about human nature … we are none of us so far from behaving like wild animals … it is simply a matter of circumstance. Doing what you believe to be right at any given moment.' A silence falls.

'And what say you?' asks Al of Colin, who looks slightly surprised to be addressed. 'You look like you've seen a bit o' life. You must have an opinion on it.'

'Well, I may be forced to agree with our friend,' he says in his smooth baritone, with a rueful smile. His eyes dance intelligently behind the heavy frames of his glasses. He turns to address Dan and 'Sephone. 'But, I would hope that young people would look at the world ... and see a world that needs changing for the better. And I would hope that they understand that it *can* be changed for the better, *if* they so choose. It's a social *construct*, d'you see? What *you* construct, will decide humanity's fate ... by what you do, and do not do. But why would you know this? Those that hold power do so by shutting down enquiry, making decisions in the dark, having you follow without question. To church, to the shops, into battle. Politics? Well, you get an *illusion* of choice. But this question of *why* ... it's the most important word there is. As well as love, honour ... integrity, truth. So, perhaps it's the most important *question*. And you should particularly ask why when it comes to war. Sending the youth to die ... it only makes sense if you don't question it.

'That's all very well, sir, but some wars are *necessary*,' says Stuart.

'Which ones?' asks Colin playfully. 'Vietnam? Iraq?'

'Help me out here,' says Stuart to Arthur. 'Can you explain to our *friend*-'

'It wasn't for us to question it.' Says Arthur. Stuart looks somewhat pleased. 'But maybe we should have.' Stuart looks less pleased. 'Thing is, when the bombs start falling around your ears ... you're ready to do what you 'ave to. There's no politics ... but we were lucky to have leadership in them days.' He shrugs. 'And you got no choice in the end. Every one of us was ready to give his life for family, friends ... country. I can't speak for all wars ... but I can tell you that when they start in your back yard, you got to be ready to finish them.'

Anna looks at the teenagers, who appear several years younger in this moment: somewhat out of their depth. She feels it rise up in her, the urge to protect them, but she thinks of Colin's words. Maybe it *is* best they hear this.

'So, let's hear the voice of the youth.' Al looks from 'Sephone to Dan and back again.' Dan has that perpetually unsure look about him, the kind that makes a certain kind of woman throb maternally in its presence. The kids look at one another, and a glance from Dan is taken by 'Sephone as an invitation to start.

'If you ask me for an honest appraisal of the state of the world, I would say that, if we are to inherit it, as Colin suggests, then we could scarcely do a worse job.' She waits for the initial round of responses, and just as her father draws breath to comment she continues. 'At university, most of my peers are concerned only with what they wear, how they look, what they drive, what phone they have, where they travel to, and mainly, what other people think of them. There are plenty who are politically interested, but they are certainly in the minority, overall. Of the political discussions, many are academic, but a few are about direct action. Those students generally seem to have highly politicised backgrounds, and wish to actively attempt to change the world. But they too are as split as it's possible to be. Some think political evolution is the only way, others say there is no time, and that revolution must happen immediately. The others say yes, *but*, all political, cultural and economic change takes time, and that they must bring the majority of people along with them in the process. The others counter that access to power is the problem that must be deal with, and the old guard will never allow this, and so must be thrown out. The other guys say no, this would cause anarchy and expose and pressurise every fault line in society ... and so it goes. Meanwhile, we watch the news and realise that all the lessons Colin refers to, well, they appear to be comprehensibly ignored, do they not? I am fond of the saying, that if we've learnt one thing from history, it's that we've learnt nothing from history.'

'Well, I'm glad I asked,' laughs Al. He glances at Stuart and nods towards 'Sephone with a grin. He is evidently tickled by her performance, and knows she and her father must have these same conversations over and over again.

'Young lady, the *old guard* are not as evil as you may suspect,' says her father. 'We love our children, we obey the law, we do our best for our family.'

'Oh aye? But you don't mind exploiting *other* families to do it, I suppose? That's just business, is it?' says Al.

'What *are* you talking about?' says Stuart irritably. He shoots a glance at Arthur, beetling his brow, perhaps hoping for some understanding.

'He may be referring to sweat shops,' says 'Sephone, who appears to be biting back her anger. 'All those throughout Asia for example, who work for starvation wages.' She takes a breath. 'I'm sure I hardly need point these things out.' She looks at the others. 'My father and I have been around this particular block many times.' He also gives them a weary look. Al nods – *thought so.*

'So you've not got a lot of hope, is that what you're saying?' asks Anna. 'Dan? What do you think?' He shifts about in his chair for a few moments, clearing his throat and tapping at the Coke bottle.

'Well, it's pretty hard to feel confident about the future, like. If you watch the news anyway. I mean, there's no good news, is there? It's all shi- ... er, it's all bad. Like *she* said,' he says, motioning towards 'Sephone.

'So, what *are* you aiming to do with yourself, Dan? Your dad told me you're in school?' says Anna, kindly.

'I'm doin' film.' He looks around the half circle, perhaps to see how this is received. Most of the adults nod neutrally, but 'Sephone smiles at him, and it lights him up. 'I s'pose I want to make the world, the way *I* want it. Well, some of the time. Sometimes I just want to look at a *tiny* little piece of it. Might be summat good, might be summat awful. I mean, it's all pretty amazing, right? *Life*? That we're here at all.' Anna feels a strange warmth as she sees Dan finally find his voice, and want to be heard. 'I know there's a lot of ... *awful* stuff goes on too ... tragic ... waste of an opportunity ... to make a world that *everyone* can enjoy. It *has* to be possible, don't it?'

'Well, I hate to be the one to tell you this, but it's not entirely *plausible*.' Stuart seems genuinely sorry to be breaking the news.

'Well, maybe if people *believe* that story about humanity, that's half the reason that it defines so much of our lives,' says Colin.

'I simply think it's human nature,' says Stuart. 'I'm sorry, but if you look at our history as a species, it has ever been thus. I've watched what humans will do to one another over a piece of earth.'

'If anything, Dan, it may simply be that the world is a mess because we all want something different,' says Colin. He and Dan share a look that makes Anna think that her father could be a great dad.

'I hadn't thought about that ... but surely a lot of it's to do wi' how the media picks its stories, and tells 'em.' says Dan. 'It's right grim it is. But there's loads of good stuff 'appenin' here, and elsewhere – you just don't get to hear about it. What's that about?'

'The media is connected intimately with the corporate and political worlds,' says 'Sephone, echoing her father's clipped delivery. 'It's all the same thing. Like the military-industrial complex. And let's face it, the mainstream media *is* a business. They want ratings, page views, advertising revenues. You can't trust any institution of this type. Private profits will never deliver true public goods.' She looks across at Dan, and a kind of sad, desperate look is shared between them. Anna wants to say how heart-breaking it is to hear the voice of youth so forlorn, so painfully aware of these brutal realities. Everyone looks uncomfortable, drained, and for the first time this evening, no one has anything much to say.

Maggie and Arthur tell everyone they are heading for bed, and Kenny goes to give them a hand up the stairs. They are given a warm send-off by the others, wishing them a happy anniversary again. Those remaining then close the circle a little more around the fire. 'Sephone says she and Dan are going to check on the weather from the big upstairs window and Stuart looks uptight, but he waves them off. Anna observes his discomfort. She watches him wrestle with both his desire to say 'Don't be long,' and his understanding that if he does he will embarrass everyone in the room.

'Don't be *too* long,' says Al. 'Need some kip at some point.' He avoids Stuart's eye, sparing him. Anna notes a subtle shift in Stuart's demeanour, a battle between gratitude and resentment. Dan nods and follows 'Sephone across the bar and up the stairs. Anna again sees the gentle amusement in Colin's eyes, as though he wants to comment but doesn't. She wonders if he wants to say something about how wonderful children are but feels he can't, under the circumstances.

A silence falls over them and after a minute or so of quiet drinking and reflection, Al says. 'So what about our hostess? Penny for your thoughts, on the ways of the world.' She smiles and points at the sign over the bar which says 'Don't discuss politics with anyone you haven't seen naked.' 'Oh aye,' he says. 'That 'ow it is?'

'A rule to live by, *especially* if you run a pub,' she says, looking immovable.

'Well, you're off the clock now, love. You must have an opinion. You're enigmatic as the Sphinx you are.'

'Well, what can I say? I've watched a lot of men come into bars and drink their sorrows away. But there are always more sorrows, always more nights on the barstool.' She looks around the pub. 'And then there are some nights ... like on New Year's eve. This place, provided people can *get* here, it'll be crazy. Singing and dancing all night, through to dawn. Like ancient Rome. The best of times.' She shrugs, looking into the flames. 'We make our own heaven, and our own hell.' She smiles toward the fire, watches the flames for a few moments. 'You ask me what I *make* of it all? Life in general? Well, tonight ... I met my father. This is Colin.' He beams at them from the depths of his beard, his eyebrows arching merrily. Al and Stuart look caught out, as though unsure if she's being straight or not. 'Yeah. *That's* my point. Life is like that. We're all just makin' it up as we go along. Tryin' to go with the flow. You never know what's around the corner, so all you can do is try to ... *be here. I* think ...' she takes a sip of her tea, 'that it's not a race. You can't take anything with you ... I

moved around like crazy all my adult life, till I fetched up here. And
… I guess I found a kind of peace here. You ask me what I would do,
if this was it? The sun never came up? Last night on earth and all that?
Well, there's worse places. And I would've … *yeah*, I would've found
my family, right at the last possible moment. Like I said, you never
know what comes next. All you can do … well, you just gotta be the
best version of yourself you can be … be a friend to *yourself*, give
yourself support and good advice … look after yourself so others don't
have to … and try not to screw anyone else over in the process. Try to
enjoy your life, while you have it. Like Dan said, it's pretty amazing
that we're here at all.' She takes a moment, staring into her cup, then
glancing at her mother, then at Al. 'How was that?'

'Aye. Right good. You must be chuffed, Colin. Turns out your
daughter's a bit special, like.'

'Oh *my* yes. Absolutely.' He grins again, looking slightly clownish.

'To think … she was such a tiny little thing once,' says Sue. 'But
always *bright* as a button.'

'She still is tiny. Slip of a girl,' laughs Al.

'Before the internet, she was a complete mystery, my daughter.
Maybe having hippy parents … maybe that wanderlust … she got
from us. Somehow. For *years* she was just a string of postcards, and
the occasional polaroid, on the kitchen pinboard. Of course I worried,
but she had this inner strength. She just kept at it, wouldn't let life beat
her down or put her off. I knew she had integrity … soul … a good
heart. And it made me weep with happiness whenever she called.' Sue
dabs at her eyes with a tissue, blows her nose daintily. 'Oh dear. We
do hold *such* a lot back, don't we? Parents, I mean.' She looks from
one to the other, and the whole room seems to soften as she does. 'It's
not easy, is it? Never. Not for a day. But it's beautiful. It may be the
best thing in life, having children. As long as they're not a *complete*
horror.' She laughs, peering back through time. 'Yes, I knew she was
special, my daughter. I knew all I wanted was for her to be happy, to
be healthy, to choose wisely. And in the end you just have to trust that
they will. I wish she'd wanted to have children, but …' she holds up
her hands. 'I'm just thankful she is who she is.' She presses the tissue
to her eyes again, and clears her throat. '*Well.*' She laughs and rolls
her eyes. 'Okay, that's it. I'm off to bed. Need my beauty sleep before
doomsday. Goodnight, gentlemen. Goodnight, love.' She leans down
to kiss Anna's forehead, then to his evident surprise, she leans down to
plant one on Colin's forehead too.

'I'll give you a hand,' says Anna, and takes her mother upstairs, leaving Al, Stuart and Colin with their drinks.

They talk for a half hour about how awful their children's music is, about how it was so much better when they were growing up. The first thing the men have agreed on all night is The Rolling Stones. Eventually, the talk turns back to the moment.

'I imagine,' says Stuart. 'We could be stuck here for several days, if it's as bad as Anna says.'

'It won't stay frozen for too long, don't you worry' says Al. 'Like the young lady said, you never know what's round the next corner.'

'Oh *indeed*,' muses Colin. 'Your children could wed, and you two fine gentlemen could become brothers.' He looks at them levelly, as their features scramble for order.

'Do you perhaps derive *pleasure* from the discomfort of others?' asks Stuart, testily brushing invisible specks from the sleeves of his jacket.

'Why would that make you uncomfortable?' says Al. 'What's wrong wi' my son?'

'*Really*, Al. I *know* when I'm being baited. And I'm sure your son is a fine young man. You don't set a *terribly* bad example for him, I suppose.'

'What's that supposed to mean?' demands Al, with some weight in the words. Stuart holds his finger up.

'Got you,' he says with a smirk.

'Right *you* are,' says Al with a magnanimous laugh.

'Well, gentlemen, it's been … *interesting*, but I must turn in, and find my daughter.' Stuart tosses back the last of his gin and tonic, shakes the hand of Al and Colin, and sets off for the stairs, with the alcohol, and the hour, dragging at his legs.

Two minutes later, he comes back down with greater energy.

'They aren't up there,' he says blankly.

Anna and Kenny are called down to help them search, and Anna soon discovers they have gone out the back door and into the snow. The doorway is in the lee and has escaped the snow drifts. Further out, on up into the beer garden, their footprints are deep and clear. The sky is now empty, swept of clouds, and the wind has fallen away. A half moon makes the landscape shine, a soft white glow stretching out towards the hills. A silence falls over the five adults. The scene is too delicate, somehow, for fear, for shouting and hurtling into the night. Anna tells the others to wait, says she knows where they will be, she is the only person with wellington boots, and she doesn't want to risk an insurance claim. She flicks on her torch, heads up the steps. The tight crunch of fresh snow, and the yellow beam of the torch, recede.

She can hear the fathers muttering unhappily, and Colin's voice interjecting, stopping the others dead. She couldn't hear what he said, but she chuckles, knowing it was probably something random, and with that oddly teasing delivery. The garden rises up about ten feet, and goes back over sixty feet. At its end is a conservatory that she never locks, which on a clear day has a good view of the mountain. She shines the torch ahead, giving them plenty of warning. By the time she gets to the glass, they are standing at the entrance.

'Look at you guys. Rabbits in the headlights, if ever.'

'I saw this place earlier, and I wanted to show Dan,' says 'Sephone, with a breezy confidence that Anna admires. She imagines that it must build character, having Stuart as a father. Dan looks rather more caught out. Anna notes that he appears to be holding up his trousers with his hands, thrust deep in the pockets of his coat. She quickly looks back at 'Sephone, who has a little uncertainty in her eyes now. Anna smiles reassuringly.

'Guys, take a moment, then head on back, okay? Your folks got a little worried there.'

''Sephone told me about the end of the world,' blurts Dan. Anna cocks her head, eyebrows aloft, waiting for more, but he shuts his mouth and shifts about awkwardly.

'Right. Well. That's serious stuff. Two minutes, alright guys?' She walks back, composing herself. She reaches them, offering an easy smile. 'Everything's cool. Just stargazing, talking doomsday. You know, teenager stuff. They're on their way.' The fathers avoid each other's eye, and they all head back into the bar for a nightcap. As promised, Dan and 'Sephone quickly appear, stamping their feet and looking pretty much at peace with the world, and they join the others for a round of brandies.

'Well, here's to another day on earth,' says Anna, raising her glass.

'To the children,' says Colin.

'To the parents,' says Stuart.

'To the brewers,' says Al.

'To peace,' says 'Sephone. They all look at Dan, waiting. He raises his glass, biting the inside of his mouth.

'To love,' he says quickly. They all do a double-take. Anna and Colin exchange glances, trying to conceal their amusement. They all chink glasses with a weary brightness and take a sip.

'Some night,' says Al.

'You wait for New Year's eve,' says Anna.

'Please God we'll be home by then,' says Stuart. He catches a couple of looks and waves a hand dismissively. 'No offence meant. I have a rather enormous business matter bearing down on me, and I really *must* get back to London.'

'Well, if God loves you the weather'll give you half a chance,' says Al, nodding sagely.

'Why did you come up here at this time of year if you had to be back down there?' asks Anna.

'*This* young lady said she wanted to see Snowdon. She's a terror with a camera. Got the idea into her head ... and I couldn't say no. It gets harder to spend time with them, doesn't it?' he looks at the others, who nod heavily. 'It's just ... well, *you* know. Life gets in the way, things change. I have to get back. Couldn't have foreseen it.'

'Well, you'll remember it, eh?' says Anna.

'Certainly will,' says 'Sephone quietly, tugging at one of her long brown curls.

'So, that's that then,' says Anna quickly. 'I gotta lock up, get some shut eye.'

They all finish their drinks and get ready to head for bed. Stuart and Al shake hands with respectful smiles, pausing to hold one another's eye, and nod. They say no more, but bid goodnight to their children, then wave to Anna, Colin and Kenny, and take their leave. Dan and 'Sephone walk slowly upstairs behind their fathers; Anna notices them sharing a glance and a shy smirk that melts her heart. Kenny begins emptying the trays and cleaning the bar down, allowing Anna and Colin to try to find a final response to the day.

For a short while they converse without words; they remark on Al and Stuart parting almost as friends, their children going them one better; and they share their amusement at their own situation. With a subtle inclination of the head, and a particular kind of shrug, and smile, Colin tells her that he can't believe he left it so long, almost until it was too late, and that he is overwhelmed that they finally know one another. Anna has too much to say, and just shrugs, laughing and throwing her hands up, conveying how bizarre and unexpected and wonderful it all is. He says nothing, but grins at her, those big eyebrows arching, and he embraces her. She finds it strangely easy to do. She thinks, well, he really *is* a likeable guy. And half of my genes. He lets her go, raps on the bar three times, enigmatically, and makes his way up to the rooms without another word.

The landlady sits down on a stool, taking a moment, while Kenny quietly cleans the bar. She thinks about the perpetual half smile Colin wears, as though he finds it all slightly amusing, as if he gets the joke and is waiting for everyone else to start laughing too. She tries the word 'father' on him, but it doesn't stick, it slips off. He is a different breed, she thinks. He is an island. An odd strength about him, a sort of resilience. She imagines he could be dropped anywhere, and he would find a way to survive. He'd be an instant hit with the locals … a kind of effortlessness about him, a gentle true spirit. Just as she thinks this, she wonders what her life would have been like if she'd known him, if he'd been there. She wonders if thinking about it all now is such a great idea, or maybe she should let it percolate overnight. Even for someone who runs a pub, it's been a new one. And, life will never be quite the same, no matter what comes next. She opts to park it, does the restocking instead, but makes a mental note to straighten up in the conservatory before anyone else gets there tomorrow.

When she's finished, she goes to sit on the sofa by the fire, as she does most nights. But tonight she sits and thinks of Maggie and Arthur, and the endless challenges they've made it through. She feels humbled by this, and it makes her heart swell in a way she can't find words for. After a few minutes Kenny joins her, puts his arm around her and pulls her close for a cuddle. She takes a breath to say something but Kenny tightens his arm around her neck, shushing her, and she subsides with a laugh.

'That's enough for one day. You did good, darling.' She rubs his trouser leg companionably, and nods. 'Especially with your new father. He is funny.'

'You think so?'

'Take it from me, if your parents make you laugh more than cry, you are fortunate.'

'Right on. Well, if the apocalypse doesn't arrive in the next few hours, I'll find out, won't I?'

'Huh?'

'11.11 am.'

'*Now* you tell me,' he says, shaking his head and tutting at her.

'Well, I've got a feeling we'll all still be here this time tomorrow. Feels like things *have* to carry on. You know what I mean?'

'*Yes*, chicken, of course! They *have* to! And take my word, when you wake up in the morning after you think you gonna die, the world is new. *You* are new.'

'Where there's life, there's hope, huh?'

'Yeah. Is just getting interesting.'

It's About Time

What do you believe? In your heart of hearts, what, in your life, do you believe one hundred percent? For example, do you believe that you will grow old? That there is a you out there, some way down the road in time, waiting for you to make good choices, because their life depends on it? Or do you believe instead that there is only now? Only *right now* – the only moment you are alive, or ever will be? Can I be honest with you? I don't think I'd ever thought about it. Not until a month ago. And now? I think about it round the clock. When you hear what I have to tell you, you'll understand exactly why.

I was in a bar, I think I'd been there before ... but I'd just hit whatever bar looked dark and quiet, and anonymous enough, you know what I mean? Maybe you know. I was a drinker. I drank. Every day. I'd just slip in, order, and get into it. Maybe I'd remember leaving, maybe not. And sometimes you get someone join you. Could be a hustler, a hooker, could just be someone who needs to talk at someone. And oftentimes, that's all it is. But, once in a while, it's someone who actually needs to be *heard*. And that's different.

So, on that particular day, that particular bar, I guess I slid in there some time after noon. The heat that pounds the streets of L.A. in August has weight to it. You get into a bar with the AC on and the lights off, you spring up about two inches. Once you're in, your face gets lit up like some carnival freak by the neon. The barflies too, sitting at the bar in their jackets, mostly silent, intent, kinda like monks. You feel respectful around them, leave 'em to it. I guess I got a different vibe, but folks'll come right up to me and start in, no problem.

Sure enough, there I was, minding my own business, when I feel the weight of someone behind me. I'm at a table near the back, as far from the door as I can manage, facing away so I don't have to squint when the door cracks open and the place is blasted with that light from outside, like an angel just walked in. Anyway, I'm a couple of beers deep, just getting started, when he says, 'Mind if I join you?'

I turn slightly, see if he's got a blade, but he's just some old white guy, fidgeting his way into a chair next to me. I give him a once-over and shrug. Grey hair and beard, but not shabby-looking. Dressed okay, an unfussy coat, a shirt with a collar that looks freshly pressed. And he's no lush. Eyes are too bright, movements too sharp. But he's got this nerviness, he won't look right at me, starts playing with his beer bottle, turning it round and round on its base, looking kinda jumpy. I take another slug and mumble, noncommittal. He looks over his shoulder, then moves around to sit in front of me. He kind of hunkers down in his chair, like he's trying to hide behind me. I get that sober feeling. The guy's trouble after all. I look up at him briefly, and he catches me full in the face with a smile. There's something in there, and I'm not quite sure what it is. I get some strange feeling from when I was a kid, like when someone'd say, usually with a little music in their voice, 'I know something *you* don't know!' This guy has something to say. I figure I can always leave if it gets ugly.

A few more moments, I just stare at the table in front of me, one arm on the table, a hand around my beer, I don't move. I got that move down. Only someone who drinks or gets high a lot can be a statue like that. Or someone who has religion. I guess those meditating monks could hold their own in a sitting contest with me.

Finally he says, 'Friend, can I tell you something?' I've heard this line *many* times before. Talking of religion, people will come up to you in bars and confess all kinds of things. They have some crud to wipe off their slate, and once it goes through the ears of a drunk it comes out purified, like spring water. And it's so little effort to oblige them, you just sit there. So, I say the only thing I *can* say.

'Sure.' He breathes your genuine sigh of relief. And another. He looks like he might cry, puts a hand to his eyes, but he goes another way.

'Okay, what I'm going to tell you … well, you may never be the same again afterwards. Are you ready for that?' I look up, I run the God detector over him again. Looks clean. He's twitchy, but sincere. This is something else.

'Ready as I'll ever be.' I play that line loose, not too sarcastic. Just enough to put a little buffer right there on the table. His eyes dart around again, he's looking everywhere but at me. After a second he opens his mouth, but then just keeps sliding his jaw side to side, weighing it up. He raises an index finger, wags it. Finally he speaks.

'I guess I'm gonna give you a piece of advice.' Right before I can speak he carries on. 'It's about *time*, okay?' He laughs suddenly, kinda rolls his eyes, like he just got the joke. 'Yeah. *Ha!* My friend, it's about *time*, I told someone about *time*.' He cracks up again, this wheezing laugh, his shoulders bouncing up and down. He slaps the table with his palm. 'God *damn!* God damn ...' he trails off, shaking his head. I want to know what the fuck, but don't want to encourage him, you know what I mean? 'Okay, listen up.' He clears his throat, shrugs, puts his fingertips together on the table and leans in a little. He fixes me with this look. 'I am in a *unique* position, to tell *you* ... about *time*.' He points at me and lifts his eyebrows. '*Mm?*' Cocks his head to one side. I get the feeling he's waiting for me to catch on.

'So, go right head, friend.' I play that one pretty straight. He takes a breath, looks away for a second, then back at me.

'Alright then. You watch movies and stuff about time travel? I mean, you've seen a few. Am I right?' I nod. 'Good. Then you know how it goes. Wish fulfilment, all that kinda stuff?' I nod again, taking another slug. 'Well. I'm here to tell you ... it's *very* different.' He sits back, looks me up and down. He's giving this the big production. I figure, why *not* indulge him? Could be quite a show. I nod again.

'How so?' I turn to catch the bar guy's eye, wave my beer bottle. I turn to my man. 'Another?' He shakes his head, but I hold up two fingers anyway, and wait for the guy to bring them over. 'Okay, we're set. Shoot.'

'Okay.' He leans in again, gives me these tiny little expressions that say, okay, I'm trusting you to take this on board, and hoping you can keep up. Then he says, 'As far as I know for *sure*, I am the one and *only* human being ... that has *ever*, successfully travelled back *and* forwards in time. *Mm*? Huh?' He tips his beer towards me and nods, then winks and takes a mouthful.

'Okay.' I give a little shrug, like, yeah, *and*?

'*Yeah*. You know how *long* it's been around?' He smacks his lips, waiting for me to shake my head. 'Since the mid 1960s. Before you were born, I'm guessing.' He tilts his beer at me again and laughs, friendly, then leans in. 'The *military*,' he says, glaring. '*Obviously*. NASA guys too, picking up on work done in Germany and Austria during the second World War. *Yeah*.' His eyes kind of *flare* as he says that. '*I* was picked,' he says proudly, tapping his chest. 'Well, me and a bunch of other kids,' he says more modestly. 'We were meant to be heading for 'Nam, but they sent us to ... *another place*.' He eyes go kinda nervy again at this, some fear there. He looks up, around, towards the door again. 'Anyway. They split us up ... one by one we get carted off ... there were rumours ... *crazy* ... you'd have to be *nuts* to believe them ... but they were *true*. Holy God in heaven, they were *true*.' His eyes glaze up, he's staring way back.

I figure I might have lost him altogether after maybe ten seconds of nothing. Then he comes back. 'So, yeah ... anyway ... *my* turn comes, after maybe three weeks, dying of boredom, under ground. I get briefed by a couple of guys in suits, a couple in uniform. They tell me I'm gonna serve my country ... that I'm gonna make the world safe from the *scourge* of Communism. I'm just sat there nodding, trying to figure out what I'm meant to say or do ... finally they open a brown folder stamped top secret. The files inside are all stamped top secret. Part of me's excited, you understand?' I nod, slightly dazed. 'So I'm gonna just ... *go along* with whatever, right? Serve my country? You're *damn* right I'm gonna!' He goes to slap the table again but pulls up, and pats it instead. 'There's such a thing as doing *right*, isn't there?'

He takes a moment, but it's apparently rhetorical. 'So, I keep nodding like a frickin' ... *somethin'*, while they tell me about the program I'm involved in. It's scientific stuff, physics and energy and particles and Christ knows what ... I can't take it in, can't stop my brain trying to skip ahead, figure out the punch line. And then they get to it. Me and the guys are testing a new technology that will not only help us win the war in Vietnam, but win every other war, and create *permanent ... American ... hegemony.*'

He flashes that smile at me again. This one's kinda cheeky. 'You *believe* that? That's *just* what they said to me. Like *that*. They figured they'd come up with a fool proof plan to rule the world, *forever*. Even to me – a rubber-faced recruit, destined to be cannon fodder, take my last breath in some steaming hundred-degree jungle, *for my country* – that sounded fuckin' *crazy*. But, sure enough, they take me along what felt like a mile of corridors and tunnels, and finally to this huge room. Holy *shit* it was big! It was a dome, maybe two hundred feet tall at the centre. There's cables and pipes, and walls of lights and switches, and generators and control rooms, and everywhere, there's guys in every kind of uniform and suit you can imagine. There are big screens around something in the centre, and around it, only the guys in the big white suits with these *huge* helmets. The MPs take me to a long cabin off to one side, where they strip me down, stick me in a weird shower kinda thing where they wash me and zap me with some light gun, then

I have to dress alone, put on this sealed white suit and helmet, in an air-tight room, while some guy the other side of a window is giving me instructions. Finally, he comes in and checks my gear. I'm good to go. No one looks me in the eye. Part of me … well, I just want to say no thank you and just *walk* … and keep *on* walking. But I have to let that go, you know?' He pauses, to look for some understanding. I pull a face like I understand.

'Sure,' I say. He nods, a brave little smile. He's grateful.

'So, *then* they take me to the centre of the big room, where all the pipes and everything else lead to, where *everyone*'s now looking. Behind the screens … it's a kind of metallic sphere, about the size of a VW bus, in a kind of harness … with these big red digital clocks next to it, one set at 60 seconds, and another with the time, hours, minutes and seconds, ticking away. It was just before 10.00 hours. It's open, and there's room for one in there, plus luggage. You have to walk up a step to get into it, and that step was the biggest I ever took. Felt like I weighed a freakin' *tonne*.' He pauses again, giving me a look. 'Biggest step I ever took.'

The air kinda goes out of him, he shrinks, right there in his chair. I want to say something like, look buddy, you don't want to talk about it no more: don't. It's cool. And right *then*, I realise I'm actually *buying* it. I sit back too. I think, *damn*, this guy's really something. I don't know what *kind* of something, *but*. I don't know what to say, so I just gave a little 'mm.' He kinda picks up then.

'Er, where was I? Right, the *step*. So anyway, I get in there, and this guy in one of the big white suits tells me that they'll open the door after a few seconds, and my work will be done for the day. I say okay, and in I go. It's totally black in there when the door closes. I didn't even look up as they were closing it, I was shiftin' about, trying to get comfortable. A few seconds go past, it's dead silent. I just feel the sweat beading down my forehead, I want to wipe it, but I can't, 'cos of the helmet. I start to get a little freaked. It's so damn hot in the suit. I can't hear anything. Then there's this vibration, it just keeps building up. It starts to get kinda noisy in there, then *deafening*. It was hell. I don't know how long it went on, I'm just holding on to these little handles, either side of my butt, grittin' my teeth … but then it just stops. And sure enough, the door opens. I climb out, they're all kinda gathered there, the guys in white suits, and about fifty feet back, maybe twenty guys in all these different uniforms, a few of them looked like brass, and a guy in white asks me how I feel. I give the thumbs up, and the place goes nuts, whooping and hollering and handshakes and high-fives. Then they catch the dumb look on my face and point behind me. I turn around and all I see is the clock. 09.55. I look back, shrug, and it's like I'm Bob fuckin' Hope, they're laughing their asses off.'

'No shit.'

'No shit, I *assure* you.' He leans his head down and strokes his fingertips gently across his forehead, back and forth, face expressionless. 'No shit.'

Well, I just take another swallow, I don't know what else to do. I'm hooked.

'So anyways, there's much rejoicing … and they want me to go again. They tell me they think they've banged the kinks out of the system, and we're really onto something now. That night, one guy lets it slip in the mess hall that eventually they'll have a way bigger capsule, half the size of the whole dome, big enough to fit a battalion or two. I figure, he's only telling me this 'cos he thinks I'm never gonna make it out of there alive.' He looks me in the eye again, spreads his hands like a magician and pulls a face. 'But here I am.'

'Some story.'

'Just gettin' started, buddy.' He smiles. I smile back. Hard not to like this guy, crazy or not. We all like a good story. 'So I make a few more small jumps. Back and forward, a few minutes each time. Then it starts to get serious. They try some other guys, but for some reason, when they send them back … they don't come back again. They open the door and there's no fucker in there! They lose a couple of special forces guys, and everyone starts getting nervous. These guys were going to be sent on missions to win the Vietnam war.' He takes a sip of beer, then a longer pull. Then he just keeps going, finishes the bottle. He shivers then, like someone just walked over his grave. He's gone someplace else again, looks kinda shook up. I want to say something, but I got nothing. I take another drink, and I start to feel real awkward. I want to split, but no one ever spun me a story like this one, and I gotta hear the end.

'So what happened, man? You're still in one piece ain't ya? You got out of it okay?' He seems to hear me, but it's like he's having this internal conversation, and I'm butting in. After a few he looks back at me like he's never seen me before … then recognition.

'Oh, right. Well, ah … *yeah*. So … okay. Seems like I was the only one who … well, I was like their rabbit's foot, you understand? For some reason, I kept making it. So they decided to train *my* ass. Combat, infiltration, intelligence, surveillance, languages, all kinds of stuff, all over. They figured I could go back any time, and I'd get the job done. But then, just as I was about to go back, my first mission, it seems like the lid was blown on the program. I heard Nixon finally got wind of it, and freaked. Asked a lot of questions. Over the months I'd gotten friendly with a guard on the base, and he told me the eggheads and the brass were having to have endless sessions to try to map out the *repercussions* of the work, to prove it was actually workable. Apparently they had all these huge walls of charts and diagrams. Drove 'em cuckoo tryin' to figure it all out. The big question was, if I went back and changed the course of World War II, maybe there would never be a case where the research would have come to light, so that we continued to make the machine that went back and won the war. You follow? Or without Vietnam, the programme would never have had the go-ahead. There was this idea that however things *are* is the only way they *can* be. Any attempt to make changes will nullify the *possibility* ... of *making* the changes. Understand? Well, in the end, there's a lot of covert testing, a lot of trial and error. Some things are *worth* changing, they figured. The timeline would alter accordingly, they hoped. But, for the future, that's *different*. Less messy, in *theory*. I could go into the future and come back with intelligence, and see how America needs to change its policies around the world to stay on top. You know, shuffle its cards. *Problem* for the guy *doing* it is, it's hard to keep your mind in one piece once you start going back and forwards. Believe me kid, it gets so you can't get a grip on anything. And everything starts to look flimsy, kinda meaningless, like you get infinite do-overs. You fuck up, just call a Mulligan.'

'Right.' I nod slowly, taking it in. 'So ... so what happened next?'

'Oh *man*. I had years in the service ... did shit that'd make your head explode. Assassinations, up close and personal, or with the sniper rifle, or C4. Stock and currency market manipulation, coups, even some lobbying work. Amazing what changes the course of history. Made a tidy few laying bets. I mean, why not? No one lookin' over *my* shoulder! So far, so good, you might think. But now, they say, the Chinese got themselves the tech. The only *good* thing about that? That I can *possibly* think of? Now maybe I'll have someone to talk to about this shit who'll actually *understand*.' He drinks again, stares at the door. 'Believe you me, son, there's nothing that'll make you as lonely as being one of a kind. Those queers in one horse towns up and down this great country? Even *those* guys can hop a Greyhound to some place bigger and find themselves a pole to smoke. History's littered with people who were the last to ever speak their language. No one left to talk to. All those creatures who find themselves with no one left to fuck. And me, the only person I ever met who knows what I know.'

'And what's that?'

'That humanity's got a *real* problem with time. Seems like we won't, maybe *can't* learn the lessons of the past, to plan for a *better* future. We're not *built* for it. We're real good at wasting our lives, regretting the past, worrying about the future ... *or* we live in the now so much we don't look up the tracks even the tiniest bit, and figure out that we better be ready. Doctors that smoke ferchrissakes ... driving without a seat belt on ... running out of cheap oil ... climate change. You'd think that enough smart people are out there trying to do something about *that* one. Well, maybe the U.S. has done squat 'cos the few who *really* pull the strings figure we can always go back and do something about it. But I *seen* what's comin' ... and in less than a century the whole world's practically unrecognisable. I shit you not.'

'That's ...'

'Yeah. Ain't it? Well, friend, I've been everywhere, every*when*, and believe you me, we fuck up so much I'm not even sure we *can* do any different. Makes you wonder about fate. God. *Something's* gotta be pushing us *this* hard off the cliff. Can't be *just* us, can it?'

'Right ... so ... so why aren't *you* going back to help fix things?'

'Too old, they say. I'm too damn *old*.' He laughs dryly, strokes his beard. '*That's* bullshit. Well, it ain't just that, anyways. I guess they don't want guys like me around for ever ... too much baggage. Seen too much, done too much, think too much. But they got new blood, that's true enough. They've had me train younger guys for years. Hand picked out of the secret service. They're *athletes*. You think *astronauts* have the right stuff, you should see *these* guys in action. *Machines*. But take it from me, there's *nothing* behind those eyes. They're kinda creepy. Well, who knows. They may be gearing up for something big ... I mean, everyone's useful for somethin', right?'

'So why are you telling *me* all this? Aren't you worried they'll catch up to you? I mean, this is *serious* shit!' I start to feel pretty nervous right there. You can imagine.

'Ah, don't worry about that, friend. I guess if there was anything came of it, they'd go and change it, and it wouldn't have happened in the first place.'

'*Ouch.*' I rub my head.

'Yeah, it drives you nuts. Well, there's a point you go past. Like learning anything new, first the confusion, then all the work to deal with it, the ups and downs, but sooner or later, it's just how it is, your mind adjusts. Whether that's its *own* kind of madness, I don't know. I *do* know that even though I've lived this way a long time, and I can handle it on most levels, one of the hardest things is talking to guys like you and knowing that for the rest of your life ... you'll never *quite* believe me.' He kinda squints at me, as if trying to figure out how much I buy it. Then he winks. 'In the end, what does it matter? I tell you the truth because if there's *one* thing that *really* scrapes away at the soul? When you live like this? It's the lies. The lies you tell, the lies you get told, the truths you can't tell, the deception, omission, the bluff, the silence ... the way it cuts you off from other folks. Lies are like a nest of vipers. You understand? They obscure the truth, and you try to get to the truth, *through* those lies? You're gonna get bit. Lies ... *man*, you get so *sick* of them. But the truth? The truth *wants* to be told. Do you know that?'

'I guess.'

'You *guess*. You guess *right*. But you want to know something that'll really freak you? Bring all this home?'

'Uh huh?' I don't really.

'You know when the second world war was won?'

'It was ... '45.'

'Until 1986, the second world war was won in *1950*. Five more years.' He sits back, shaking his head. You know how much of history changed *overnight*, 'cos of that? Everything that you *think* you know about world history since 1945 ... has only been that way for less than 30 years. What's fucked up is that I can still remember the *original* timeline. Maybe I survived all this time 'cos I have some kind of immunity to schizophrenia!'

'Oh *God*.' I got my head in my hands. I look up at him ... I guess in my eyes I'm begging him to tell me he's putting me on. He reads it, holds up his hands.

'I'm sorry, friend. I'm just sayin'.'

'*Why?*' I hiss at him. Now I'm actually getting kinda pissed. He holds up his hands again.

'Well, go ahead and think about it. It's hard at first, trying to get your head around the idea of a whole other reality, something you can't *see*. But you can *feel* it, can'tcha? That something's just not as it seems? If I got you in a room with half the eggheads I met on the base, they'd scramble your brains once and for all. All that quantum relativity and shit? The uncertainty of *everything?*'

'But ...' I can't find the words. I take a long swallow of beer and just call over my shoulder for two more.

'Listen, you can drink like a madman all your short life, or you can open your mind, and actually live the life you got given. The you that's hanging around up the road is waiting for you to work that out. *His* life's in *your* hands.'

'But why *me?* I don't understand why *me.*' The beers come and I just pile one straight down. My throat's got that cold burn. I can't manage the next one right away. The mist settles in, and I feel a little better, but I'm vexed as fuck.

'Think about it. Just hit the streets and think about it. Go home and think about it. And pay it forward.' The old man stands up, raises his bottle to me and throws down the last of it. He places it down gently, then pulls out a hundred and slides it under the bottle. He takes one more long look towards the door and heads for it without another word.

I sit there, dazed, for maybe half an hour. The second beer's warm by the time I put my hand on it. I get up and just walk out.

Out on the street, I look around. It all looks, sounds, smells and feels normal. The summer sun baking the cars, people, streets, sidewalks, buildings, slowing everything down. But then it hits me: maybe until yesterday, California was wiped out by Soviet nukes, or until six months ago, Al Qaida wasted L.A. with a dirty bomb, or some other bunch got us with smallpox ... or God knows what else. Should I feel safer, or less so ... or just the same?

I'm sober again by this point, and tired and hungry. At least my body feels normal. I drift along the street to a Wendy's, get some cheap carbs inside me. The people all look normal, the Mexicans, other African Americans, the whites. But *I* don't feel normal. I'm carrying around the most mind-bending story I ever heard, and I can hardly fit it between my ears. And yet, after an hour, it doesn't seem so crazy. I mean, look at all this. How much of our technology, architecture, civil engineering ... how much of that would look like magic to folks in the middle ages? I'm saying: why *not?* Why *can't* we travel through time? I read shit in the news about it, how some bunch of scientists over here say it's possible, another bunch over there say no way. Who knows? And, would a nation *not* try to use such technology to advance or protect their position in the world? Isn't that just how we roll? All of us?

By the time night comes around I'm just lying on my bed with the window open, listening to the rhythms of the city. There's a little breeze, mercifully, but it's still damn hot. Obviously, I can't get this guy out of my head. Well, he told me to think about it. Maybe it's just his thing. Makes himself feel better, telling drunks this story, just in case they get it into their heads to shape up. He told me to think on it, and I spend all night doing just that, wondering what might be going on out there.

It hits me that it's no more amazing than the fact that we're here at all. Even being able to lay awake all night thinking about this guy's story ... that's incredible in itself, never mind the time-warp business.

Is God or some other being or mechanism controlling things? Is that where this new toy came from, to change the past, or the future? Is it *meant* to be part of our trip? Or is the point that we should make better choices, think further down the road? I mean, How *can* you know what's right, except what seems right at the *time?* You can go round and round in circles, back into your past, off into your future, but like that guy, you'll just keep coming back to today. I guess it'd be great if you could somehow get it all to make sense, like a nice neat story that runs from beginning to end, but that ain't how life is. You go ahead and *make* your plans, if it makes you feel any better, but then stand back and see what happens.

I've been tempted to go back to that bar, see if he's in there – 'cos I still got a head full of questions – but it's a month now, and I've been sober since that day. I don't want to put myself in reach of temptation, know what I mean? But I feel like he's out there, trying to adjust after all that craziness. Being out of the bottle now, I guess I relate a little. Maybe the Chinese'll grab him, and he'll sing like a bird for 'em, just for the sake of talking to people who know what he's talking about. I do it, twice a week at AA. It feels good, like we're getting the lies out of us, as much as the drink. It's like he said. Somehow the worst truth is never quite as bad as the lies, like a nest of vipers, that cover the truth.

Printed in Great Britain
by Amazon.co.uk, Ltd.,
Marston Gate.